CW00336421

PsychoAnalysis

V. R. STONE

Saturday August 10th 2013

He's been staring at the blonde for ten minutes now. He can't tell whether they're making eye contact – she's wearing sunglasses – but he's sure she just raised an eyebrow. And those tiny shorts … it looks like she's applied them with a spray can, one that didn't contain much paint.

'Target engaged,' he says to the friends by his side, bumping fists, then pushing his way across the crowded dance floor.

He leans on the bar next to her, chest slightly puffed out. He purchased the T-shirt this afternoon – tight over his slim waist and white to show off his forearms, tanned and toned from working on the site.

In heels, though, she's taller than him.

'What you drinking?' he shouts over the thudding bass line of a generic RnB track.

'Really?' she says. 'You came over to ask me that?'

He frowns and glances at his pack of leering friends. One of them smirks.

His gaze returns to her, his mouth slightly open, nothing but air coming out. Other men watch with interest – there are five for every woman in the club. The place is stuffed with cheap-looking expensive clothes, slick hair and testosterone.

'No more lines ready, no Plan B?' she says. 'Do I seem like the kind of girl who can be bought with a vodka and Coke?'

'I–'

'What do you want for breakfast?'

The creases in his forehead deepen; still no words. He can't see her eyes and that question leaves him shaking his head.

'To have breakfast, we'd need to spend the night together, but that's only implied,' she says. 'It's clever – subtle. That's how to impress someone.'

'Breakfast … So–'

She grabs him by the waist, leaving him no time to react before she leans in and firmly presses her lips to his. When he moves his mouth, she's already backing away, smiling. She lowers her sunglasses for a second.

Perhaps it's the lighting, but her eyes – he can't quite tell whether they're green or blue.

'School's out, home time,' she says. 'Are you coming?'

He gulps, suppressing the urge to salivate.

'Follow me,' she whispers in his ear, grasping his wrist, guiding him from the bar, out of the doors and up the stairs to the cloakroom. She collects her coat and they walk out together into an evening that requires nothing more than short sleeves.

'What's your name?'

'I'm Sarah,' she says. 'Want to tell me yours? You don't have to.'

A tentative smile spreads across his lips. 'Gary.'

They walk silently up Dean Street and out of Soho, dodging groups of boys brawling and laughing, stepping off the pavement to move past slow-moving couples with arms around each other, heads resting on shoulders. Past the shuttered chain stores and souvenir shops in Oxford Street now, the hordes of bargain hunters long gone. And Fitzrovia, with its office buildings old and new, is deserted, just the odd drunk stumbling home or bewildered tourist searching for their hotel.

A tatty green Nissan Primera approaches. It slows and the driver lowers his window. 'Minicab?' he says. No phone number on the doors, no sticker in the window.

She looks up and down the street, hesitates, then gives the driver a nod.

* * * * * *

They've been in the car for more than half an hour now, up the Western Avenue, escaping London on the M40.

Gary's sitting next to Sarah, palms on knees, the same stiff pose he'd strike when waiting for the door to the headmaster's office to open. He's not much of a talker; all he can manage are sporadic glances in her direction. She's a bit older than he thought. *You can never see properly in clubs. Must be at least thirty with those little creases when she smiles. And there's no way she's a natural blonde.*

She could have mentioned her place was out of town. He had three pints at the club, his stomach is turning like a cement mixer and they've passed at least twenty kebab shops, greasy tubes of meat glistening in the windows. He thinks about asking to stop for a bite. *No, best not to, Gary. Might make you look like an idiot.*

She's just tossing the driver directions, telling him where and when to turn. Gary slips his hand into his pocket, fingers the eighty quid he has left. It will cover the fare, if they arrive soon, if he has to pay.

He should be having a grope, squeezing her arse while the driver has a peek in the rear-view. She gave him the big come-on and now she's clicking away at her BlackBerry. Gary can't even play with his own phone – he's sure it was in his pocket when he left the club, but it wouldn't be the first time he'd dropped it somewhere after a few drinks. Unless this is a wind-up. Maybe the boys put her up to it, slipping her a few notes so she dumps him in the middle of nowhere in his boxers with no way of calling anyone.

They peel off the motorway and drive through a posh town – banks with bay windows, plenty of trees, no concrete in the high street.

'Here's fine,' she says. The street is lined with brick houses – newly built, waiting for lawns to be laid. Gary reaches for his cash but Sarah taps his hand and tuts. She passes a couple of crisp fifties to the driver.

When the minicab's out of sight, they walk through a few tidy residential streets until they come to a single track lane next to school playing fields. Sarah opens the passenger door of a polished black Mercedes S-Class parked there and gestures for Gary to get in.

'Where now?' he says, hanging back. It's been an hour since liquid touched his tongue. They passed a taxi rank in the town centre ... the lads will be in the club until it closes.

'Home. Just need to be discreet.'

She's famous? He doesn't recognise her, but he's not going to pry. He didn't realise the girl he was chatting to in a club a few months ago was a minor pop star. Asked her what she did for a living and she poured her cocktail in his lap. Fucking expensive cocktail it was too.

'Gotta be honest with you, er … Sarah. I thought we were gonna cab it to some flat in Chelsea. For a, well …'

'Quick one?'

Gary is suddenly fascinated with the car's tyres, poking at one with his toe.

'You've got plans for the morning?' she says.

'Not exactly.'

'I haven't, I'm free all day. And maybe we won't make it to work on Monday,' she says, holding his gaze, unblinking, as she speaks.

Gary ceases his tyre kicking.

'Might even get that breakfast I promised. I think you'll need it.'

He grins, then slips into the passenger seat. Sarah gets in the driver's side, closing her door with a *thunk*.

'There's a cooler in the armrest,' she says, accelerating hard, driving out of town.

Gary flips it open and lifts out a bottle of champagne. Not Stella or Bud, but it'll do.

'Glasses are in the other compartment,' she says, her eyes meeting his. The sunglasses are gone and the way she looks at him … somebody's going to get tied up or spanked tonight. *I'll have a story to tell the boys on Monday. Or Tuesday.*

He pops the champagne and his heart leaps as the cork hits the roof, but only vapours escape the bottle. He manages to pour himself a glass without spilling anything on the beige leather seats.

Soon they're back on a motorway, leaving Buckinghamshire, into Oxfordshire. Then they're driving through villages, deeper and deeper into the countryside. They go for minutes at a time without meeting another car or passing a house with the lights on. There's just the occasional flash of fox eyes in the headlights.

They pull up to a set of wrought iron gates in the middle of a high, rough stone wall. Sarah pushes a button on the dashboard and the gates swing open.

As they cruise up the tarmac drive, there's no house in sight. The full moon and the headlamps illuminate seemingly endless open space, with a few scattered trees. Then, emerging from a tunnel of tall trees, they come to a halt in front of a sandstone mansion.

So she's a rich girl, fancies a bit of rough – like that Italian woman last year ... Gary was building an extension to her house in Kensington. She made the workmen use the Portaloo outside so they didn't make a mess in her bathroom, but she was happy to have one of them in her bedroom. She made him take his boots off before coming upstairs, though.

Sarah opens a huge oak front door and Gary follows her into a hallway the size of his Croydon flat. She leads him to a room – what some of Gary's clients would call a drawing room: white linen-covered sofas, giant marble fireplace, no TV. 'Take a seat. I'll get you a drink.'

'What you got?' He turns away to do a chalky champagne burp into his fist. *No more fizz.*

'Whiskey, vodka, gin–'

'Whiskey.'

'Bourbon or Scotch?'

'Don't mind.'

'I've got Irish, Jameson, if you'd prefer?'

Bloody hell, just pour me a drink, love. 'Anything,' he says through clenched teeth.

She smiles and removes a bottle from an antique cabinet, unscrewing it and sloshing in a couple of inches of dark amber liquid.

'Ice?'

'Yeah.'

She smiles to herself again and brings his drink in one hand, a lacquered black box in the other.

Gary takes the tumbler and sips, grateful for something to do with his hands. He's no expert, but it tastes good – smooth and woody. 'You need to catch up.'

'I don't drink.'

'Got plenty of booze for someone who doesn't.'

'I do a lot of entertaining.' Sarah kneels on a Turkish rug next to a coffee table and opens the box. She takes out a small packet of white powder, tips it onto the smooth surface of the table and cuts it into fat lines with a black credit card.

Gary isn't a drugs man – alcohol only – never even smoked a joint. But if that's what she likes, it's fine with him.

Sarah offers Gary a silver tube. He holds up his glass. 'I'll stick to this. You go ahead.'

'It's not for me.'

'Not for me neither … either.'

She puts a hand halfway up his thigh. 'This will keep you awake, keep you up all night.'

There's that smutty sparkle in her eye again. And what she said … the phrase – it escapes him now – French for double meaning.

He leans over the table, hoovers up a line, passes the tube back to Sarah and finishes the whisky.

Sarah takes his glass and returns to the cupboard.

Gary feels a dull ache below as she glides away – those legs that curve in and out just a little from calf to knee to thigh, the same way as her chest and hips. And those tiny shorts …

Sarah comes back, picks up the tube, gives it to him. He does another line. A hand on his shoulder. She pushes him, turns and sits on his lap, writhing against his crotch. 'Want to watch me get undressed?'

'Do it,' he says, his voice assertive now.

Sarah walks away with an exaggerated swing in her hips. She clicks on a stereo. Notes on a piano, a female jazz singer's voice: husky, slow, sad.

Gary is buzzing – jaw tight, teeth grinding, fists holding on to the fabric of the sofa.

What'd she do if I pushed her to the floor and ripped her clothes off? No, let her play her game – they like to feel sexy, don't they?

The shorts come down, showing a lacy black thong. She turns around, slides the straps of her bra off her shoulders, revealing small, pert breasts. When she flicks the thong at him with her toe, he thinks: *Collar and cuffs, they don't match.*

As if reading his mind, Sarah plucks off her blonde wig, revealing coppery-red locks underneath. She removes the band and pins holding them in place, and shakes out the straight shoulder-length hair.

'I hope you don't mind, but I have more luck as a blonde.'

Gary's not going to complain. This girl could be in any of the magazines scattered around his bedroom. No fat on her: where she should be flat, she's flat; where she should be round, she's round. Almost a six-pack, arms toned but not veiny, the only imperfection a horizontal scar above her neatly trimmed pubic hair. And the way she's put so much thought and effort into getting some – without seeming desperate – well, it makes Gary think she's going to be good, will know her way round the bedroom.

'Your turn.'

Gary stands up too quickly, yanks his shoes and socks off, T-shirt over his head, wriggles out of jeans and boxers together. He flattens his hair. He's had plenty to drink, but he's hard, pointing at the ceiling. When he gazes up at that ceiling, though, he has to shuffle his feet a little to prevent himself from toppling over.

Sarah points to the coke. Gary shakes his head. 'What?' he asks. She's staring at him like she knows something, her eyes slightly narrowed.

Her fist connects with his jaw. Gary drops to the rug on all fours, white lights bursting in his eyes. There's a cloth wrapped around her knuckles. She steps forward, knees close to his face. Her legs bend and a swinging fist hits him in the side of his torso. His ribs crack as the air is forced out of his lungs.

'Wha … what the fuck,' he says wincing, then coughing. Gripping the sofa, he drags himself up. 'Why you doing this?'

'You're not having fun?'

He frowns, lowers his head like a bull about to charge. 'I'll show you "fun", you ginger–' He lunges at her but she catches him with a ramrod jab to the nose that sends him lurching backwards, arms flailing until he thumps into a wall and collapses.

'Oh, Gary,' she says, hands on hips. 'Maybe you can outrun me?'

'You're fuckin' nuts,' he says, rising unsteadily to his feet and running into the hallway. His heel touches something greasy and he slips, falling sideways and cracking his knee on the stone tiles. Reaching a door jamb and pulling himself up, he fumbles with the chunky steel lock and flings the door open.

The warm night air rushes over his naked skin as he runs across a large square lawn, lit by security lights, towards a rising slope and then darkness. The adrenaline and the booze and whatever else she's given him take the edge off, but every breath is like another smack in the ribs, every stride stiffened by the warm throb in his knee.

From behind him, the thud of feet, faster than his.

He makes it to the slope and scrabbles up, fingers and toes slipping on wet grass. A few times he falls, sliding on the muddy incline. At the top, he pauses to catch his breath. He checks – she's not behind him.

He stumbles along a dirt path cut into the downward slope. There's a cluster of trees at the bottom. All the lower branches have been sawn off; no stray ones to use as a club. The turf is clean like a new carpet; no sticks or stones to use as weapons. The grass on the hill is sopping wet, even though it hasn't rained for weeks.

A chill passes over him. He looks up at the sky, half expecting to see giant people, waiting to move him like a piece in a board game.

Heart and mind galloping, he sprints between the trees but her forearm connects with his sternum, knocking the breath out of him again. Back on his hands and knees, he vomits, each heave sending spasms through his battered torso.

He staggers to his feet and she lands a punch on his ear. It's like he's under water now, doesn't know which way is up or down. He rolls around, feels his elbow connect with something soft. She's hobbling.

Gary rises slowly, arms out to keep his balance like he's walking a tightrope. He takes a swing, but the angle and distance are wrong – he misses her by a foot. She grabs his forearm and sweeps his legs from under him. She stamps on one wrist, then the other.

Now she's grappling with him on the ground, turning him on his side, sliding one leg under his waist, the other on top, an arm around his neck. He tries to scream but she's crushing his throat, and when he strains, attempts to wriggle free, it's like he's in a strait-jacket. Her chest is hot against his back, sticky sweat glues them together. Between his heartbeats he can feel hers pounding against his body. Moist, fast breaths blow in his ear.

Light gradually recedes from the edges of his vision. The moon and the stars dim until the black, the darkness, is all there is.

Sunday August 11th 2013

Martin removes the joint from his old tobacco tin. It's a three skin because this is a special occasion. He puts on his bulky, old-fashioned headphones, selects Hendrix's 'All Along the Watchtower' on his smartphone and lights the joint with a silver Zippo, taking a long, deep puff, then blowing a cloud of smoke up to the clear blue sky. He'd like to sit, eyes closed, enjoy this moment. But it's a new section of the cemetery so there are no tombs or monuments to lean against, only rows of upright shiny slabs and the occasional carved scroll, heart or angel. No benches.

A mound of fresh soil covers the grave. Martin wonders what happens to it. Does someone pat it down? No headstone yet, either. Who'll arrange that, pay for it?

He lies down next to her.

The grass is dry, tickles his neck. When he shuts his eyes, the sun shines through his eyelids. If he listens to more than three songs, he'll get burned.

'I kept your secret,' he says. 'I didn't tell a soul.'

Jimi's guitar fades out. The next song on the playlist, specially prepared for this day – a kind of memorial – is The Who's 'Won't Get Fooled Again'. The sound of Townshend's keyboards swirl around Martin; he plays the drums without moving his arms.

'I should've been there at the end, though, to see you die.'

Something casts a cool shadow on his face. He opens his eyes. An elderly couple loom over him like a pair of tight-lipped, wide-eyed ghosts.

He stands up but has to put his hand on the old man's shoulder to steady himself. He offers the joint to the man, who recoils. Martin stubs it out on a headstone, slips it into his pocket. 'I was just saying goodbye,' he says.

The old man frowns – it's unlikely he was expecting the ripped jeans and Led Zep T-shirt to belong to someone so well-spoken; probably thought he was some kind of tramp. But up close, you can see Martin's the son of a ruggedly handsome rock musician and a waif-like model – grey eyes that are never bloodshot and skin that's always clear no matter how little sleep or how much alcohol he's had. Even the unruly greying hair appears to have been carefully styled that way. It looks like the past forty-two years have been kind to Martin, even if the opposite is true.

The old woman shakes her head and the couple shuffle off.

Martin's strolling back to the main gate when he sees an old acquaintance.

Of course – it was August, two years ago.

She doesn't hold flowers; she's standing, talking to the headstone. Acting without an audience.

It's too exposed for Martin to hang around without being seen, so he hurries to the gate. He'll take a chance and wait for her at Kensal Green tube station. Although it's not much of a gamble – he knows where she lives.

She doesn't spy him waiting at the ticket machine. He follows her down the escalator.

The first time they met, she wasn't wearing any makeup, her hair was unwashed and she wore a baggy grey tracksuit around the house. Now she has a golden tan, glossy hair. Her black dress is crisp and clean.

As expected, she changes to the Hammersmith & City line at Paddington. Martin follows her all the way from Ladbroke

Grove station to the white, three-storey town house in Notting Hill. He watches her approach the front door, half hiding behind a tree.

A man – olive-skinned, curly black hair tamed with some greasy product – opens the door. No shoes or socks.

They kiss.

Martin should return in a couple of hours, after he's had an espresso, cleared his head, got the smell of weed off him.

That's not going to happen. His lips tingle, his throat feels tight.

He rings the doorbell.

'Hello, Lucy, do you remember me?' he says, with all the charm he can muster.

'Detective Inspector White? You … what do you want?'

'Mind if I come in?'

'Who is it?' says a man from inside. The accent is Italian.

'The police,' she says, her eyes boring into Martin's, her voice flat.

'Lucia, what is it they want?'

'Lucia?' Martin says.

'It's what he calls me,' she says, continuing to glare at Martin. 'And like he said, what do you want?'

'I was in the area, thought I'd pop in for a little chat. Maybe a cup of tea.'

She turns and walks along the freshly painted hallway, duck egg blue, leaving Martin to follow her, closing the door behind him. There's a stack of mail on a small table next to the telephone. The top letter is addressed to Maurizio Agustino.

Lucy perches herself on the end of the red leather sofa where Maurizio's lounging, watching the news on a brand new, razor-thin flat-screen TV. He doesn't greet Martin, just glances at him.

'Mind if I take a seat?' Martin says.

Lucy shrugs but she's chewing the inside of her cheek.

'I like what you've done with the place,' Martin says. 'Very stylish, very … Italian, wouldn't you agree, Maurizio?'

Maurizio sits up. 'How you know my name?'

'Are you aware of what Lucy did?' Martin says. 'Did she tell you about that?'

Maurizio picks up the remote and switches off the TV. 'She tell me all about you, Mister White.'

'*Detective Inspector* White. What exactly did she tell you? That I believe she murdered her husband so she could have all of this to herself?' Martin gestures around the room.

'Why are you here, Mister White?' Maurizio says.

'When I saw Lucy was living with a new man, I thought I'd better warn him. Do you have a large life assurance policy?'

'What do you want from me? What?' Lucy asks, fists clenched, tears welling in her eyes.

She always puts on a convincing, if slightly over-the-top performance, Martin thinks. 'I may not be able to prove it, but I know what you did.'

'How can you be certain when you are ignoring the evidence?' Maurizio says, still calm, looking Martin in the eye without blinking.

An even better actor. 'Just an old-fashioned hunch. I hope for your sake, Maurizio, that I'm never proven right.'

'You're just going to sit there and … and threaten us?' Lucy says.

'I would love to stay, but I suppose I'd better be getting home.' Martin pats Maurizio on the shoulder. The stray black hair on the collar of the white shirt had been visible from across the room. He picks it up as he says, 'Good luck.'

* * * * * *

Sarah raises the garage door and climbs into the old grey Land Rover.

Last night she returned to the house, got dressed, drove to the wood on the other side of the hill and loaded up Gary's body. Usually the physical exhaustion and the fading euphoria after a hunt would send her into a deep sleep, ten hours or more. But last night she lay awake, checking the clock like an insomniac keeping score. Rolling on to her side, her front, her back. *Again. I want to do it again.*

Over the years, she's learned to savour the thrill for longer, replaying events in her mind for weeks, until the hunger is overwhelming and she has to go again. But recently, during this hot summer, she's hunted every fortnight; now the gap has dropped to a week.

The UK has been good for her – the cameras everywhere and the skilled police force controlling her appetite like a stapled stomach. Although the staple seems to be coming loose.

She pulls up at a crumbling single-storey sandstone building, goes inside and comes back with a wooden handcart. She slides the bag out of the jeep and onto the cart, then wheels it inside.

Sarah shovels different grades of coal into the pit of the old blacksmith's forge. The varying densities will ensure that each layer is exhausted after igniting the one below, with the heavy, tightly packed chunks at the bottom providing enough heat to finish the job. An oven would be more suitable – this is simply a raised, open fireplace – but it still generates enough heat to burn a body down to the bones in a few hours. She doesn't know exactly how long it takes; she won't wait around to watch and let the smell of burnt flesh embed itself in her hair and skin.

She places a bundle of kindling on top of the coal, lights a match and holds it to the spindliest, driest looking piece. She could use firelighters, but it seems right to do it the old-fashioned way. These quiet Sundays, with their nods to ritual and tradition, are an appropriate end to the hunts, a respectful method for the disposal of the men.

After all, Sarah isn't a wacko or a pervert. She doesn't mutilate the bodies or keep souvenirs. It's a chase, a sport. Then cleaning up.

The twigs crackle and whine, smoking lazily. When the flames spread, Sarah opens the bellows door below to help things along.

She unzips the bag and takes a last look at Gary. She closed his eyes last night. He's bruised, but still beautiful.

The fire roars and Sarah removes her jacket. She pulls the bag away from Gary and rolls him onto his funeral pyre.

* * * * * * *

A woman wearing a headset counts in Roger, the host.

Karl pushes up his rimless spectacles with an index finger. He had the makeup artist apply powder to his bald dome so it won't shine in the studio lights. *Don't be patronising, Karl. Or aggressive.* British people don't warm to his German accent.

'Welcome back,' Roger says. 'Our next guest on *The Week* is psychiatrist and author Doctor Karl Gross. Good afternoon, Doctor Gross.'

'Good afternoon, Roger,' Karl says.

Roger's smile melts away. His face is stony now, eyes penetrating. 'As ever, your latest book is attracting mixed reviews and plenty of controversy.'

Karl gives him a small nod, says nothing.

'Your most vocal critics accuse you of dragging psychology into the gutter and exploiting your role as therapist to a number of celebrities.'

'I write about human behaviour and it seems the book-buying public find sexuality fascinating.' Karl leans forward in his seat. 'As for exploitation, all my patients consent to their case histories being used – with the names changed, of course.'

'But in the past you've complained your work isn't taken seriously. What do you expect when you write books about sex addicts and serial killers? Why not publish in scientific journals? Why not conduct proper studies?'

'Freud wrote books about his patients.'

'I think Freud's work has been largely discredited.'

If Karl leans any further forward he'll slide off his chair. 'Very good, Roger, very good. You parrot someone else's uninformed opinions, expressing your views on a subject you have absolutely no first-hand knowledge of.'

'Well–'

'Freud has *not* been discredited. He's been abandoned by psychologists who aspire to be physicists, and who haven't discovered techniques to test his theories in the traditional hypothetico-deductive framework.'

Roger's eyes are blank.

A cheap trick, Karl admits to himself, bamboozling the man with jargon, but he deserved it.

The studio crew, though, and the pretty researcher who asked Karl to sign her copy of his latest hardback – their eyes are blank too.

Karl smooths his tie and gives Roger a tight smile. 'What I mean is that human behaviour is complex – you can't measure it the way you record the mass of an atom or the speed of light. You have to travel through a person's life like a story, identifying the turning points in the narrative, decode the meaning. Only then can you help them.'

'How do stories of serial killers and celebrity sex-addicts help the average person? How do they assist the millions who suffer from depression and anxiety?'

Karl leans back now, hands on the arms of the chair. 'All human behaviour lies on a continuum of some sort. Being depressed or anxious isn't black or white, on or off. Some people are a little unhappy, some struggle to get out of bed in the morning, others are permanently suicidal–'

'–Serial killers, though. How are they relevant?' Roger is speaking quickly now, almost shouting.

'Please let me finish,' Karl says. He waits for Roger to nod. 'By repairing a machine that has broken down, you can learn how it works and make it function better, stop it failing the next time. So in studying extreme human behaviour, we learn about the human mind, we further our understanding.'

'Do the nicknames upset you – "Doctor Death", "The Dirty Doc"?'

So you're going to get personal. 'The media love snappy headlines and over-simplification.'

'You don't shy away from the limelight.'

'Perhaps. But I object to the ill-informed nonsense that is written and spoken about me.' He jabs a finger at Roger. 'Yes, I write about controversial subjects. But the same newspapers who print this nonsense about me are more than happy to dedicate their pages to violence and … sexy gossip.'

A couple of the studio crew chuckle. Roger's eyes flick over to them, then return to Karl. 'Let's set aside the mainstream media for a moment. There are many in the medical community who are just as critical.'

Karl sighs. 'I hate to use the word "envy", but that's what a lot of my critics are motivated by. These so-called intellectuals turn their noses up at my work - they believe it's on a par with pornography and crime fiction. We all have sexual desires, though, we all fear violence and death. I write about real people and real people buy my books, millions of them.'

'Well, I can't argue with the sales figures.' Roger swivels his chair and looks at the camera. 'We're going to take a short break. Then we'll be back with our round-up of the Sunday papers.'

They stand up and Karl unclips the mic from his lapel.

'Tell me,' Roger says, smiling again. 'Is it true that "Miss B" is–'

'As I told you in the interview, patients must remain anonymous. I am a doctor.'

'But between you and me–'

'No!'

'Listen,' Roger says, taking a step towards Karl. 'I helped you look good out there, just made it *seem* like I was giving you a rough ride.'

'You didn't have a choice. You're no Paxman, are you?'

'You bloody–'

'He's erudite, skilled. Do you even know what erudite means?' Karl still holds the microphone. He searches for someone to give it to.

A slight, sandy-haired man appears next to Roger, placing a hand on the host's elbow, and tries to guide him over to the other side of the studio where a politician and a journalist wait on a sofa. 'Forget about coming on here to flog your next piece of trash,' Roger says, stubbornly refusing to move. 'This show sells books, but no more of yours.'

'I've sold enough without your help,' Karl says, pushing his microphone into Roger's hand. 'I'm sure I'll survive.'

* * * * * * *

Sarah doesn't watch TV while she waits, doesn't own one. If it's not raining, she'll pull on hiking boots and walk around her parkland, occasionally glancing towards the forge to make sure the chimney is still smoking. Since she's alone, and she doesn't eat meat, there's no point cooking a traditional Sunday roast. She reads company reports and monitors the news all week, so a couple of hours with the papers is no treat.

When she tires of walking or it's wet outside, she lies on a sofa in the drawing room, listening to jazz, mostly female singers, or sometimes the less challenging instrumental stuff from the sixties. Miles Davis's dreamy trumpet is a favourite, filling the house with a slow, mellifluous sound. She doesn't know where she got her taste in music from – certainly not her parents or one of the few men she's had a relationship with. But those albums have an ethereal quality that makes them perfect for a Sunday afternoon spent alone.

Occasionally she'll switch to something classical, bombastic – a piece with loud horns, dramatic strings and kettle drums – that will take her back to the moonlight, running, chasing, hunting.

At around four o'clock, the music ends and Sarah slips her Barbour jacket and wellingtons back on and drives to the forge. She removes the charred bones with a pair of tongs and places them in a clean, stainless steel box, leaving only the ashes, free of all traces of DNA.

It's a short drive to the river, across the bridge to the water mill. Sarah's had the wooden wheel and system of cogs and shafts restored, but the mill will never be open to the public or visited by historians.

She slides the steel box out of the Land Rover and hooks it up to a pulley hanging from the top floor.

After climbing the stairs, she brings up the box using the pulley, drags it inside and empties it into an oversized mortar so she can break up the charred pelvis and skull with a stone-tipped pestle, as well as snapping the larger bones and rib cage. The opening at the top of the millstone – meant, of course, for small pieces of grain – is the size of an adult hand, but anything the rough, grooved stone gets a grip on is dragged inside and crushed into powder.

Originally the flour would have flown down to bins, but now Sarah attaches a pipe that takes Gary's remains out of the window on the floor below and into the river, where he'll flow along tributaries, into the river Avon and out to sea.

The process won't eradicate all traces of her victims, even after she's thoroughly washed the pipe, the pestle and mortar, and the steel box. But they won't be discovered by accident – no dog walkers will come across a shallow grave; no decomposing corpse will float to the surface of a lake.

* * * * * * *

Martin has delivered Maurizio's hair to forensics. It's black and should match the oval cross-section of those found in Lucy's husband's fist, indicating they belong to a person of European origin. The lab will probably find traces of the same styling wax and maybe the cocaine present in Maurizio's hair two years ago; that will be enough to bring Maurizio in, get full sampling done and compare his DNA with that of the hair and follicles Lucy's husband ripped from his murderer's head, when Maurizio posed as a mugger and stabbed him.

Enjoy the house and the money, Martin thinks. *You won't have them for much longer.*

He fumbles in his pockets, finds his key and lets himself into the four-storey townhouse in Hammersmith.

The TV is on in the lounge, an interviewer harassing some bald man. Charlotte is napping on the large corner sofa, their two-year-old daughter Molly snuggled up next to her – two heads of matching black hair in a sea of beige fabric.

He creeps along the hallway, his old film posters and framed album covers long since replaced with reproduction Impressionist paintings. In the kitchen, he finds the space in the fridge door where his gherkins should be. There's a Post-it note that says, 'They were past the "Best before" date'.

You put food in vinegar to preserve it, Martin thinks. *What kind of bacteria would grow in that jar?* He imagines him and Charlotte in a marriage counselling session: 'When I first met her, she was too busy to touch my gherkins.'

He takes the stairs to the attic, unlocks the door to his study and sits behind the desk piled high with files. Lucy's case is an older one with no recent developments, so the papers are halfway down one of the stacks. Martin pulls out the file and places it on the shredder. He'll wait until Maurizio and Lucy are arrested before he destroys it, but it no longer belongs on the desk or in his mind.

Of course, all the information is available by computer, and he shouldn't have files at home, but a tower of paper is hard to ignore, it's tangible.

Right now, though, the height of the stacks and the dust on the shredder is a reminder that he's slowed down lately, ever since he found out about her cancer, the terminal prognosis.

He realises he didn't finish his playlist at the cemetery. He walks to the shelves of vinyl LPs – his father's – and picks out Cream's *Disraeli Gears*, dropping the needle on track two, 'Sunshine of Your Love'. He takes out the joint, lights it and picks up where he left off.

Clapton gives him goose bumps, and he wonders why the songs people say were the favourites of his dad, a drummer, were guitar tracks. Like his peers who made it – Charlie Watts, Ginger Baker – he listened to the jazz drummers, but it seems as if his real love was another instrument. Maybe that's why he ended up as more of a hanger-on, following bands instead of playing in them.

Martin finishes the joint sitting at the old drum kit, playing along until the vinyl runs out, clicks and pops coming from the speakers.

Charlotte stands in the doorway, wafting smoke from her face. 'We need to talk,' she says.

It's not going to be a discussion of the utility bills or replacing the carpet.

'What time is it?' Martin says.

'Want me to come back when you're not stoned? Next week?'

'I was visiting my mother's grave.'

She's shaking her head, or it could be a shiver. 'I … When did she–'

'Last week, they buried her on Friday. I didn't go, paid my own little tribute this morning.'

She gives him that look, open-mouthed disbelief followed by a smile with gritted teeth when she remembers who she's talking to. 'Well … I've contacted a divorce lawyer.'

'On a Sunday?'

'No, I was waiting for the right time–'

'This isn't it.'

Charlotte looks up at the ceiling then back at Martin. 'Why do you have to be so flippant? Can't you take me seriously for once?'

Martin puts his drumsticks down. 'Sorry. You'll let me see Molly?'

'Of course.'

'I'll make it easy if we get that down on paper, that I can spend time with her.'

Charlotte smiles, just a little.

'I'll need a flat, I suppose,' he says. 'We'll have to agree on the financial arrangements.'

'I'm going back to work.'

Of course she is, Martin thinks.

When she was pregnant, Charlotte looked forward to abandoning her career in corporate finance with its long hours, demanding clients and competition for partner spots at the pinnacle of the accounting firm's pyramid. But her romantic ideas of days spent baking cupcakes, playing in the park and keeping house turned out to be someone else's dream. She needs deadlines, pressure, praise. 'If we split everything in half I can buy a smaller house and find an au pair,' she says.

'You've got it all planned, as ever.'

'Someone's got to,' she says, sighing and leaving the room.

* * * * * * *

'Very good, dear, as always,' Liz says. 'You made him look a little silly.'

Karl can always rely on his wife for a favourable review. He follows her as she wheels herself along the hallway and into the kitchen. The early afternoon TV appearance in

Manchester has pushed their usual Sunday lunch back to supper. 'What is it today?' he says.

'Lovely bit of lamb.'

It will be dry and tasteless. But Karl, watching his wife moving so efficiently across the kitchen, never complains.

It's his fault she's in the chair.

A female patient less than half his age became attached to him, as so many people do when they find someone who will listen, appears to care. He wasn't even conducting a psychoanalysis, in which she'd experience transference, redirecting feelings for her father to Karl.

He ignored the warning signs, never confronted her about the times she 'just happened' to be in the park near his home, but nowhere near hers. He took the weekend phone calls – all because he wanted to gaze at her for an hour on Wednesday and Friday afternoons.

It was too late, really, when he recommended she see a colleague of his, a woman.

'Mind setting the table?' Liz says.

Karl reaches down and opens the cutlery drawer, fishing out two knives and two forks. 'What's for pudding?'

'Apple crumble.'

He picks up two spoons, nudges the low drawer shut with his knee and walks over to the table, the wood warmed by the sun shining through the skylight.

Just two places to set now that Josh is in New York. Amelia hasn't passed through London in months. At least they had them before the accident, Karl always tells himself, in a weak attempt at positive thinking.

The squeal of tyres from behind, the over-revved engine. He saw the car mount the pavement, heading straight for him. Karl dived into a garden, leaving Liz to take a tonne and a half of steel on the hip, instantly making everything below limp and redundant.

She's never shown any sign of blaming him, though. She has that straightforward, rational style of thinking some well-bred English women from the countryside possess. Generations of farming accidents, crippling falls from horses and hunting mishaps. 'These things happen,' she'd said with a breathtaking casualness that he wished all his neurotic, obsessive and depressed patients could witness. 'In your line of work you're bound to come across the odd loony, aren't you?'

* * * * * * *

The sun has retreated behind the hills and Gary is on his way to the Atlantic via the Severn Estuary, the Bristol Channel and the Celtic Sea.

Usually Sarah would switch her phone back on now, grab her laptop and catch a train to London. But she's sitting at the kitchen table, face lit by the computer screen. She tries to persuade herself that it doesn't bother her

Every few months she goes to Facebook and types in 'Oliver Brown'.

She doesn't have an account – who would she add as a friend? The kids at school knew her by a different name, university classmates another. She always used the first name that popped into her head when introducing herself to fellow backpackers.

Oliver's profile is visible to anyone, though. And last week it changed. No longer an action shot of him snowboarding in the Alps. Now three faces crowd the frame: Oliver, a grinning blonde and a bald baby … boy?

Sarah slams the laptop shut and, with a flick of the wrist, throws it at the wall. It bounces off and falls to the stone floor. The screen springs open and now the Facebook page is looking at her, taunting her.

I bet your relationship with her is nothing like what you had with me.

She picks up her mug, drains the last of the coffee and flings it at the computer.

It misses.

She's still for a while, then pushes herself out of her chair and trudges upstairs to bed. She'll go straight to work in the morning.

Tuesday August 13th 2013

Martin rings the bell of an anonymous grey door nestled between a sandwich bar and a newsagent in Soho. The street is quiet at this time of the morning. The restaurants and many of the shops are closed, people are at their desks in the offices above and the tourists will still be scoffing hotel breakfasts. This particular building's grubby gothic façade looks a little eerie next to its smart Georgian and Victorian brick neighbours. The door clicks open and he hears the DCS say, 'First floor,' over the intercom.

Detective Chief Superintendent Terrence Cook – new head of the Met's Homicide and Serious Crimes unit – didn't explain why he wanted to meet in Wardour Street, hanging up before Martin could ask any questions.

Now Cook sits behind a tired desk, the plastic pine-effect veneer chipped and dirty, only a laptop and a few stacks of paper in front of him. There are two more desks pushed together against the wall facing him, each supporting an ancient PC with a boxy monitor. The carpet is grey, balding and coffee-stained. Cook has removed his jacket and rolled up his sleeves – the air-conditioning is either broken or switched off.

Martin takes one of the seats in front of the DCS's desk.

'The hair wasn't a match and the Italian bloke was out of the country at the time.' Cook says. 'Now this woman,' he picks up a piece of paper, 'Lucy Reid. She's made a complaint. Says you're harassing her.'

Martin sighs. 'She had her husband killed. There was a seven million pound life assurance policy.'

'And?' Cook has interrogator's eyes – blank, betraying no emotion.

'When you know, you know. I don't think I need to explain that. Talk to her. You'll see what I mean.'

Cook scratches the side of his head with thick fingers, lightly ruffling his closely cropped granite grey hair. 'We're not in the business of just identifying suspects.' He picks up more sheets of paper, scans them. 'Your record – it's ... patchy. No good only getting the deer in your sights. You've got to hit the target. And it looks like your aim's getting worse.'

Martin pictures the stacks of files in his study.

'Seems to me you're not as … indispensable as you used to be.'

So the new man at the top is having a clear out.

'I've been thinking about leaving the force,' Martin says.

'Again?'

'What do you want?'

Cook grunts, then stares at his watch, counting down the seconds.

The intercom buzzes.

He stands up and limps across the room, dragging his stiff right leg. He presses the door release and sits back down with a wince. Everyone calls him 'Captain Cook', as if he's a pirate with a wooden leg, not after the explorer. One of the things Martin knows about the DCS: never let him catch you staring when he walks.

Heavy footsteps ascend the stairs and a man enters the room. The neatly trimmed beard and slim-cut, expensive suit worn with a narrow wool tie help to disguise his age and identity. Martin guesses he's only in his late twenties and that

– because he's joining the meeting with Cook – he's a police officer.

'DI Martin White, DS Phil Burton. Phil, grab a seat,' Cook says. Phil removes his jacket. He searches unsuccessfully for somewhere to hang it, folds it in two from the collar and carefully places it on one of the desks at the rear of the room. Then he takes the remaining chair, in front of the desk.

Martin sighs. There's only one reason why the DCS is introducing him to a junior officer.

Cook lifts a stack of paper from a desk drawer. 'On Saturday night, Gary Burke goes to a club, down the road from here, with a few mates. They say he approached a girl and, five minutes later, they walked out. Nobody's seen him since.'

'Have we traced his phone?' Phil says, dropping the first "H" with a softened Yorkshire accent that suggests he's been living in London a while.

'Found a couple of streets away, no prints,' Cook says.

'Any cash withdrawn from his account?'

'Not even a tenner.'

Phil leans back in his chair, staring at the corner of the room where the ceiling meets two walls.

'Why are we talking about a missing person,' Martin says, 'in an office in Soho?'

Cook points at Phil. 'Why didn't you ask that question?'

'I was thinking–'

'Good luck with that.' Cook takes a few sheets of paper from a stack and passes them to the detectives. 'Saturday before last, another bloke – Darren Burns – went missing from a club in Stoke. A fortnight before that, Ricky Cox in Derby.'

Good-looking boys, Martin thinks as he flicks through photos. Pretty boys.

'Same girl?' Phil says.

'Always different. Happened a few times last year and the one before. But this summer it's stepped up.'

'The weather makes people crazy,' Phil says, unfastening his top button and loosening his tie. 'I read about it the other day. Heat waves increase your riots and murders.'

'This isn't crazy, though,' Cook says. 'Well-planned.' He taps a few keys and rotates the laptop so Martin and Phil can view the screen. 'CCTV in the clubs and bars, mostly crap.' There's footage of blondes and more blondes. One of them has sleeves of tattoos, another wears a tight black Lycra t-shirt over a bulging bra.

'Do we ever see the eyes?' Phil says.

'Nope. But the images from Saturday are sharper – keep watching.'

Another blonde standing at a bar. A man approaches; they exchange a few words. He looks around, appears to be struggling for words. She speaks again, leans in, kisses him, pulls away. They walk off camera.

'Got more shots from around the club,' Cook says, 'but none of them are as clear. Take a look anyway.'

The girl enters through a door, climbs the stairs to a cloakroom, leaves with the man.

'The one time she lowers her sunglasses,' Phil says, 'she's facing away from the camera. She probably knows it's there.'

'Whoever these girls are, they know what they're doing', Cook says. 'No leads for any of the disappearances.'

'Wait a minute,' Phil says. 'Let's go back through the videos.'

They watch it all again.

'The hair,' Phil says. 'None of the girls is wearing it up in a ponytail, anything like that. It's always a do – chunky fringe or something short. And look, when she's got big tits... they're covered up, no cleavage so they could be padding. Tattoos could be fake.'

'So the girls are disguised?' Cook says.

Martin sits up straight, a previously dormant region of his brain activated. 'The mannerisms are the same – the way she drinks, the way she grabs the men. And if you're using a different girl each time, you can't know how she'll react. Pay a woman to go into a club and bring someone out – they'll look around, play with their hair, drink too quickly. But here it's always the same. Casual, quick, no faffing about. Professional.'

'So?' Cook says.

'It's the same girl,' Martin says.

Cook smiles and points two fingers at Martin, like a gun.

Phil frowns.

'Private joke,' Cook says.

'You didn't answer my question, sir,' Martin says. 'Why aren't we discussing this in your office?'

Cook holds Martin's gaze for a few seconds, then switches to the other detective. 'Loads of jurisdictions. Missing persons, no corpses. Nobody noticed Shipman was offing little old ladies, and if we're right about this, nobody's noticed that at least ten blokes have disappeared after meeting the same girl.'

'Nobody's noticed?' Phil says. 'You mean *we* haven't noticed.'

'This didn't happen on my watch,' Cook says. 'I was working counter-terror–'

'You're not SO15 any more, so open it up, get pictures in the papers–'

'You know how difficult it is to kill someone every two weeks?' Cook says. 'Fred West took years to rack up the numbers we're talking about. Dennis Nilsen ended up flushing body parts down the toilet 'cos he couldn't get rid of them fast enough.'

'So … maybe we're dealing with a team, people who are organised.'

'Organised? Fucking understatement,' Cook says. 'She strolls in there and strolls out. Couple of forces thought about the cases being linked, but there's no evidence. No car seen in both places, no bloody nothing.'

'That means the team's good … We need to throw resources at this,' Phil says.

Cook scratches his chin, although Martin gets the impression the DCS isn't really considering anything. 'One more thing. Mistakes happen, but there's been way too many. Club on the outskirts of Birmingham, used to have drug problems so they installed new cameras, bloody good ones. Night of a disappearances last year there's no recording. Can't tell if the cameras weren't switched on or if somebody wiped them.' He pauses, inviting a reaction from the detectives. 'Year before that, in Southampton, she used a minicab, caught on CCTV. When they went to interview the driver, he'd scarpered, jumped on a plane to Bangladesh, three hours earlier.'

'You're not saying they're getting inside help,' Phil says.

'It'd explain a lot, if they've got someone to sort things out when they make a cock-up.'

'I don't buy it,' Martin says. 'The inside angle. The video could have been a mistake. The minicab driver probably heard we were looking for him, perhaps he had immigration problems.'

'Those were the best leads we had. I don't believe in coincidences.'

Martin frowns. 'But, sir—'

'We're not taking any chances with this. It goes back to the logistics. This stuff isn't impulsive – it's bloody well planned. They've got resources. Far as they're concerned, we don't know what's going on. Chuck a hundred uniforms at it, splash it all over the papers and they'll change their MO, we'll have to start again.'

'So you throw two detectives at it? *Fookin' two*?' Phil says, his accent slipping.

'Three.'

'No disrespect … surely you're busy with—'

'Meetings, paperwork, presentations?'

'Well … yeah.'

'I can spare an hour or two a day. I'll get anything you want – access to everything on the disappearances, all the national databases, whatever you need.'

Phil makes a steeple with his fingers, rests his chin on them.

'You're a betting man,' Cook says. 'We solve this we're heroes. We fuck it up and nobody knows. You like that gamble?'

'When you put it like that …'

'Two computers over there,' Cook says, pointing to the additional desks. 'One's connected to HOLMES and everything else. Other one's got no network connection – that's where you record details of the case. You need forensics, reports from another force – it goes through me.' He picks up a newspaper from his desk. 'One more thing. Today's *Telegraph*: "Last night the Westminster Police released this photo of a woman seen with builder Gary Burke, 27, shortly before his disappearance from the Glass Club in Soho. Mr Burke was drinking with friends and has not been in contact since …"' Cook runs his finger down the paper, mouthing a few words. "'Police would not comment on any possible link with the disappearance of Ricky Cox under similar circumstances from a club in Derby last month.'"

'I thought we weren't releasing photos?' Martin says.

'Westminster put it out,' Cook says.

'Should we be worried about the journalist?'

'They missed out the one from a week ago. Don't reckon they've got anything to go on.' Cook checks his watch. 'I'm late. I want an update tomorrow.'

* * * * * * *

By ten-thirty a.m., European stock markets have been open two-and-a-half hours – enough time for buyers and sellers to settle on a price before the banks in New York and the hedge funds in Connecticut start throwing their money around a couple of hours later and the American economic data hits the screens. Until then, traders in London can take it easy, perhaps spend an hour in the gym or browse online for Porsches and Aston Martins.

Ten-thirty is also when Derek, risk manager at RTC Capital, often visits Sarah for a chat.

He perches himself on the edge of her desk, trousers riding up to reveal five inches of hairless calves above his striped socks. 'Good numbers, eh, Sarah? From Japan. You're in for a strong day.'

Sarah keeps her eyes fixed on her screen. 'Derek, remove your bony little arse from my desk. Now.'

'Er ...'

She turns to face him. 'Which part of what I said, which bit *exactly*, made it unclear what I meant?'

The research analysts on either side of her resist the urge to stare, willing their fingers to continue typing without a pause so they can pretend they're not listening.

Derek scuttles away, back to his glass box, and Sarah returns to her screen.

She always reads the news after a hunt – people don't simply vanish without someone wondering where they are. Adult men, though, who were out drinking on a Saturday night, aren't as newsworthy as children or attractive women in their twenties, all of them the potential victims of paedophiles or rapists. Men can disappear for any number of reasons: debts, affairs, drink, drugs. Drunks stumble into rivers, family men run off with younger women. A man falls asleep in a bin in Brighton and a rubbish lorry crushes him. You can construct many scenarios in which a man gets himself into trouble. Less so a twelve-year-old.

And if the man happens to be ordinary – not a 'promising student' or 'successful lawyer' – well, there'll be no press conferences, no tearful appeals from the family. So photos of Sarah's prey just appear in the local papers or they receive at most a couple of inches in the nationals.

Now a picture of *her* is featured prominently in the online edition of the *Telegraph*. Nobody has ever suggested a link between one disappearance and another, until now.

Sarah's cursor hovers over the 'Book' button on the British Airways website – a direct flight to Hong Kong.

She'd have to abandon the houses, but most of her cash and investments are offshore – there must be $70 million after the recent market moves, years of bonuses aggressively invested.

But for all her efforts to avoid attention, her departure will create a ripple, maybe a wave. She's been profiled as one of the *Financial News*' '40 under 40 Rising Stars'. *Trader Monthly*, before it folded, mentioned her as one of the best – male or female. CNBC and Bloomberg frequently ask her to appear on TV, although she always turns them down. As soon as the traders and analysts at the desks around her discover she's gone, news stories will hit the wires.

But then all this is why nobody would identify her as a suspect. Serial killers are losers, men on the edges of society. Not self-made women.

So what – there's a photo, with a wig, eyes behind sunglasses, resolution so bad the nose is a blur?

Sit tight, Sarah. Sit tight.

* * * * * * *

'Nice car,' Phil says, pushing aside crisp packets and Coke cans with his pointy-toed shoes. 'I love old BMWs. The air-con even works. Could do with a tidy, though.'

'I always catch hipsters like you looking at it,' Martin says.

'*Hipster*? The Met's running courses for old gits so they can talk to kids?'

'I'm a couple of decades off my bus pass yet.' Martin stops at a traffic light on Piccadilly, letting a herd of shoppers and tourists stream across the road. Americans shopping for English clothes, English for American, Chinese for everything. 'My sources tell me that's the name for young chaps with beards.'

'What do you call that?'

'Stubble isn't a beard,' Martin says. 'I haven't got round to shaving for a couple of days. You probably comb that thing.'

'Hipsters wear second-hand suits,' Phil says as the light turns green. 'So who's this Dr Gross?'

'TV psychiatrist, writes dirty books about celebrity sex addicts and serial killers.'

'That fella?'

'He's actually pretty good. Seems to understand these people, helped me a few times.'

'And serial killers, you think that's what we're dealing with?'

'I believe that's the technical term for someone who commits three or more murders, Philip.'

'It's just Phil, says so on my birth certificate.' He opens the glove box and pulls out a handful of CDs. 'I think Cook's jumping the gun – talking about murder. The girl could be – what's the word? – "procuring" these pretty boys for someone. Keeping them locked up in a mansion somewhere, maybe sending them to an Arab's palace.'

'If you want human slaves, there are places around the world they're much easier to obtain.' Martin stops at a pedestrian crossing. 'What made you think the girl was disguised?'

'I play a lot of poker.'

'Any good?'

'I came thirty-seventh in the World Series last year.'

'Meaning?'

'Hundred and ninety-one thousand dollars.'

Martin can feel Phil watching, waiting for a raised eyebrow. He keeps his eyes fixed on the road as he pulls away. 'What's that got to do with it?'

'When someone acts strong, if they're a beginner, assume they have a weak hand. A raise announced in a loud, confident voice is a bluff. They whisper and they're holding a monster.'

'Always assume the opposite?'

'Assume that they're doing some … false advertising. I like to wear headphones at the table without any music playing – people think I'm not listening to what they say.'

A teenage boy darts out from between parked cars; Martin gives him a blast of the horn. 'Why join the force, then, if you've got the poker?'

'There's this FBI agent, learned to detect lies. Now he writes books and teaches people to detect bluffs.'

'So you thought you'd take your poker skills and use them to catch bad guys?'

'Yeah.'

They sit in silence for a while, the wheezy engine and the hum of traffic around them the only noise.

'The real reason?' Martin says. 'Not the bullshit you gave them in the interview, some kid playing detective.'

Phil remains silent, examining one of the CDs closely.

'Me too,' Martin says.

* * * * * * *

Sarah's been staring at the photo in the *Telegraph* for nearly fifteen minutes when her phone rings; her knee strikes the underside of her desk, almost toppling a cup of water.

An internal call.

'Hi, Dan,' she says. *Has he seen the picture?*

'Can you step into my office?'

She walks along the spacious aisles between desks piled high with screens displaying rapidly changing numbers and zig-zagging charts.

Dan's is a corner office that overlooks the Thames from thirty floors up. He closes the glass door behind her and points at the seating area where two grey sofas face each other.

He sits, his bulky frame causing the leather to creak. He's a jolly, bearded fellow who looks like he enjoys ale and hearty food. 'I hear you were a tad unfriendly towards Derek.'

'That little shit, I'll snap his neck.'

Sarah's wearing an ivory sleeveless blouse and Dan glances at her exposed, sculpted shoulders. 'I have no doubts that you could. But that's not the way we do things here, is it?'

Dan has built one of the world's largest hedge funds, despite the fact that, or perhaps because, he's a stickler for rules and fairness. His clients have come to appreciate the fund's absence from the newspapers and the regulators' hit lists.

'Oh, come on,' Sarah says. 'He stops by my desk ten times more than anyone else's.'

'You're our biggest trader, with twice as much capital as anyone else – over a billion dollars. Have you considered that?'

She takes a deep breath, then exhales through her nostrils. He's right. She certainly hasn't hit a glass ceiling here. Dan has fulfilled the promise he made in the interview.

'Are you married?' he asked her six years earlier. 'Some women find it necessary to hide their rings.'

'Not married, don't have a boyfriend. Not a lesbian. And I can't have kids, if that's what you're worried about. Can we return to my track record?'

Dan smiled, then chuckled, then shook his head. 'Sarah,' he said. 'I've already offered you a job. And I don't know what you've experienced, but RTC is like a family – my family. Yes, we're here to make money, but quite frankly, I could do that without any of you. I take an interest in my staff, and we will occasionally discuss subjects other than the market.'

Sarah nodded, her cheeks now warm.

'This is no gentleman's club. If you make twenty per cent a year, I'll give you more capital. If you lose twenty per cent, you're out. Whether you have a cock or not.'

'That's good to know.'

Dan glanced past Sarah towards the trading floor. 'In my experience, women make excellent traders. But I receive applications from fifty men for every woman. Based on that, the "fairer sex" is over-represented out there.'

* * * * * * *

Dr Karl Gross makes the detectives wait seven minutes before he lets them into his office – the oak-panelled library of an Arts and Crafts mansion near Windsor. He repeats this little ritual every time Martin visits him on business, even though the doctor was always punctual back when the appointments were personal. *A very transparent way of communicating who's doing a favour for who*, Martin thinks. *Although, knowing Karl, the transparency of the message is intentional.*

'Detective Inspector White, good to see you again,' Karl says, gripping Martin's hand. 'How are you?'

'I'm fine.'

'And the family?'

'They're fine.'

'So,' Karl says, gesturing to the seats in front of his elegant, spindly-legged antique desk. 'What can … You didn't introduce your colleague.'

'DS Burton,' Phil says.

'What can I do for you?' Karl says while eyeing Phil.

'Give the doctor an update,' Martin says, enjoying the sight of Karl's wrinkled brow. *He'll be wondering why I'm no longer working alone.*

Phil squirms in his seat. 'Er … What am I allowed to say?'

'If I couldn't keep my mouth shut,' Karl says, 'I'd very quickly go out of business. People come to me to discuss deeply private matters. It's my job.'

Phil hesitates, then describes the Gary Burke disappearance, the belief that it's related to others. He shows Karl a few photographs. 'But we're struggling with a motive.'

'Do you have reason to believe the case is appropriate, that it is compatible with my principles?'

'Principles?'

'The doctor,' Martin says, 'isn't a fan of ours. He has a few issues with the way we go about our business–'

'–It's not the police, specifically,' Karl interrupts. 'It's the entire system – justice, political, social.'

'Right,' Phil says, looking at Martin with a frown.

'Offenders were often victims in their youth,' Karl says. 'Sexual abuse, violence, drugs, poverty, mental illness – they feed off each other. You can either disrupt the cycle with the appropriate therapeutic interventions or you can exacerbate the problem with incarceration.'

'Can we have a quick word?' Phil says to his colleague, standing up, straightening his jacket. 'Outside.'

Martin raises his eyebrows at Karl and follows Phil into the waiting area.

He knows about the intercom – he spoke to Karl over it when he was a patient. The setup seems a bit weird – no receptionist or other staff, just Karl in this big old house. All the celebrities probably appreciate the discretion, though. Perhaps there are a couple having a lie-down upstairs.

'You sure about this?' Phil says.

'Why wouldn't I be?'

'The boss seemed pretty clear … he wanted to keep things as quiet as possible.'

'The doctor won't be a problem.'

'I … what about these … "principles" he's going on about? Sounds like he'll fuck us over if he thinks the killer's daddy liked a drink.'

'Listen, Cook understands how I work. You? Well, I'm not sure how knowing whether a royal flush beats four of a kind will help us.'

'He knows how I work too, fella.'

'And maybe he thinks you need to learn a couple of things.'

'For your information–'

'And how do you think this makes us look? Gross knows we're arguing out here, he's a psychiatrist.'

Phil gives Martin a long, hard stare as the DI opens the door to Karl's office and waves the DS back in.

Karl stands looking out of the window, distancing himself from the desk speaker he was no doubt using to eavesdrop. 'Shall we continue?' he asks the detectives as they sit down.

'Please,' Martin says.

Karl doesn't turn around to speak. 'A woman picks up a man in a bar and he's never seen again. What's going on?'

'Yeah, that's what we're trying to figure out,' Phil says.

'I'm framing the question,' Karl says. 'Have a little patience – I am, after all, the one offering my services to you, for no charge.'

'Right,' Phil says. 'Go on.'

'The typical profiles of females involved in serial murder are the black widow – who kills for financial gain – and the acolyte, who is doing the bidding of her male partner,' Karl says. 'But a profile is only a loose collective description of people who have been caught in the past. Occasionally they can be useful, but they're no help when you're confronted with a case which requires a little … imagination.' He finally turns around and looks at Phil. 'What are your thoughts?'

'Well … there's no sign of her taking money from the victims. I think maybe she could be working for someone who has a taste for pretty boys or who sells them on.'

Karl shakes his head. 'There are cities where human slaves are far easier to obtain than London.'

Martin smirks at Phil.

'Detective Inspector White,' Karl says, 'I'd like to hear your observations.'

'On the videos, she seems calm, in complete control.'

'Control. It's interesting you say that.' Karl raises a finger to his chin. 'There are various mental disorders where a sufferer may be detached, or experience inappropriate emotions in a given situation. And a classic psychopath can appear restrained, then shock you with their impulsive behaviour. For your information … Sorry, I'm afraid that I've forgotten ...'

'Phil.'

'Yes,' Karl says with a tiny smile. 'For your information, Phil, although we can't fully explain the roots of their behaviour, true psychopaths are almost certainly not the product of broken homes and poverty. For that reason, I'm happy to aid you in capturing one.'

'You think she …' Phil says. 'You've worked with women – violent psychopaths?'

'They're rare. Men are more prone to emotional detachment, aggression, risk-taking. And women typically find non-violent ways to harm others.'

'You should see some of the girls rolling out of the pubs on a Saturday night,' Phil says.

'Well,' Karl says. 'There's a belief that women are becoming more like men. Violent crimes committed by them are increasing. We hear about girl gangs, drunken fights, generally loutish behaviour. There are various theories about this, many of which are nonsense.' He sits back down behind his desk, as if he's finally ready to get down to business. 'She's attractive, which suggests she isn't the most basic type of serial killer, who is really just a rapist trying to eliminate the key witness.'

'What you're telling us is all a bit ... general,' Phil says.

Karl tuts. 'How many serial killers have you met?' he says. 'My number's seventeen. I've spent many thousands of hours studying still others.'

Phil says nothing.

'I assume that your silence means you haven't met a single one. I'll continue,' Karl says, obviously straining to prevent a smug grin spreading across his face. 'What do the victims have in common? Any indication they're into S&M?'

'They're all very straight. Good-looking boys,' Martin says, feeling a little self-conscious as he uses those words in the doctor's office.

'And she's attractive enough to make them leave without a word to their friends?'

'Doesn't make sense, does it?' Phil says.

Karl rests his elbows on the desk and leans forward. 'Some of my clients – rich, famous men – have no trouble attracting women. Yet they pay for sex because they crave the things normal girls won't do, or they're simply aroused by handing over money, owning someone.' Karl picks up a photo of the woman. 'Now I'm speculating here ... She could be doing this for someone else, simply be the bait. But if she's the killer, and it's not about money, then she must need something she can't obtain from a normal encounter.'

'And that would be what?' Phil says.

Karl stands up again, palms on his desk, looming over the detectives. 'Human desire, sexuality. It can manifest itself in particularly dark ways.'

There's a moment of silence as all three men ponder those words.

'Asphyxiation, disfigurement, torture. Sadism, vampirism, cannibalism. Sex and violence. Pleasure and pain. When boundaries are crossed, when fear of punishment or empathy for one's fellow human beings is absent, and all that remains are obsession, delusion and gratification … well,' Karl says, 'in those cases … the possibilities are endless.'

* * * * * * *

Martin returns home without Phil, who went back to the office to review files on the disappearances.

The house is empty – Charlotte's at her mother's in Surrey with Molly – but he still closes and locks the door to his study. He slips a DVD into his laptop and watches the CCTV footage again.

The blonde walks into the club and up the stairs to the cloakroom. She doesn't look around, for cameras or eyes, but she's not straining to avoid them either. When she waits for service – the glass, of course, being washed an hour later, erasing any fingerprints – she doesn't tap on the bar or wave a credit card. And her body language when speaking to Gary: no crossed arms or leaning away. When they leave, she leads.

He sits through the film another five times. She seems confident, in control. That's it.

The dark things Karl spoke about – the psychopathic tendencies – are they the key? Is he looking at a woman unable to understand the moral implications of what she's doing, someone with a taste for brutality and death?

He switches from the DVD to the internet.

There are thousands of videos involving 'dominant' women, whipping gimp-masked, skinny men; pinching their nipples; squeezing their balls. Perhaps the camera causes the wooden speech and over-acting, but the performances are unconvincing. The women aren't really into it, losing themselves in a frenzy that could become fatal. And of course, the men are willing participants, experiencing discomfort that will be over within minutes. They're not fighting to stay alive.

The vampire stuff is soft-focus, stagey and self-conscious. The men are usually in control. Even the genuine role reversals – women with strap-ons, penetrating men – are unconvincing. No passion.

None of this stuff could escalate to murder. He has to look further, not accept the obvious.

The photo of Molly on his desk catches Martin's eye. He kisses his fingertips, touches the picture, then turns it face down before trawling through more porn sites.

He discovers another video. The woman is huge, a bodybuilder, tanned skin stretched over thick arms and breast implants. Her frizzy hair and the man's moustache suggest it's an old film, probably copied from VHS. It starts slowly. She lifts him off the ground in a bear hug, throws him on the bed. She lies on him, smothering him with her chest, making him stroke her muscles. But when she gets on top, one hand around his throat, pinning him to the bed while she pumps up and down – it's clear that *she's* fucking *him*. She's in control.

The woman in the CCTV footage has the same definition in her shoulders, the same curve of the bicep, albeit on a much smaller scale. *Am I onto something?* Martin wonders.

There are more videos of the bodybuilder, but most of them are simply wrestling matches. She throws men around like they're crash test dummies, pins them, taunts them. Martin isn't sure whether his curiosity is purely professional when he googles the woman's name, Amazon Kara, and 'contact details'

The first result is a website, listing women who wrestle men. There are photos, stats (biceps, bench press, cup size), email addresses and phone numbers. Martin scans the list of women who operate in the UK. There are a few bodybuilders, but also girls who are five foot four and a hundred and twenty pounds, which is – he takes a minute to calculate – eight and a half stone. He searches for videos of these smaller women. There's plenty of fantasy stuff – he's learning the lingo – but also competitive matches where the women show off their martial arts skills: complicated arm locks, chokes and throws. Some of them even go up against each other, cage fighting, drawing blood.

These women, Martin thinks, *they're violent.*

And they're not acting.

* * * * * * *

Less than five minutes after Dan releases Sarah from his office, he fires out an email, inviting everyone to a bar in the City.

She always tries to avoid these events, with their need for small talk: 'Good weekend?' 'Yeah, picked up a guy in a club on Saturday night, stripped him naked, hunted him through the grounds of my estate and killed him with my bare hands. Sunday I just chilled out and disposed of the body. You?'

But the timing isn't a coincidence. Dan wants to bring the RTC family together – he'll no doubt wave Sarah over when he's chatting to Derek.

The entire firm is crowded into a roped-off area of the bar, ordering drinks from slim European waiting staff in maroon aprons that match the wallpaper and the livery of the booths. Occasionally men in their early twenties stop and point at Dan – if money is their religion then he's at least a demigod. Sarah's relieved to receive attention purely for the way she looks; a cheeky grin is more welcome than a knowing nod.

'Any plans for the weekend?' Amanda says. Sarah's been cornered by Marcus from sales and his latest girlfriend.

'Relaxing at my place in the Cotswolds,' Sarah says, smiling and staring into the distance.

'Ooh, that would be lovely, wouldn't it?' Amanda says, turning to Marcus. 'I could do with a break from London every now and then.'

Marcus flares his nostrils. 'I took you away last month, forgotten about that?' he says.

'Oh, yeah, we went to Dubai, stayed in an unbelievable hotel. We got our own butler!' Amanda says, waiting for Sarah's eyes to widen at the thought of such luxury.

A waiter approaches Marcus, who holds a full glass. 'I think we're OK here. No, wait. Sarah – what are you having?'

'Nothing. I don't drink.'

Marcus smirks. 'Of course not. The trading robot, always in control.'

Sarah gives him a Terminator glare.

'A small glass of Chardonnay?' he says. 'Or a sherry? My granny used to like sherry.'

'Just doesn't agree with me,' she says. *Has Marcus heard about the Derek incident,* she wonders, *the reason Dan summoned us here tonight?* Maybe that's why he possesses the confidence to speak like this to someone infinitely more important to the firm than him.

'We all wake up with a headache the morning after.' Marcus winks.

Amanda nudges him with her elbow.

'No, it's ... you know the film *Gremlins*?' Sarah says. 'When they get wet, bad things happen. I'm like that with alcohol.'

'I don't recall any of the Gremlins dancing on a table and ending up on the toilet floor with their knickers round their ankles.'

Amanda elbows him hard.

An image of Marcus – eyes wide, mouth twisted – flashes across Sarah's mind. She can hear his sobs, and her laughter.

Sarah snatches his drink and swallows it in three gulps, the soapy gin and tonic almost making her gag. She sucks an ice cube for a few seconds to prevent the alcohol coming right back up, before crunching and swallowing it.

Marcus's hand still clutches a glass that's no longer there.

'Bring me another one of those,' Sarah says to the waiter. 'And one for him.'

She retrieves her phone from her bag and sends a message.

Half an hour and two G and Ts later, her phone vibrates. She excuses herself and steps outside to find Jake already halfway through a cigarette. This is his only addiction, which makes him a reliable coke dealer.

'Sarah, Sarah, Sarah. Been a while – what can I do for you?'

She looks around. A couple of girls in short skirts and high heels are smoking a few feet away, but they're too deep in conversation about a male colleague to overhear anything. 'I need something very specific.'

'Why doesn't that surprise me?'

'I remember a while back some pills–'

'*Pills?*' he says, making sure she's talking about ecstasy, not the tablets you get on prescription.

'Yes.'

'Not so popular anymore, kids only want the MDMA powder,' he says with a nostalgic look in his eye.

'I know. Anyway, apparently these were … fast. Comedown arrived in a couple of hours, like … tumbling off an infinite cliff. Horrible.'

'And you want them why?'

'Just want to speed things up, for convenience.'

Jake nods, although there's no way he could begin to imagine what she means. 'How many?' he says.

'One.'

'And you need it …'

'What time is it now … six-forty-five? Has to be by nine-thirty.'

Jake gives her a weary smile. 'You're asking me to track down something that may or may not have existed for many years, something that is, essentially, crap that nobody would willingly buy? And you want it now?'

'I pay for time and effort. You know that.'

Jake takes a long drag on his cigarette, flicks it into the road and pulls a pack from his pocket. 'How much?' he says, tapping another one from the box.

'Before nine-thirty, a grand. After that, a hundred.'

'You're killing me.'

'We have a deal?' Sarah says, fixing him with a flirtatious look and a little smile.

Jake sighs, slips the cigarette back in the box and pulls his phone out of his jacket pocket. 'Deal.'

Sarah kisses him of the cheek, then says, 'One more thing. A gram of coke, the good stuff.' She smiles again. 'It's for me.'

* * * * * *

Martin straightens in his chair and rubs his neck. The streetlight outside his window flickered to life an hour ago. He's eaten nothing since breakfast, watching video after video, scrolling through hundreds of forum posts and photos. He needs to stand up, get out and talk to someone, face to face.

The wrestling site with the reviews and contact details is American, but there's a European section of the forum, moderated by someone called 'fbbguru1'. He's posted thousands of times, the last only ten minutes earlier, and it seems as if he lives in or near London.

Martin sends him a private message: 'CAN I ASK YOU A COUPLE OF QUESTIONS?'

The response is instant. 'BEFORE YOU ASK ME ANYTHING, HAVE YOU SEARCHED THE SITE, CHECKED OUT THE FAQS?'

'I WAS WONDERING IF WE COULD MEET UP.'

'THAT YOU SUSAN?'

'WHO'S SUSAN?'

'A FORMER MISS UNIVERSE WHO DOESN'T LIKE WHAT I'VE BEEN SAYING ABOUT HER ON THE INTERNET.'

Martin smirks, his fingers hovering over the keyboard for a few seconds. 'I'M A DETECTIVE WITH THE MET.'

'RIGHT. WHAT DO YOU WANT?'

'I CAN'T SAY HERE. WE SHOULD MEET.'

'IF YOU'RE REALLY WITH THE MET, YOU CAN FIND ME.'

That might take a while. 'YOU SUGGEST A PUBLIC PLACE.'

There's no response. Martin picks up his phone and scrolls through his contacts, wondering if he should go through Cook to get an ID on fbbguru1 or start the wheels turning right away.

A new message pops up. 'OK, YOU'VE GOT ME CURIOUS NOW,' fbbguru1 says. 'IF YOU DON'T TALK TO ME, YOU'LL GO TO SOMEONE ELSE. YOU'RE IN LONDON RIGHT NOW?'

'YES,' Martin says, standing up as he types.

'CAN YOU BE AT THE HARE & BILLET IN BLACKHEATH IN AN HOUR?'

'I'LL SEE YOU THERE.'

* * * * * * *

Sarah returns downstairs and stands with Marcus, Amanda and a couple of men she vaguely recognises. A minute later, the two strangers drain their drinks and depart.

'So how long have you two been together?' Sarah says.

'It's been, what …'

'Four months,' Amanda says, beaming.

Marcus shifts from one foot to the other.

'How did you meet?'

'I caught this naughty boy checking me out at the gym.'

'I think you were checking me out too,' Marcus says, flexing a bicep.

'Have you met the parents?'

Marcus's smile evaporates. 'Not yet,' he says, watching Sarah warily. He examines his drink for a few seconds, then the flicker of a new thought spreads across his face. 'Oh, by the way, I've got a client who keeps pestering me to arrange a meeting with you. Runs a wealth management firm for women.'

'How much is she good for?' Sarah's not interested but recognises the opportunity.

'If you're going to talk shop, I'll search for fun somewhere else,' Amanda says.

Sarah waits for her to disappear to the bathroom before speaking. 'If I asked you to leave with me,' she says, 'what would you do?'

Marcus's glass stops short of his mouth.

'I know, you and Amanda …'

He takes a gulp of his drink, lowers the glass slowly. He scrutinises Sarah for a few seconds. When she gives him a small smile, he grins. 'I'll tell her I've got an early meeting. You want to go now?'

'No, no, I promised Dan I'd stay for a while. And it's too early to be making that sort of excuse, if you need a decent alibi.'

* * * * * * *

It doesn't take a detective to spot fbbguru1: somewhere near fifty, bald on top, thick forearms and powerful hands gripping a pint of Guinness. He's the only one sitting on his own – at a corner table – in the newly refurbished pub: white tiles on the walls, pale stripped wooden floors.

'Hi,' Martin says, holding out his hand.

The man looks up without smiling. 'Got any ID?'

Martin hands his warrant card over.

The man takes a photo of it with his phone and gives it back. 'You don't look like a copper.'

'That's the idea.'

The man thinks about this for a second, then gestures for Martin to sit down at the table. 'Colin,' he says. 'Want a drink?'

'I'll pass.'

'Oh, you're on duty, something like that. Anyway,' Colin says, looking around the pub and then back at Martin, 'what's this about? Somebody get hurt?'

'Maybe,' Martin says.

Colin takes a sip of his beer, places the glass on the table. 'Listen, *you* asked to see *me*.'

'I did,' Martin says, taking his turn to scan the pub. None of the twenty-somethings are interested in him and Colin; the roar of alcohol-fuelled conversation and laughter will make it difficult for anyone to overhear them. 'What I'm about to discuss, well … it might seem like gossip but it's important that it stays just between us.'

'Understood,' Colin says, looking suitably solemn, although his eyes widened when Martin said 'gossip'.

'I'm working on a murder investigation.'

'Murder?' Colin says, a little too loud. A young couple nearby halt their conversation for a moment and look over. 'Oh, er … sorry.'

'Perhaps this was a mistake,' Martin says, getting up, although he's only playing a little game.

'I can keep a secret,' Colin says, his eyes pleading.

'Looks like you swap of lot of stories online.'

'Yeah, well … that's less serious. A hobby.'

Martin stares at Colin for a few seconds and then sits down. 'We think a woman might be involved. A violent woman.'

'Involved how?'

'I can't say.'

'So what do you want from me?'

Martin lays his hands on the table. 'I've just got this hunch, this feeling, that it's a kind of dominance thing, you know?'

'You think whoever got killed was into wrestling?'

'No … but that's not something we've checked. Interesting.' Martin pulls a notebook from his inside pocket. 'It seems, at least from the CCTV footage we've got, that the victims don't know her.'

'Victims? There's more than one?'

'We don't know that, either.'

Colin leans back in his seat and takes a couple of sips from his pint. 'Seems like you don't know much. Seems like you're just fishing. Or worse …'

'Worse?'

'Happens in the sex trade, a lot. Some bloke posing as a copper, or maybe he is a copper, shaking down the girls, looking for freebies.'

Martin frowns. 'Why would I be talking to you then, why not go straight to the girls?'

'Maybe you want me to introduce you to them, make you look legit.'

Martin looks Colin in the eye, as seriously as he can. 'Listen, I'm sure you get a lot of weirdos on your site, hear plenty of stories about dodgy characters. But just take your phone out, search for my name, or search for the "Knightsbridge Killer" case. I've been a homicide detective for fifteen years.'

Colin does as he's told, scrolling through the old news reports, raising his eyebrows or nodding occasionally. 'I'll give you the benefit of the doubt,' he says, putting the phone away. 'So this hunch you've got, about dominance, what's the story?'

'Some wrestling videos I saw online, I could imagine her in them.'

'Sure you're not imagining you and her in the videos?' Colin says, grinning.

'I'm not into that stuff.'

''Course not.'

Martin smiles – he knows Colin is only teasing. 'But they opened my eyes a little, suggested certain things,' he says. 'Now some of the women in the videos look like they're having fun, and others are obviously going through the motions–'

'Yeah, I know the type.'

I'll bet you do, Martin thinks. *Probably write sniffy reviews of them and get yourself in trouble.* 'But a few of the women were really into it, violent, maybe even a little sadistic.'

Colin closes his eyes, takes a deep breath. 'A fight to the death, the ultimate way to go.'

'Well … Have you ever heard any stories about that, credible ones?'

Colin opens his eyes and nods. 'It's talked about a lot. A lot. But … not good for repeat business.'

'Did you ever get the feeling, though, that given the chance anyone you've met would go all the way?'

'That would probably be wishful thinking.' Colin says. 'But …'

'Go on.'

Colin stares into the distance, squinting a little. 'There was this girl, must be about ten years ago. Went by the name of Bellona.'

'Sounds Italian.'

'No, she was definitely English. The "real" Bellona was a Roman goddess of war. Women wrestlers often use fake names. Anyway, she had an edge, a certain … brutality to her.'

Martin takes a few photos from his inside pocket, hands them to Colin. 'Could this be her?'

Colin examines the pictures one by one. 'I can't say. Long time ago and these aren't great.'

Martin takes them back. 'Can you describe what she looked like?'

'Black hair, but really black, like it was dyed. Five foot seven, maybe eight. Pretty tall. Her eyes … I don't remember.'

'Any marks, moles?'

'Sorry, it was years ago.'

Martin scribbles more notes. 'This edge she had …'

Colin leans forward and places his elbows on the table. 'Most people who work out, do martial arts, they like to feel strong, you know. Maybe the big kids pushed them around at school. But for a woman, a certain kind of woman, she gets a massive buzz out of physically controlling a man, showing him who's boss.'

'What was different about Bellona?'

'Well, the wrestlers, they're business people. You pay them by the hour, whether you want to feel their muscles a little bit or fight. And I'll save you asking – some of the girls will go all the way, but most won't.' Colin stops, drains his beer and looks at Martin.

'I'll get you another one,' Martin says.

He watches as the barman pulls Colin's Guinness two thirds full and lets it settle. Martin can almost taste that creamy white head. 'Make it two,' he says. He tries to tell himself that having a beer with Colin will build some rapport, get him to open up more, but really, he just wants a drink.

'Where was I?' Colin says when Martin sits back down. 'Oh, yeah. Some of the women, especially the professional bodybuilders who are getting on a bit, they won't wrestle you in a competitive way – it's too easy to get injured. But Bellona would only wrestle, and hard. You wanted to do anything else and she'd stop answering emails.' Colin takes a sip of Guinness then wipes his lips. 'You agreed a code word when you got in the room, to let her know you really wanted to stop, and she'd make you say it over and over.'

'That could be part of the act,' Martin says. 'Don't take this personally, but I'm sure this went down pretty well with some of you.'

Colin smirks. 'You remember that James Bond film, *Goldeneye*?'

'I saw that one.'

'There's the villain, the woman – Xenia Onatopp. Bloody good name, by the way. Anyway, she's fighting Bond and she gets him between her legs, she's squeezing and she's moaning like she's in a porno.'

'I remember,' Martin says.

'I bet you do. Now, Bellona, when she had a man saying the code word, screaming or trying to scream while she was choking him, she'd be panting, her cheeks red. Like yours,' Colin says with a conspiratorial smile.

'How many times did you see her?' Martin says, not sure whether it was the first sip of Guinness or a blush that's got him feeling warm.

'Once – that was all I could get and … well, maybe she was a bit much for me.'

'Really? Sounds like she's about as good as it gets.'

'We're not all into the same thing,' Colin says. He leans back, seems to be chewing on something. 'When I was ten, my big sister's friend caught me peeping at her when she was getting changed. She chased me, pinned me down and pulled all my clothes off.'

Martin wonders whether Colin's telling him this for a reason.

'So … I'm not into the pain stuff, more like humiliation. And anyway, Bellona was bloody hard to meet, asked a lot of questions. And expensive.'

'How much?'

'Towards the end it was five hundred quid an hour. She went overseas a lot – probably Japanese businessmen, Arabs. She'd only meet in hotels, give you the address just before the appointment. And the room was dark, just one lamp, with a cloth over it.'

'Any idea why?'

'This girl was private. Can't always believe these stories, but I heard she broke someone's arm when she saw a camera in their bag.'

'I don't suppose she ever talked about her background, anything that might place her?'

'No chit-chat. You agreed the code word and that was it, apart from trash-talking, calling you names, asking where it hurt.'

'Any rumours about who she was?'

Colin holds up his hands. 'Loads of them. She was from a rich family, she had a high-profile day-job, she was wanted by the police ...'

Martin hesitates just as he's about to sip his pint. 'Really?'

'Just rumours. Only thing that seemed believable was her being a student. She was probably early twenties and did her overseas tours for a few weeks at Easter, Christmas and over the summer.'

'So what happened to her?'

'After about eighteen months she just disappeared.'

'She paid her way through university and then quit?'

'Maybe,' Colin says. 'There was one bloke, we spent a lot of time together. After she vanished, he posted on the forum, swore he'd seen her in Thailand. I can show you.' Colin takes out his smartphone, taps the screen, hands it to Martin. 'Says she walked right past him in Bangkok. She'd changed her hair colour, but he said it was definitely her. She looked right through him.'

Martin reads the post, scrolls up and down looking for more. 'Where can I find him, he's still in Thailand?'

'Oh, no. Graeme used to go there a couple of times a year, wasn't just into wrestling, dirty bugger, but, anyway, he's dead.'

'What?'

'Before you get your knickers in a twist, it wasn't her. He smoked like a chimney, drank all day. We were down the pub when he keeled over. Massive heart attack.'

Martin taps a finger on his pint glass, stares at the bottom. 'Maybe she set herself up somewhere else.'

'No way. She's a legend, worldwide. There are blokes with plenty of cash that want to spend it on her. Heard a couple hired private investigators – they couldn't find a thing.'

'They might have something I can use. They're on the forums?'

'Nope. These rich types like their privacy as well. You'll struggle to even find out who really saw her. Lot of fantasists. And if you did see her, she told you not to post a review. People obeyed her orders.'

'How do you know so much about her then?'

'One bloke tells someone at his gym or a bodybuilding show, Chinese whispers.'

'So it could all be nonsense,' Martin says. 'She could have just settled down, had kids, became a primary school teacher.

Colin shakes his head. 'I only met her once, but I'm telling you: she was mean. I'd give her the code word and she'd wait a few seconds, put on more pressure, inflict a bit of extra pain.'

'She's a sadist.'

'She … came alive when she was fighting. And I got the feeling that she really, really didn't want to stop squeezing, didn't want to let go.'

'So …'

'This girl is either dead or … she's gone underground – and she's hurting men.'

* * * * * * *

Sarah is observing herself in the glass partition that separates her and Marcus from the taxi driver, as if the reflection is of someone else – a reckless twin over whom she has no control. Back at the bar, she insisted on drinking shots of tequila – before tonight it had been over ten years since she'd had a drink.

'I'm sorry, about the drinking … I shouldn't have pushed you,' Marcus says. 'I was like a little boy pulling your hair to get your attention.'

'Don't worry about it.' She reaches into her bag and finds the pair of two-inch-square paper packets Jake delivered just in time. 'You're lucky,' he'd said. 'Someone tried to flood London with this crap a few years ago. Nobody could shift them once word got out. I don't even know what it is. And it's old, so no guarantees.'

Sarah opens one of the packets, pours a short line of coke onto her thumb and snorts it. Then she takes the pill out and shows it to Marcus. He leans his head away from her, as if assessing the situation from a slightly different angle will explain this unexpected development.

'Trust me.' She places the pill on her tongue, leans over and kisses Marcus, pushing it into his mouth. She pulls away.

He hesitates, letting the pill sit on his tongue, then swallows.

'You've had it before?'

He shakes his head.

'You'll enjoy it.'

Marcus relaxes in his seat and smiles. 'You're full of surprises tonight.'

Sarah glances at her reflection again. 'I haven't even started yet.'

* * * * * *

Martin's back at home, in his study, hunched over his laptop.

Colin didn't exaggerate – Bellona's a legend. There are pages of discussions, written by people who tried and failed to meet her, or came to the scene too late. There are no photos, but Martin finds a thread where people post drawings of what she might look like. There are beauty spots, furry warrior queen outfits, huge breasts. Blue eyes, red eyes. Dark skin and light.

Am I chasing a myth?

Colin's met her and seems convinced she's capable of extreme violence. Perhaps all the speculation and fantasies have twisted his ten-year-old memories. And nothing, except an athletic physique, links her to the crimes.

He ignores Phil's calls, letting them go to voicemail.

Another day has passed, bringing the next disappearance closer and he's trawling the internet, looking for a fantasy woman who disappeared a decade ago.

The only real lead – no, the possibility of a lead – is in Thailand, backpacker central. He can imagine how that investigation would go: 'A woman, in her early twenties, in Bangkok. She was here a few years ago. No, I can't tell you what she looked like.'

Martin sighs, closes his laptop and says goodnight to the photo of his daughter.

* * * * * * *

Marcus sits on a modernist black leather sofa in a dazzlingly white room. The fireplace is black marble, but the curtains, carpet, furniture – all white. There's no clutter, none of the knick-knacks women seem to love. The paintings on the walls are abstract, monochromatic. 'Nice place you've got,' he says, shivering, although he isn't cold. *A big house like this,* he thinks, *in Holland Park. Must be worth fifteen million. Maybe twenty.*

'I don't spend much time here, between the office and the house in the Cotswolds,' Sarah says, sprinkling a line of coke onto the table.

'Yeah … I … er.' He takes a couple of deep breaths, exhaling through his mouth. He's shaking in the same way he does when he's about to close a big deal. 'I … yeah, something's definitely happening.'

Sarah finishes off the coke, then looks up. 'Oh yes,' she says. 'It's happening.'

Marcus rubs his palms on his trousers. 'Wow, this … unnn.'

She passes him a stick of chewing gum. 'Tell me when you need more.'

'Righto,' Marcus says, popping it in and chomping furiously. 'You know what?' he says.

'What?' Sarah says, smiling the way you smile at an excited child who's infected you with their enthusiasm.

'I can't believe I'm here, you know. I mean, I can believe it because I'm here, we're here together, you know, but I can't believe it.'

'You're going to be a talker, aren't you?'

'Is that OK? If you want me to be quiet I can be, but I feel like I really need to talk to you, I've got so much to tell you. Is it OK if I stand up for a minute?'

Sarah nods.

Marcus stands. 'Whoa, I'm going to sit down now. What was I saying? Oh, yeah, I was shocked when you said, "What would you do if I just said let's go?" because my whole life, I mean obviously not when I was a baby, but my whole life since I was a bit younger, no matter who I've been going out with, there's always been someone, who I thought: Say the word and I'll drop anything and travel anywhere with you.'

'You're a romantic.'

'Maybe, but it's ... yeah, I go from one person to the next, but it's not cynical, you know – if anything, it's naïve – I always think there's something better, for me, out there. And maybe, especially with these fantasy women, it's just that. Like with you, I don't know you that well and I've constructed this idea of you. I mean you're hot, oh, my God, you're so hot and I know it's inappropriate but your body ... and those eyes. I think about you a lot. A lot.'

'I'm flattered,' Sarah says, then does another line of coke.

'God, I'm talking a lot, I hope you don't mind but it's all coming out. You're tough, you know, won't take any shit. I don't get involved with that kind of girl, I like to be the boss, maybe that's why you're the fantasy, you're unknown, different. When you wear those boots to work, you know the ones I'm talking about, I imagine you in nothing but, wow, I've crossed a line now, that line is a speck in the distance, it's light years away, it doesn't even exist any more ...'

Sarah gets up to turn on a stereo. The music, it isn't really dance music, it's the kind of stuff they play in bars, in the background.

'So with Amanda it's OK, she's nice, you know–'

'Marcus.'

'But she can be annoying–'

'Marcus.'

'Did you hear that? My voice is loud in my head!'

'Marcus!'

'Yeah?'

'Close your eyes and listen to the music.'

'Oh, OK.'

He's sitting by a hotel pool, watching the sun setting over the ocean. Sarah lies on a sunbed next to him. They're surrounded by tanned men and women, youthful and slim, their hair thick and luxurious, and they all have these eyebrows that look like they've been drawn with a marker pen. The women's bodies are identical: long, caramel-coloured legs; breasts threatening to spill out of white bikini tops. And Marcus recognises the men's bodies – the hours he's sweated and pushed himself in the gym, the sunbathing in Dubai.

One song melts into another and everything – the hotel, the people, the sun-reflecting waves – moves in time with the beat.

The music stops.

Marcus opens his eyes. 'How long was I listening for?'

Sarah sits on a sofa opposite. She checks her watch. 'An hour and forty-nine minutes.'

'Wow.' Marcus grins and shakes his head. 'You want to know what I was thinking about?'

Sarah raises a finger to her lips, stands up and puts more music on.

Marcus recognises the song: 'Fever' by Peggy Lee.

His heart vibrates with every bang of the drum; the female vocals send tingles all over his scalp.

Sarah slips off her shoes. She keeps her eyes on Marcus's, doesn't blink once as she undresses, rolling down tights, unbuttoning her sleeveless shirt.

Marcus shifts from one buttock to the other, taps the arm of the sofa with his fingers.

The skirt drops. She's in her underwear now – black, lacy, small. Her bra hits the carpet and suddenly Marcus's skull is cold, the leather of the sofa slimy against his fingertips.

Has the music stopped?

No, it's … slowed down. The singer's voice is deep; the drums sound as if they're skinned with elastic.

She's still staring at him as she steps out of her knickers.

Please don't look at me.

'This is what you wanted, isn't it?' she says.

'I …feel …wrong.' His thoughts, his speech, his breathing – inertia diffusing throughout his body stifles them all.

'Follow me.'

'I … can I stay here?'

'You can lie down on my bed.'

Marcus heaves himself up, shuffles out of the room after her and up the stairs.

Another white room. Old-fashioned brass bed, antique-style furniture – all white.

'Remove your clothes, fold them up and place them neatly on that chair.'

Marcus follows her orders.

'Everything.'

He steps out of his briefs, lays them on top of the pile. His cock has shrunk, small as he's ever seen it. He wishes somebody would hand him a blanket so he can hide.

'You can get on the bed now.'

He lies on his side, knees to his chest, watching her.

She opens a wardrobe – the lining is vivid purple. Handcuffs and strips of leather hang from the door.

'I'll be going now,' Marcus says, pushing himself up on his hands and knees.

'Stay on the bed.'

He goes to the chair where he left his clothes.

Sarah rushes past the bed and shoves him against the wall. She wraps an arm around his bicep, the other hand gripping his wrist.

'You feel the pressure on your elbow?' she says. 'I apply a little more and you'll need surgeries – plural.'

Marcus's eyes are wide. He's unable to speak.

'I can't promise not to hurt you, but if you behave yourself, then nothing will get broken. You have my word.'

She lets go of his arm and steps back.

He leaps over the bed, grabs the door handle.

'It's locked,' she says, walking up behind him, landing a sickening punch – a liver shot – to his lower back. Marcus has to grip the door handle to stay on his feet.

Sarah shoves him back onto the bed.

She takes a large mahogany box from the shelf in the wardrobe.

If she wants to tie him up and hold a gun to his head while they fuck, well, there's nothing he can do. But if she's going to cut him, or pull out a syringe and give him more drugs, he's going through the door.

She flips the lid and there it is: shiny and red, a ball on the end of a gently curving, ribbed shaft. Leather fastenings are attached to the base.

Marcus has seen strap-on dildos in videos, but not one like this. He looks frantically around the room. There are keys in his pocket, shoes on the floor. Weapons.

He manages to get off the bed for only a second before she lands on his back, arm around his throat. She slides off him and he feels a knee jab his left thigh, then the right. Her foot connects with his ankle and he's on the floor again.

Sarah walks to the wardrobe, returns and cuffs Marcus's wrists in front of him. She grabs him by the hair, pulls him up and shoves him face down on to the bed. She climbs on the bed and, pulling his arms above his head, ties the cuffs to the bed frame with a short length of black rope. 'I was going to start gently, work my way in, but not now.'

A distant voice urges Marcus to fight.

But another voice speaks louder. *There's no point*, it says. *Everything is inevitable.* Whatever was in that pill has robbed him of hope.

She stuffs a pillow under his stomach.

'Watch me put it on.'

He feels tears well in his eyes and half-closes them so the liquid stays in his lashes, blurring his vision. But he can't ignore the angry red stick protruding from her silhouette.

Music starts. Marcus knows this song too: Madonna's 'What It Feels Like for a Girl'.

Giggling. 'It was the first thing that came into my mind when I heard this. How could you possibly think of anything else?'

The bed creaks as she climbs onto it.

Something cold brushes the inside of Marcus's thigh, high up. She puts her knees between his, spreads his legs a few inches wider.

'Please don't. Please.'

Sarah lies on him, her small, strong hands gripping his wrists. He buries his face in a pillow and wails.

'Not what you had in mind, is it?' she says.

She prods him gently, then he feels her pulling her hips back. He braces himself.

He waits.

And waits.

But the pain doesn't come.

He hears her slide off the bed.

'This was a mistake,' she says, leaning over and removing his cuffs. 'Put on your clothes and go.'

Marcus looks at her for a second. *Is she playing a game?*

'Out. Before I change my mind.'

Marcus hurries over to the chair and pulls his clothes on while Sarah watches. He struggles to button his trousers and shirt with shaking hands.

When he's done, Sarah unlocks the bedroom door, waving him through.

He hobbles down the stairs, one by one, gripping the bannister, his legs aching from the blows she landed.

How will he make sure she's punished for this?

He won't.

He has to keep this a secret. Whether he goes to Dan or the police, details will emerge. It will be all over the City. The story – female trader drugs and almost rapes salesman – it will define him forever.

'Turn right and walk for a couple of minutes, you'll find a taxi rank.'

He pauses at the front door, glances back at her.

Sarah stands halfway up the staircase, looking down on him, naked.

There's a flash of rage in her eyes.

Then disappointment.

Wednesday August 14th 2013

Martin reluctantly pulls off the covers, grabs a dressing gown in the darkness and shuffles downstairs. He smoked a couple of joints to help him drift off to sleep last night and isn't ready to greet the day quite yet. But somebody's pounding on the front door, and they've made a conscious decision not to use the doorbell or the knocker.

If it's another delivery for next door, that package will soon be heading straight to the bin.

'Thought you'd be out, following up a lead, not having a lie-in,' Phil says, framed by blinding daylight on the doorstep. 'And I like the dressing gown, fella. Pink's your colour.'

Martin looks down and confirms that, yes, he's wearing one of Charlotte's old dressing gowns. He pulls a false grin and lets his colleague in. Then he trudges back upstairs with Phil following. 'I was up late, doing some research, had to go and meet someone,' he says over his shoulder.

In the study, Martin casually removes the files from his desk and slips them into a drawer as Phil walks over to the drum kit and points at a framed photo on the wall. 'Who's that, with Mick Jagger?'

'My dad.'

'He's a musician?'

'Was. For a while.' There's only one chair for the desk, so they have to share the sofa. Sitting side by side, Martin opens his laptop and shows Phil a few of the videos he watched the day before.

'Right … research, that's what this is,' Phil says.

'Yeah, yeah, very funny. Dirty videos on the internet and all that. But look, these women are beating the men. They're more skilled, more aggressive.'

'So what? You get women doing UFC now, boxing in the Olympics. And every fella who's ever got in a scrap is a murder suspect?'

Martin shakes his head. 'You know there's a difference. Violent women, really violent ones, are rare.' He hands Phil the laptop, then pulls the robe down to cover his knees. 'Google the name "Bellona" – B-E-L-L-O-N-A.'

Phil does as he's been asked. His eyes dart around the screen. He smirks – must have found the drawings.

Martin describes the meeting with Colin.

'So we've got a suspect who was around a decade ago,' Phil says. 'Last seen in Thailand. Fucking Thailand. You been there?'

'No.'

'I have. Forget it.'

'I know, I know,' Martin says. 'But it's all we've got.'

'Then we've got nothing.'

Martin gets up and sits behind his desk, grateful for the cover it provides. 'Approximately, to the nearest ten, how many murders have you solved? And I'm not talking about the easy ones.'

'You sound like that bloody doctor. How many murders *haven't* you solved?'

Martin glances at the spot on his desk where his files had been stacked. 'I don't stop until they're done.'

'I'm no golfer, but give me a club and I'll eventually get that ball in the hole.'

'Bad analogy. I've solved more cases than I haven't.'

'OK, OK, your record's good. But you've followed leads that turned out to be nothing, right?'

'This is why I work alone.'

'So nobody's there when you get it wrong?'

Martin sighs and leans back. 'You want to be like everyone else, going with the obvious, following procedure, that's fine. You won't make a difference, though, won't solve a case that a hundred other detectives couldn't solve. I thought you were better than that.'

Phil sits up a little straighter. 'Look, we agree it's the same girl, and she's probably getting away with it because she *is* a girl. That's logical. The wigs, the confidence … But this Bellona thing is a massive, massive leap. When you get down to it, we have a woman who's killing men, or maybe she's just bait. And we've got another woman, last seen ten years ago. One possibly violent woman. "Mean", according to your contact. No link between them.'

'This Bellona is worth investigating.'

'Why?'

'Sometimes you have to trust your instincts.'

'I prefer numbers,' Phil says, 'probability.'

'You've never been in a situation where you knew what was going on, you could just feel it?'

'Yeah. But I wasn't always right. A few times it cost me a lot of money.'

'Maybe it was a lack of experience.'

'Or just getting overexcited by a couple of videos.' Phil raises an eyebrow.

'What are instincts?'

'You're the psychologist now?'

'Do you think about walking, analyse every breath you take?'

'Of course not.'

'It's instinctive. Do this job long enough, meet enough murderers, and spotting them becomes just like walking or breathing.'

Phil leans back with one arm across the back of the sofa. 'Maybe your instincts are right. But here's the thing: Thailand is a timewaster. When I was there, everyone swore their hostel room smelled like a dead body. And even if ninety per cent of it's bullshit, all those stories and rumours will waste your time.'

'There'll be records of unsolved murders.'

'Yeah, fucking loads of them, I'll bet.'

'Life there's cheap, maybe that's why she went.'

'Doesn't matter if she went, it's a dead end.'

'What have you got that's better?'

'We've got the wrestling thing,' Phil says. 'We'll go back to the victims, check their web searches, talk to their pals. Maybe they were into this stuff, maybe that's why they approached a girl in that kind of shape. And if she's as tough as they say, somebody must have trained her. We talk to the karate schools, university martial arts clubs. There'll have been competitions, with weight categories, photos of winners.'

Martin rubs his jaw. Objectively, Phil's right. This is the way to approach things. But Thailand... perhaps she was less careful there, didn't feel the need to cover her tracks.

Maybe, maybe, maybe ...

That's the problem with instincts, Martin thinks. They're inaccessible, part of the subconscious. Any logic they possess comes after the thought, when you're trying to justify them. Following procedure – you know exactly why you're doing it. But the type of grunt work Phil's talking about is time-consuming, boring. And sometimes you need a different approach, when the correct answer may not be the obvious one.

'Hello, what's this?' Phil says, picking up an ashtray from the floor. He selects the butt of a joint and rubs it between his finger and thumb. 'You've got to be joking.'

'You've never smoked one?'

'Not any more, fella. No wonder your thoughts are a little … cloudy. This stuff's all right for that lot,' Phil says, gesturing at the photos of musicians. 'But I like to feel like I can trust my judgement.'

'So it would be better if I had a couple of drinks in the evening?'

Although, if he's honest, that happens quite a lot too.

'Well …'

'Maybe I have a couple more,' Martin says. 'Then I get called to a scene. Or I give my wife a whack, my daughter. Maybe I smack around a suspect–'

Martin's phone vibrates on the desk. He stares at Phil for a couple of seconds before picking it up. 'He's here too,' Martin says. 'Really?'

Phil leans forward, straining to hear who's on the other end of the line.

'We'll be right there.'

'What is it?' Phil says.

'Gary and the girl got in an illegal minicab on Saturday night. Cook's found the driver.'

* * * * * *

Sarah's spoken to her research analysts about every stock in the portfolio. They should be able to cope without contacting her for a few days. She lies on the sofa and closes her eyes.

Five minutes later her phone rings. It's Dan.

'You're taking a couple of days off – everything OK?'

'Yes … I'm just … a little tired after last night. And you're always telling me to take a holiday.'

'You're sure that's all it is? Nothing else?'

I work so hard to go undetected, Sarah thinks, *and then I do something to a colleague. I'm a big game hunter – I don't pull the wings off flies.*

'Sarah?'

'Really, I'm fine. Are you?'

'Well, it's just that Marcus called this morning, resigned. He won't even come into the office. Then you say you're taking a couple of days off, which I'm sure you'll appreciate is a little strange, and I start to worry that someone is raiding us, stealing our best people.'

'I'm not going anywhere, I promise.' Sarah sits up. 'But Marcus, why … why did he quit?'

'It's very suspicious. What was he talking about last night?'

'Why do you ask?'

'I saw you chatting to him and his girlfriend. You left at the same time, didn't you?'

'I don't think so.' *I left five minutes after and we met two streets away.*

'If he said anything, anything at all that might explain his leaving, then I'd like you to tell me.'

'It was all just small talk, you know, about their relationship, my place in the country, that sort of thing.'

'You're sure he didn't drop any hints?' Dan says. 'Ask if you were happy with us? Because if he's planning on setting up on his own, stealing our clients … I'll have lawyers climbing up his arse.'

Sarah almost laughs at that but also with relief. Marcus hasn't talked, yet. She moves the phone away from her mouth and covers the mic with her other hand.

'Are you still there? I keep losing you?' Dan says.

'No, no, I'm here.'

'Good. Well … enjoy your time off.'

Sarah walks to the kitchen, opens a door and descends the stairs down to the basement. There she unlocks another door leading to a tunnel that runs under the garden. She emerges in the cellar of the mews house behind, which she bought along with the main house. Then she's in the garage, which would have been stables a hundred years ago but now contains today's equivalent of the workhorse: a four-year-old white Ford transit van.

She opens one of the rear doors and climbs into the back, which is sealed from the cab by a metal sheet. Crouching down, she unscrews a piece of plywood trim and lifts the lid of a compartment that sits above the wheel arch. Inside are five sets of registration plates, all matching those found on other white transits of a similar age. A thorough search of this van would, of course, reveal the plates, but there's no reason for anyone to stop her while driving this most anonymous of vehicles.

She attaches one pair of the plates to the front and back of the transit and drives out of the garage, heading west.

* * * * * * *

The boys sit in Connor's bedroom, curtains closed and walls plastered with posters of sportsmen. Mostly footballers, but since he failed to make the Bristol City under-14s team, Connor's been watching more basketball.

A *Call of Duty* game plays on the PS3 that he grabbed in the riots two years ago. He puts in at least three hours a day on it, and he's delegated Luke, who isn't skilled enough to act as his back-up, to sit and watch.

'Con-norrrr,' his mum shouts from the kitchen with her thick West Country accent.

'What?'

'Why don't you two go out for a bit?'

'We're playing,' he says, dispatching a pair of enemy soldiers with two clean shots.

'You been in there all day.'

Connor looks over at his chubby friend and rolls his eyes.

A minute later, his mum shouts again. 'Dean'll be home soon.'

'Make us some tea and we'll go out.'

'I ain't got food for the two of you.'

Another clean kill. 'Give us some money then.'

A pause. 'Alright.'

In the kitchen, the microwave hums, filling the room with the smell of gravy. Connor's mum opens the tall, round silver tin where she stores her cash. She's handing her son a five pound note when the front door slams and Dean strolls in.

'Finally paying your way?' he says to Connor.

'They're going out,' Connor's mum says. 'Right, boys? Won't be back 'til late, will you?'

'Maybe look for a job while you're out there,' Dean says.

'He's only fourteen. He's got school.'

'I done a paper round when I was twelve,' Dean says. 'What's for dinner?'

'Steak and kidney pie,' Connor's mum says, waiting eagerly for a reaction from her boyfriend.

'Nice.' Dean winks at Connor, then walks into the lounge where he slumps into an armchair and picks up the TV remote.

Connor grabs a basketball from his room and the boys leave the flat, walking across the vast square of concrete between the four tower blocks, then over the road to the parade of shops. All but two of them are boarded up, just a chip shop and a pawnbroker left. They try to figure out what they can get for their money. Luke suggests three battered sausages. Connor says it's his money and orders a portion of chips and half a chicken to share.

'Dean's a prick,' Luke says as they sit on a wall down the road.

'Wanker,' Connor says. 'My dad would fuckin' do him.'

'When's he getting out?'

'Dunno, not for a couple of years at least.'

They sit in silence as they finish the greasy food, then walk over to the concrete sports pitch at the edge of the estate. It's another warm evening, school holidays, but the place is deserted. They take it in turns to dribble the ball towards the basket, while the other one tries to defend. Most of Luke's shots miss by a foot; Connor makes about one in every two.

* * * * * * *

Frank Attafuah blocks almost every inch of the doorway to his flat on the top floor of a low-rise block in Bethnal Green. He wears a cheap grey suit that somehow manages to be a size too large. 'Yes?'

'Frank, I'm DI White, this is DS …'

'Burton,' Phil says.

'Anyway, we have a few questions about last Saturday, the tenth.'

'You are meaning Tuesday,' Frank says. 'Yesterday night – that is when the police are stopping me.' He's Ghanaian – one of the few basic details Martin knows – and arrived in the UK nearly two years ago.

'No,' Martin says. 'We want to talk about two of your passengers on Saturday night–'

'There are none,' Frank says, showing no sign of moving from the doorway. 'Yesterday is the first day I am doing the taxi driving.'

'You're on camera.'

'Oh,' Frank says, briefly shifting his gaze to Phil. 'I am needing a lawyer, I think.'

'Relax,' Martin says. 'You're not under arrest. Tell us about Saturday, then we can make your other problems disappear.'

A huge grin spreads across Frank's face, exposing a gap between his top front teeth. 'Come in, come in, please,' he says.

They follow him into a yellow lounge, furnished with a brown velour sofa and another one in cracked red leather. Shelves sag under the weight of textbooks. A lanky West African is folded into a chair at the dining table, more textbooks scattered around him. He peers at the detectives through large 1970s glasses.

'Please, sit down,' Frank says, then fires instructions in a foreign language at his flat mate, who hurries from the room. Frank glares at him on the way out and then smiles at the detectives again.

You never really get to know someone if you don't speak their language, Martin thinks, reminding himself to examine everything Frank says with that in mind.

'So, Frank, you're here on a student visa–'

'Business studies.'

'Right. And you're paying your way through university with a little driving in the evenings.'

'I am needing to send some money, to my wife, for the children.'

'Why not get a legal driving job?'

Frank frowns. 'You say we are going to talk about Saturday?'

We will. Good to know there's something I can use if I need it, though. 'CCTV from an office near Tottenham Court Road shows two people getting in the back of your car at around one-thirty a.m.'

Frank looks at the ceiling.

'A man and a woman,' Martin says. 'She had blonde hair and wore sunglasses.' He hands Frank a few CCTV stills.

'Oh yes, how can I forget?' Frank says, then laughs, his belly shaking.

'Where did you take them?'

'I am remembering it exactly. It is a very nice place, outside of London. Marlow.'

'What address did they give you?' Phil says, flipping open his notebook, almost dropping his pen.

'No, no. The woman, she directs me. Turn here, go there.'

'Where did you drop them off?' Phil says. 'Could you show us the house?'

Frank waves his finger. 'I leave them in the street, they stand there while I am driving away. I watch them in the mirror.'

Martin sighs. Unlikely that Marlow was the final destination.

'Could you describe them, the couple?' Phil says.

'She is … the boss, you know? The man is saying nothing, he is nervous. And … she pay me with fifty pound notes.'

'Still got them?' Phil says.

Frank shakes his head. 'I transfer some money to my family yesterday. I use the fifties.'

Phil slumps backwards on the sofa.

'What else can you tell us about her?' Martin says. 'What did she say?'

'They do not talk very much.'

'Anything unusual about her appearance?'

'She has a good …' Frank laughs again, cupping his hands below his chest. 'A good body, you know. I think she is working out.'

'Her hair, what was it like?'

Frank closes his eyes. 'Blonde … thick.'

'Did she ever scratch her head, play with the hair?'

'I do not think so,' Frank says, opening his eyes again. 'Who is this woman?'

'That,' Martin says, 'is a very good question.'

* * * * * * *

Sarah stops briefly outside a village off the M4 and changes to a new set of registration plates. She rejoins the motorway, heading for Bristol, a city she hasn't visited before.

There's no plan. She doesn't know what will happen or exactly where she'll go. *But maybe a little impulsiveness is a good thing*, she thinks. Her Saturday night routine is an MO, a pattern that links her crimes and makes her predictable. *A spontaneous Wednesday evening hunt in a new city, in an anonymous van, is less reckless than assaulting a colleague, isn't it?*

She cruises around the surrounding towns and suburbs for a few hours – Fishponds, Kingswood, Keynsham – avoiding the busy streets and CCTV cameras of the city centre.

Then she sees them.

A pair of teenage boys, wearing tracksuit bottoms and T-shirts. One of them bounces a basketball as they walk casually past a row of small industrial buildings. Sarah passes them and stops a little further down the road. There's nobody else in sight.

She watches them approach in the transit's side mirror, winding down the window as they pass. 'Excuse me,' she says.

The boys stop, turn, look at the van.

'Yeah?' the one with the ball says. He's lean with closely cropped hair and big brown eyes.

'I'm a bit lost. I'm trying to get to Bath,' she says.

'Ain't you got a satnav?' he says, sneering.

'I'm afraid not. Could you give me directions?'

'You go up–'

'Actually …' Sarah says, stretching out the word as though she's deep in thought. 'I've got to go and pick up some equipment and bring it back to Bristol. I wonder if you and your friend might be able to come and help me?'

The other boy – shorter, chubbier and curly-haired – frowns.

'It won't take long and I'll give you fifty pounds each.'

The two boys look at each other; the short-haired one speaks. 'You're from Bristol and you don't know where Bath is?'

'Oh, no, I'm not from round here. Just helping out a friend.'

'What sort of equipment?'

'Some AV stuff, speakers, amps, that sort of thing.'

'What for?'

Isn't fifty pounds enough for a kid any more? 'A little fashion show.'

'With models?' he says, suddenly becoming interested.

'A few.'

'Can we go backstage and that?' He pauses. 'To help out with the equipment?'

Sarah smiles. 'I don't see why not.'

The boys look at each other again, shrug, then hurry around the van to the passenger door. The short-haired one sits next to Sarah in the central seat. His friend winds down the window, resting an arm on the frame.

'What are your names?'

'I'm Connor and this fat little fucker is Luke.'

Luke blinks but doesn't say anything.

Sarah gives Luke a sympathetic smile. 'Well, I'm Sarah. Now which way are we going?'

'Turn left at the end of here,' Connor says.

Sarah pulls away, following directions. She keeps her eyes on the road ahead but senses Connor looking at her, sneaking glances at her legs – exposed by a short skirt – and looking down her top. She lets him carry on, the glances getting longer, more obvious.

Sarah turns to Connor, smiles and takes his hand, placing it on her left leg, a couple of inches above the knee.

Wide-eyed, he doesn't seem so confident now.

Luke, who's been staring out of the window, notices the hand and stares at it. They stay like this for a while – hand on knee, eyes on hand – until they leave the city.

Slowly, tentatively, Connor's hand creeps higher; he watches Sarah's face for any reaction.

Her eyes remain fixed on the road.

He stops when his fingers touch her skirt.

'I have an idea,' Sarah says, her voice shattering the silence in the cab, causing Connor to yank his hand away like it's been burned. 'Why don't we find ourselves a little private place to park the van so we can all get in the back? What do you think?'

Two pairs of eyes stare at her; two open mouths say nothing.

'I'll take that as a yes.'

Sarah pulls off the main road and drives along a residential street, 1930s brick houses. She stops the van when they enter a hedgerow-lined country lane. 'Leave your phones on the seat, we don't want any distractions.'

She opens the rear door and gestures for them to climb in.

The plates. 'Actually, can you give me a minute in here, I need to … get myself ready.'

Connor shrugs.

She closes the door behind her, unscrews the wood trim again and pulls out the plates. Sarah hears faint whispers from outside – she can't hear what they're discussing but can probably guess. Connor will no doubt be insisting he goes first.

'I'm ready,' she says, opening the door.

'What you got there?' Connor says, pointing at the plates in her hand.

'Don't want anything to get in our way,' Sarah says and winks.

The boys climb in the back and Sarah slams the door, locking it.

'Oi!' they shout, fists pounding on metal. 'What's going on?'

'Change of plan,' Sarah calls back, running around to the cab, jumping in and driving away.

The boys move over to the metal sheet that separates them from Sarah – thumping, kicking and shouting.

She swerves; the van's suspension clunks as it hits a large pothole.

Thuds from behind her, cries.

She accelerates, then brakes hard. More thuds, louder this time.

'We're in the middle of nowhere. Nobody can hear you.'

The boys continue to bang and shout – louder, more frantic.

Sarah drives swiftly along the lanes until she sees it up ahead: a humpback bridge. The suspension unloads for a second as the van almost leaves the ground; the boys return to the floor with a crash. 'Think you can keep quiet now?'

They answer with silence.

* * * * * * *

Martin stands in a street in Marlow – empty brand-new houses on either side. Crime scene tape surrounds the entire development, but workmen have been cleaning away dust and dirt and laying lawns since Saturday. Uniforms go door to door throughout the town, searching for anyone who noticed a couple getting out of a minicab or walking around in the early hours of Sunday morning. CCTV footage is being collected. They're out of London now, though – there are few cameras away from the high street. No local taxi firm picked them up.

Martin suspects the trail will go cold here, the probable car swap being like the river the escaped convict wades through to escape the dogs. Two motorways pass near Marlow, linking it with London and other cities. Even in the middle of the night, there are plenty of cars and lorries travelling along them, joining and leaving at various exits, dropping on and off the grid covered by traffic cameras.

DI MacDonagh from Westminster CID is heading up the search for Gary Burke. He breaks off a conversation with a pair of local detectives and marches over to Martin.

'Where do I start?' MacDonagh says. His dark, usually lifeless eyes and doughy, pock-marked face could almost be described as animated.

'How about thanks?'

'Yeah. Thanks for interviewing my witness and telling me what he said.'

'We found him.'

'Why were you looking for him?'

'Cook didn't tell you?'

MacDonagh extends a finger, looks like he's going to prod Martin in the chest, but stops halfway. Blotches of red appear on his cheeks. 'You know bloody well I can't just pick up the phone and ask him. I could see about Commander Bell giving him a call, though.'

'I'm …' Martin checks his watch, 'working on a cold case. Minicab driver, rapes.'

'So what are you doing here?'

'Making sure his story holds up,' Martin says. 'Just because a suspect in one case got into his car doesn't mean he's not involved in anything else.'

MacDonagh stares at him for a while, then turns and marches away.

'That looked easy for you,' Phil says from behind him. 'You comfortable with this?'

Martin turns around. 'Comfortable with what?'

'Keeping MacDonagh in the dark. Doesn't feel right to me.'

'You want that idiot on the trail?' Martin watches MacDonagh take a call.

'Maybe not him … specifically, but a few more on the case wouldn't go amiss.'

'You don't think you're up to this?'

Phil smiles and shakes his head 'It's not a game.'

'Interesting, coming from a poker player.'

'That's another place where your ego will cost you.'

'Maybe,' Martin says, although his attention has switched to his rumbling stomach. 'I don't suppose you fancy getting something to eat?'

'Bit early for dinner.'

'I'll just end up getting a sandwich from a petrol station otherwise.'

'Well … I'm sure we can do better than that.'

The detectives walk out of the street, towards the town centre. A couple of lawn mowers rattle around, taking advantage of the last hours of daylight; somewhere a midweek barbecue fills the air with the smell of charred meat.

'This isn't about me,' Martin says. 'It's about keeping away anyone who'll drop the ball, let her escape.'

'There's no one else you trust?'

'What more proof do you need? MacDonagh's useless, clueless. There'll be plenty more like him. It's like Vietnam.'

Phil stops. 'You mean Thailand? You're back on that?'

'No, no. The war,' Martin says. 'The Americans sent their kids halfway around the world, fighting a battle their friends back home were protesting against. Trying to beat men and women who'd live in tunnels, give up their lives for their country, their beliefs.'

'But we've got an army, she's just one person.'

'This is her life, though. It's who she is.'

Phil steps off the pavement to let past a young mother with a pram. 'There are detectives who live for the job.'

'Perhaps, but the ones who don't will hurt us.'

Phil smiles and raises his hands in submission. 'Maybe the hunger's getting to you. Let's eat.'

They find a Pizza Express and take a table in the window. The only other customers are an old couple who don't speak but seem perfectly comfortable in each other's company.

Martin orders an American Hot pizza, some olives for while he waits and a Coke. Phil opts for a salade niçoise and a bottle of sparkling water.

'I mean this in the nicest possible way,' Martin says, 'but what on earth is wrong with you?'

'All the refined carbs in that pizza will slow down your brain. And caffeine … makes you think you're awake, but it doesn't last long.'

'You look normal, but …' Martin says, pouring his Coke into a glass and taking a big gulp. 'I don't even get the poker thing. I'd expect you to be a risk taker.'

'It's all about *calculated* risks. Waiting for the right opportunity. And sometimes it's just discipline. If you can concentrate for ten hours – cutting out the caffeine helps – you've got an edge.'

'So the Thailand angle, what's the risk?'

Phil raises his fingers to his temples, closes his eyes.

'Where's the harm?' Martin says. 'We try and get hold of case files from Bangkok, have a flick through them.'

'Meanwhile,' Phil says, 'we get closer to Saturday.'

'We're not going to catch her this week.'

Phil lets the waiter put down a bowl of olives and cocktail sticks before replying. 'No, not if we're on a wild goose chase.'

'Look at what happened here. She's too careful now. Maybe back then she was sloppier.'

Phil waves a cocktail stick in Martin's direction. 'Who says it was the same person in Thailand?'

'We have to give Cook something,' Martin says. 'All he thinks we have is the minicab driver, and he got us that.'

Phil wrinkles his nose. 'He seemed OK when I spoke to him. And you really think Bangkok will be better than nothing? If you ask me, there's more chance of him taking us off the case if we give him that nonsense.'

On that point, Phil could be right, Martin thinks. *If we want anything foreign, we'll need to go through Cook. He's already taking a huge risk, kind of a stupid risk, on us. If we're going to catch her, we'll need to delve into her past. But right now, we need a credible reason to go there.*

* * * * * * *

Connor blinks in the light of Sarah's torch. The other one, Luke, has red eyes. He cries again, when he sees the gun.

Sarah sets the torch on the floor of the van. 'Take off your clothes.'

The boys undress slowly, occasionally stopping to look at her. She nods for them to continue.

They turn away to take off their underwear; both their backs bear a leopard print of bruises.

'It's nothing I haven't seen before.'

They turn around, hands over their crotches.

Sarah picks up two sets of manacles and two pairs of handcuffs from the ground beside her. She tosses them to the boys; they land with a deafening bang on the floor of the van. 'Fasten those around your ankles, then put on the cuffs.'

When they're done, she beckons to them, watching them climb out of the back of the van, planting their bare feet in the gravel.

'You see the chairs over there on the terrace? Walk towards them. And think about how hard it would be to outrun a bullet in those chains.'

The boys shuffle over to the house, sobbing.

'Sit down.' Sarah attaches their cuffs and manacles to the chairs with padlocks and chains.

'Don't feel the need to look away,' she says, stripping down to her underwear in the cool night air. She's disappointed to see no signs of arousal from either of them, but it's understandable.

The terrace security lights illuminate the lawn, but clouds obscure the moon. If the boys make it over the slope, there's a chance she'll lose them. And they aren't under the influence of anything. *Should I strap a holster to my leg*, she wonders, *just in case? No, one of them could grab the gun when we're fighting.*

She'll see how things go with Luke – can't imagine him putting up much of a fight. She points at him. 'You're first. I'll undo the chains, put my gun down, count to three. Then I'll try to catch you.'

Luke's eyes dart around, his forehead creasing.

'In case you're wondering, if I do catch you, I'll hurt you.'

Luke slumps forward, wailing.

Sarah has the urge to put a bullet in his head. *What kind of build-up is this? There's a chance he's already given up, won't even run.*

'Luke,' she says. 'Luke!'

When he looks up, Sarah slaps his face.

'If you can outrun me, you're free. Understand?'

He nods quickly, sniffing.

'So stop blubbering and get ready to run.'

She frees his ankles and wrists. She counts to two and he gets to his feet and runs. But five shaky strides later, it's clear he sustained too many injuries in the van. Sarah could give him a twenty-second head-start and still catch him in thirty, without breaking a sweat.

She picks up the gun, takes aim and fires three shots. Two puffs of red spray from Luke's right shoulder blade, another from the back of his head. He topples face forward in the grass with a dull thud.

'Luuuuke!' Connor screams. 'No!'

Sarah points the gun at Connor's forehead. 'We're at least three miles from the nearest house, so save your breath. Hopefully you can run a little faster.'

'What the fuck is wrong with you, you crazy ginger bitch?'

Sarah laughs. 'Is that the best you've got?'

Connor glares at her.

'You should know I don't want to use this again. I want to run you down, take you with my bare hands.'

Connor's eyes narrow. Perhaps he's thinking, I could take her, I can run faster than a girl.

'So can you make this interesting?'

'How do I know you're not lying, just gonna shoot me as well?'

Sarah removes the magazine from the pistol, slips the bullets out one by one, letting them clink on the terrace's paving stones. She pulls back on the gun; the bullet in the chamber pops out.

'OK?'

'Yeah,' he says, chin held surprisingly high.

As soon as the cuffs are off, he's away. Sarah counts to three, but he's already veering off to the left, away from the light. And he's fast.

She hesitates. He's disappearing between the rosebushes.

Sarah scrabbles around, manages to pick up four bullets, pushes them back into the magazine.

She follows Connor off the lawn, through the soft earth of the flower bed, out into the darkness.

The boy is fifty metres ahead, milky skin only just visible. He disappears behind a tree and emerges again.

Sarah's legs pump rapidly but she's not gaining on him. *Should I stop and take aim?* No, if she misses he'll be even further ahead. She knows the land, every building and every possible hiding place; a high wall topped with barbed wire surrounds the entire property. Dawn is still a few hours away.

Up ahead, Connor stumbles and falls.

Sarah grips the gun tight, raises it. She fires as he's getting up.

He's still rising.

Missed.

Connor is sprinting again, approaching the stable block and the forge. If he disappears in there, Sarah will have to stop and search each building.

She takes aim again and fires.

Connor ducks.

Two bullets left.

As he enters the yard of the stable block, Sarah runs around the perimeter, to make sure he hasn't emerged on the other side.

He's not in the field leading down to the river and the mill. There are rocks down there – she doesn't want him grabbing one of those.

Sarah stops, her panting the only sound. She closes her mouth, waiting for her breathing to slow, listening.

If she goes into the yard, Connor could be watching. But there's nothing he could throw, nothing he could use as a weapon. No tools left in the forge; the stables are empty and clean. The buildings are old, though; he could loosen a brick.

Sarah stays close to one of the walls as she creeps into the yard.

The doors to the forge and three of the stables opposite are closed, but one's ajar. She creeps towards it, gun in front of her, her eye lined up with the sight.

To her right, movement.

She fires.

A fox scampers away, into the night.

One bullet left.

The distant thump of feet. Connor is running back towards the house. The van's open and the keys are in there. Could it smash through the gates? Probably. And if he breaks a window, enters the house, there are many rooms, plenty of blunt objects.

She gives chase across the parkland. That basketball he'd been bouncing when she picked him up – he probably plays for hours at a time.

The distance between them drops as they run back through the flower beds, across the lawn, towards the van. He's labouring.

He skitters across the gravel, almost falls, but manages to get into the cab. Sarah's still thirty metres away.

The engine roars, gears crunch.

Sarah stops, takes aim. The windscreen explodes.

Connor's head appears through the shattered opening as the van pulls away, heading left. Sarah runs at it and manages to grab the handle of the driver's door. It swings open, but Connor brakes, making the door flip forward, striking Sarah on the shoulder.

The engine stalls.

She catches his foot as he tries to kick her and pushes him back so he's lying on the seat. He thrashes around, but she manages to get in between his legs, kneeling over him. He covers his face; she pummels him with short, quick punches to the stomach and ribs. She's screaming, hysterical.

He drops his hands to protect his body.

She head-butts him once, twice, three times. His eyes roll back.

He offers no resistance as she wraps her hands around his throat, squeezing.

Hot tears run down her cheeks; the screams have become sobs.

She squeezes and squeezes, fingernails digging into his throat, drawing blood.

Long after he's dead, she slides off the seat, out of the cab and sits in the sharp gravel with her back against the van, head between her knees.

Friday August 16th 2013

Martin stands amid a quartet of tower blocks in Bristol, surrounded by the crackle of police radios and distant hum of traffic.

He answers the phone.

'We've got something,' Cook says.

'What?'

'A black Merc, joined the M40, junction five, at oh-one-forty-seven hours, Saturday, heading west.'

'And?'

'Similar car with that registration was written off in May. Someone's obviously cloned the plate.'

'It's not some DVLA cock-up?' Martin says, hurrying over to one of the blocks so he can lean against a wall and take notes.

'We spoke to the insurers. Car's sitting in a warehouse, waiting for investigations, probably some scrounger saying they got a sore neck.'

'Where did the black Merc go?'

'Came off near Banbury, lost it after that.'

Banbury. A map is drawing itself in Martin's head. 'Nothing similar with different plates joined further up?'

'Nothing the same colour.'

'Any Mercs reported stolen in the last few weeks?' Martin says, pen hovering over his notebook.

'A few. And there's more than you'd think on the road. Most popular luxury car, apparently. Lot of them company-owned, used by embassies, that sort of thing.'

They could attempt to locate all black S-Class Mercedes, interview the owners. But the cloned plates, and the value of the car, suggest a certain level of resources. Probably a lot of work that would involve every force in the country and would lead to nothing – Cook won't be keen on that.

'Doesn't seem like much of a breakthrough,' Martin says.

'It's something, narrows down her location. We'll keep looking for the car, see if the cameras picked it up again. And we'll go back, check on vehicles around the other disappearances.'

Cook, like Martin, is probably drawing that map in his mind. All the locations, they're in a corridor – London and perhaps now Bristol in the south, Liverpool and Leeds in the north. Banbury is near the centre of that space, a quarter of the way up.

Well, that works only if Bristol is her. This one didn't happen on a Saturday, and there were two thirteen-year-old boys who disappeared, not a man, last seen the previous afternoon.

London was an unnecessary risk, too many cameras. The earlier disappearances were from clubs in small towns, suburbs where she could escape without leaving a trail of images. And now snatching kids in broad daylight?

Maybe the piece in the *Telegraph* rattled her. There was just the suggestion of a link between crimes and the police saying 'No comment,' but those two words can suggest anything.

So she breaks her routine, does it all differently, to confuse them. Or maybe this has absolutely nothing to do with her.

One of the boys, Connor Ryan, looks her type: lean, more pretty than handsome, working class. All of the others were working men – unremarkable, without families to make eloquent appeals for information, without success stories that would win them sympathetic headlines. Connor's photo looks like it belongs in the collection, but that's all Martin's got.

The local detectives are focusing on the stepfather. They're wondering why he was eating dinner at home with the mother when the boy and his friend were last seen at the fish and chip shop.

But in this case, Martin thinks, it might just be simple neglect, nothing more sinister.

Neglect. He dials Charlotte's number.

'What have you lost?' She already sounds like a stranger.

'Nothing. I was wondering … how's Molly? Can I talk to her?'

'She's out with my parents, at the zoo.'

'Maybe I'll call back later.'

'You could come and visit her,' Charlotte says, ordering rather than offering. 'I don't want to see you, but you can collect her from my parents.'

He knows exactly how that will work. Charlotte's mother will make a big fuss, preparing sandwiches and cakes so he feels obliged to hang around the house. Then he'll spend a couple of hours sweating in their overheated lounge while she says things like, 'Such a shame … the two of you. Poor Molly, growing up without a father.'

If Martin visits, it will be a surprise attack. 'I'm a little tied up with a case.'

'Of course you are. No doubt with something that's gone unsolved for a decade or two, but you're obsessed with wrapping it up today.'

That gets a smile from Martin. 'You're not a million miles away,' he says. 'But right now … well, this case certainly isn't cold.'

* * * * * * *

The seven p.m. appointment was a late booking – Karl Gross's assistant emailed him the details at lunchtime, just when he was looking forward to an early finish to the day. A new patient: Emma Smith, self-referred.

Karl presses the intercom button and calls her name, then, as she enters, offers her a seat in front of his desk.

When he doesn't have notes on someone new, Karl tries to guess their problem.

She's slim, not striking or beautiful, but well groomed and blessed with radiant skin and well-proportioned features. It would take a rigorous exercise regime and strict diet to maintain that physique, so body image may be involved. But her posture, and the way she walked in, they both imply confidence. The Patek Philippe watch, elegant, thin-strapped white summer dress and the fact that she's self-funding her therapy all suggest wealth.

It's not enough to say she suffers from depression or anxiety, of course. He has to guess the nature of it, the specifics.

She looks too healthy to be a serious drinker, and all that bare skin rules out self-harm. She sought him out, so sex addiction is a possibility.

Is she famous?

He's not getting anything, as though her signal is blocked. The silence has lasted too long.

'How can I help?' he says, giving her a paternal smile.

'I'm an addict, I want you to cure me,' she says, not looking away, or down, or blushing.

'Admitting you have a problem is a vital step, the hardest.' *That's not actually true*, Karl thinks as he says it. *The months of therapy and a lifetime of exercising self-control will be a lot tougher. But it's best to start on a positive note.* 'It's very brave of you to come.'

'Or foolish.' She brushes a speck of something off her dress, just above the knee.

'It takes a wise head to recognise something needs to be done,' Karl says. 'What is it that you're addicted to?'

'Men.'

Karl smiles again, but this time with pride. 'So you've read one of my books or perhaps seen me on TV?'

'They almost put me off.'

'Why's that?'

'Celebrity and vanity go hand in hand. And you've never experienced anyone like me.'

'I don't write about all of my patients,' he says. *She's spiky,* he thinks. *A pleasant change from the whingers and the neurotics.*

'Oh, if you'd had the chance, you would have written about a woman like me. Guaranteed bestseller.'

What an ego. This could be fun. 'Perhaps your case isn't interesting enough, perhaps it doesn't further our understanding of the human mind.'

'Why do you think people buy your books? To learn? Or because they're gory and pornographic?'

'I write about the extremes of human behaviour,' Karl says, his tone less friendly. He drums his fingers on the desk. 'I'm happy to go on like this, but you're paying three hundred pounds an hour to give me notes on my work. Perhaps we should go back to this addiction you mentioned, to men. How does it manifest itself?'

Emma stares at Karl for a few long seconds, then speaks: 'I find pretty young men, hunt them down, and kill them with my bare hands.'

* * * * * * *

When Martin arrives at his house from Bristol, it's the first time he really senses its emptiness.

He turned off the M4, planning to arrive unannounced at Charlotte's parents' house, but hit traffic on the M25 and had to give up. No point getting there after Molly's bedtime.

Now home, he experiences a juvenile thrill when fetching his ashtray from the study and bringing it down to the lounge. He uses one of Charlotte's interior design magazines to catch the mess when he rolls a joint, and balances the ashtray precariously on the arm of the sofa.

He orders a pizza and flicks through music channels while he smokes, changing to avoid the adverts, then cursing himself when he returns to the original programme halfway through a song that reminds him of his youth.

After the sun disappears and the only light in the room comes from the TV and the red glow of his joint, Martin flicks through his collection, passing one film twice before returning to it. Finally, he slips *The Shining* into the DVD player and lies back on the sofa.

As always, he only makes it as far as the first appearance of the lifts gushing with blood before he has to hit the stop button. But it's too late – he imagines a wave of blood descending the staircase of his house, sees Molly riding across the geometrically patterned carpets of the Overlook Hotel on her pink tricycle.

When someone smashes an axe through the bathroom door, though, it's not Martin or even Jack Nicholson.

It's Martin's mother.

* * * * * *

Sarah's words hover in the air. The psychiatrist's lips are frozen a third of the way into a smile and she can see the whites of his eyes. He retains that expression for a couple of seconds, then frowns.

'Is this a joke? Who sent you?'

'I'm not known for my sense of humour.'

'Why are you here?'

'You're a psychiatrist, aren't you? You specialise in serial killers?'

Karl gives her an incredulous look that makes his glasses ride up on his nose. 'What paper do you write for?'

'Listen, Gross,' she says, 'do *not* waste my time. If this doesn't work out, then you'll have a problem.'

He stands up. 'Please leave. I don't like being threatened.'

'I hate using these things,' Sarah says, taking a small black pistol from her handbag.

Karl puts his hands up. 'Please … what do you want … who sent you?'

'If I didn't have such a thick skin,' Sarah says, 'the assumption I must be working for someone might offend me. It does make me question your instincts, though, your ability to read people.'

'But I don't know you,' he says, whining now. 'Why are you here?'

She gets an urge to slap his face, or pistol-whip him, but that won't help. 'I told you, I want you to cure me.'

The psychiatrist stares at her as if she's insane. 'I …' is all he can say. He looks around the room, eyes darting about, unable to focus on anything.

Have I misjudged things? she wonders. *Is he going to panic and do something stupid? Or just be paralysed, useless?*

'Alcohol's a pretty effective anxiety treatment, isn't it?' she says.

'Well … I wouldn't put it quite like that–'

'Why don't you do a little self-medication?'

Karl nods, slowly reaches into the bottom drawer of his desk and brings out a bottle of Scotch. Hand shaking, he pours three fingers into a tall glass next to a water jug and drinks half of it in a couple of clumsy gulps. A quick glance at the gun and he drinks the rest. He mumbles something inaudible and gives Sarah an unconvincing smile, traces of terror still in his eyes. 'I assume you've never spoken about your … addiction before,' he says.

'Correct.'

'You're familiar with psychoanalysis?'

'You get me to talk about my childhood, we discuss how my parents screwed me up.'

'We'll do plenty of talking. We'll explore your past.' Karl pours himself another generous drink, his hand still shaking. 'Now … why don't you lie on the sofa and tell me about yourself. Begin wherever you like, wherever you're comfortable.'

There are rules Sarah wants to establish, but they can wait – Karl isn't going anywhere. She lies down on a brown leather couch to the right of Karl's desk, facing away from him.

Once – when she was younger, when she was trying to figure out who she was, what she was – she wrote it all down, before burning it. Now, for the first time ever, someone else will hear it all.

* * * * * *

I always knew when my mum had a date. She'd be up the stairs before the front door had slammed behind her, washing off the smell of the bus and spending at least an hour putting on too much makeup. Then she'd ask me what I thought of her outfit. I learned to be positive, no matter what – nobody likes watching their parents cry.

She was too sensitive, though, and didn't need to try so hard. Of course, when you're five you think Mummy is beautiful, but I had noticed boys looking at her when she came to see me run on sports day or met me after a school trip.

There had been a few male 'friends' over the years, but none of them had been around for long.

It was different with Nigel. At least once a week, he would drive an hour an a half from his home in Essex to see Mum, taking her for dinner at a pub in the village or, occasionally, to the cinema in town. Mum bought an extension cord for the phone so she could take it up to her room when I was watching TV. And after a couple of months, we all had lunch at our house, including Nigel's son, Oliver, who was also fourteen. He said, 'Hello' when they walked in, 'Goodbye' when they left, and that was it.

'I've got something to tell… discuss with you,' Mum said as I took my first mouthful of shepherd's pie one evening. 'Things between me and Nigel, well … I'd like him and Oliver to come and live here.'

'I'm keeping my room?'

'Yes, Oliver will have the small bedroom.'

'I don't have to call Nigel "Dad"?'

''Course not.'

'OK.'

Two weeks later Nigel pulled up in a white van he'd borrowed from a friend. He and Oliver unloaded their clothes and their collections: Nigel, books on World War II; Oliver, boxes and boxes of comics.

Evening meals were quiet, almost conversation-free, as if everyone had arrived to a rehearsal without seeing the script. And after dinner, the boys liked to read. I often read in my room too, but that was because there hadn't been anyone to talk to when mum was washing up or had fallen asleep in front of the TV.

One Saturday the following month, when Nigel and Oliver were visiting Oliver's mum in the cemetery, I had my first chance to sneak into the small bedroom.

The bed had been made, with the sheet folded back and tucked under itself. Oliver's school shoes, polished, were next to a pair of immaculate white Adidas trainers in the corner. He was one of those boys who always tucked in his shirt and neatly parted his hair.

A narrow set of shelves was stacked with comics, and there were boxes of them on top of the wardrobe and under the bed. They were all in chronological order. I recognised some of the characters – Batman, Spiderman, Judge Dredd – but there were many more superheroes I'd never heard of.

The first row of boxes under the bed was more of the same, Marvel and DC. I pulled them out and reached for the boxes behind.

These were different – some looked Japanese, full of girls with bulging eyes and breasts, pretty boys on motorbikes, hideous monsters. The comic at the bottom of that box, well, an adult must have bought it for Oliver. There were demons with huge penises, sticking them into screaming girls.

What else do you have? *I wondered.*

The last box had a comic on the top – Fritz the Cat *– and on the cover, Fritz's paw was shoved down the front of a female cat's dress, clutching her breast. There were more like this one, filled with smutty stories, female characters bursting out of their tight outfits. And they all seemed to be wearing knee-high boots.*

The front door clicked shut and there were footsteps on the stairs. I'd only got one box back under the bed when Oliver walked in and froze.

We stood for a long moment. Then, without saying anything, he pushed past me, knelt down on the floor and started checking the comics, rearranging them so they were all the same way up.

'Sorry,' I said.

Oliver didn't respond.

He spoke even less after the incident in his room, if that was possible. I got the feeling that, despite there being no signs of it on the surface, he was in some kind of pain, tormented.

So, as a teenage girl, I decided to prod the wound.

My opportunity came two weeks later. This time it was my mum and Nigel who were out; they'd been vague about where exactly they were going.

I went into my mum's room and found what I was looking for at the bottom of a wardrobe.

A little while later, I knocked on Oliver's door.

'What?' The sound of paper rustling, bed springs squeaking.

'Can I come in?'

A pause. 'No.'

I turned the handle and swung the door open.

Oliver was lying on his bed, knees up, a comic resting on his thighs. But as he looked at me, his mouth hung open, his cheeks turned red. Finally, I'd gotten a reaction out of him.

My mum's leather boots came up to my thighs. I wore my school skirt, rolled over at the waist so it hung six inches above the knee, and my shirt tied below my chest to expose my belly button. My hair sprouted high from either side of my head in pigtails. I had thick black lines around my eyes and scarlet on my lips. I'd done a decent job of making myself look like a comic book character.

'What are you up to?' I said.

'I'm just ... reading ... What are you doing in here?'

'This is what you want, isn't it? I saw what was in those comics.'

'You shouldn't have been looking at my stuff.'

I noticed that a Wonder Woman poster had disappeared from his wall. 'Why are you so secretive?'

'Why are you so nosy?'

'We live together. Don't you want us to be friends?'

'It wasn't my choice to come here,' he said, turning his attention back to the comic. But his eyes weren't moving across the page.

'Did you have a girlfriend?'

'Go away.'

'Have you ever had one?'

He screwed up his mouth, then lifted the comic up so I couldn't see his face.

I walked over and snatched it away. 'I've never had a boyfriend,' I said.

'So what?'

'So you shouldn't be embarrassed. You can tell me.'

'Why would I want to do that?'

'Don't you get lonely,' I said, 'sitting here reading all day?'

'No.'

'But the real thing is better than a fantasy, isn't it?'

He frowned at me, as though he'd never considered that question.

'I suppose you wouldn't know …' Come on, surely that'll get a response? *I thought.* The boys at school always respond to anyone who questions their sexual experience.

But no, he just lowered his knees and lay back with his arms behind his head, staring at the ceiling.

I swung a leg over him and lowered myself so that I sat on his crotch. He didn't look at me, but I could feel his reaction. 'Don't you want to get into these?' I said, lifting my skirt a little.

'Please'. Oliver said. 'Just go. Before our parents get back.'

I slid my hand under his T-shirt and he closed his eyes tight. I got off him and left.

The following night, a creaking floorboard outside my door woke me. There was silence, then the door handle turned.

Oliver crept into my room, slender limbs just visible in the darkness. He closed the door gently behind him and stood without speaking.

'What are you waiting for?' I whispered.

He slipped under the duvet and I was on him, kissing him, hips pressing down on his, feeling him hard against me.

What I felt … I didn't intend to hurt him, just impose myself, take what I wanted.

I pulled his boxer shorts down and gripped him tight, surprised by how hot he felt.

'Do we need … you know, um, protection?' Oliver said.

'Have you got any?'

'In my room—'

'Why didn't you bring it?'

'I didn't—'

'Go, quickly.'

He returned a minute later, the condom already on.

'Lie on the floor,' I said. 'The bed will make a noise.'

I lowered myself on to him. It was mildly uncomfortable, but perhaps for many people, the first time was clumsy and they didn't have the rush of adrenaline I felt from bending Oliver to my will. I simply didn't pay much attention to the physical sensations. I just watched Oliver, as if his face was the size of a cinema screen, mouth and eyes open wide, a battle between urges to cry, scream and smile pulling his features in opposing directions.

He bucked and strained, trying to stay silent, trying to delay his climax. I leaned forward, my breasts against his chest, face in his neck, restraining him with my weight. He arched his back – lifting me, almost toppling me over – as he came. He slumped back down, his chest rising and falling, eyes closed.

'Oliver. Go,' I said, standing up.

'I'll stay here, with you. I'll leave before they get up.'

'No, go back to your room, now.'

He sat up and grabbed my wrist. 'I'll be quiet. Please.'

I took my arm away and went back to bed.

He returned the following night. I told him to go away.

The night after we did it again on my floor.

For three nights, I told him to leave. Then I got into his bed, made him watch while I touched myself.

When our parents were in the lounge, I'd beckon him into the kitchen, push him against the sink, kiss him, then pull away. When their eyes were on the TV, I'd attract his attention, flick my eyes down towards my chest, move my hands across my lap.

I ignored him for a week. He begged to just touch me, lie with him.

We took more risks, going upstairs on weekend afternoons while our parents were downstairs, or I'd expose myself in the hallway, the garden. I'd let out the occasional groan even when we weren't doing anything. Several times Oliver said we had to stop, we'd get caught. The fear on his face, that was delicious. I could make him come to me whenever I wanted.

I told him not to do his homework, then waited after school while he was in detention and took him to the woods when he got out. Some days I said he couldn't eat breakfast; on others, he had to wear my underwear beneath his school uniform.

I watched him all the time, sat in class thinking of new ways to make him squirm, make him wait and then reward him.

'Do you think we don't know what's going on?' Nigel said one night at dinner. The silence that followed was thicker than the gravy.

'We were going to wait, Nigel, we agreed,' my mum said, glancing at me.

'So she could flash her knickers at him in the kitchen? Creep into his room again tonight?'

'Don't you bloody well blame her!'

'You think he's the one who started it?' Nigel said, pointing to his son. 'He sits in his room reading comics all day, he's a dreamer. Your daughter is a dirty little cow.'

My mum pushed her chair back, got up slowly and walked into the kitchen. She returned with our huge carving knife, heavy and widely serrated. She spoke quietly. 'I think you'd better go. Now.'

'But—'

'All your things will be in the front garden when you come to get them tomorrow. Don't knock on the door, don't try to come in, don't call. Ever.'

Nigel glared at her but he couldn't penetrate her maternal force field.

'Don't you know where the door is?' Mum said, pointing at it with the knife.

Nigel looked at his son now. 'Come on, Oliver, let's not make this mistake last any longer. I'm sorry I put you through this.'

I sat in silence as Nigel and his son left, listening to the thunk *of the car doors, the engine over-revved, then fading into the distance.*

* * * * * * *

Phil stands on the doorstep, his face unmistakably apologetic as he looks up at Martin. If he was a character in a romantic comedy, it would be raining, there'd be water dripping off his nose and he'd be terribly, terribly sorry.

'What is it?' Martin says.

'Thailand.'

Martin grabs Phil by the arm, pulls him inside. 'Tell me.'

Phil waits for Martin to release his arm before speaking: 'Two weeks after that guy posted from Bangkok, that he had seen Bellona … an Austrian backpacker was found dead, strangled, at a full moon beach party on Koh Phi Phi Don. He had cash in his pocket, nothing stolen. And someone saw him following an "athletic" white girl along the beach.'

Martin looks at Phil with narrowed eyes.

'I'm sorry,' Phil says. 'I should have listened. I'll just listen from now on.'

'It's … OK,' Martin says, putting his hand on Phil's shoulder. He's not interested in how Phil feels, though. He wants to jump on a plane. 'What have you got?'

'Didn't get much press coverage here, but it was big news in Austria.' Phil reaches into his jacket, pulls out photocopies of articles from German-language newspapers: *Die Presse*, *Kronen Zeitung*, *Der Standard*.

'Not very good looking, is he?' Martin says.

'But he was small, slim. Five seven and only ten stone.'

'Did anyone see anything?'

'Nothing. No witnesses, no arrests.'

'What about before and after?' Martin says. 'Any backpackers go missing in Asia? Doesn't matter if they think they found the killer.'

'Can't find anything like this in the papers, for a year before or after.'

They stand in silence for a moment. Martin wonders what made Phil look for the backpacker murder. It must have taken some time to dig it up.

'What about the car, in Oxfordshire?' Phil says. 'We get anything else?'

'Nothing yet.'

'So it's time to tell Cook about this.' Phil says. 'The wrestling, Thailand.'

Martin scratches his head. 'I don't know–'

'But this is what you wanted.'

'I did but …' Martin points at a picture of the backpacker. 'There's still no link–'

'What are you so worried about?'

Martin examines the newspaper clippings, but the German is indecipherable. 'We've got two unrelated crimes, only linked by possibly violent females, which in the eyes of some people would be no link at all. If we give Cook this, he'll either laugh, or in the unlikely event he buys it, he'll have no choice but to launch a proper investigation with more senior officers involved. I know we're on to something, now you know it too, but we need that link, between Bellona and the disappearances. We need to show him we're on top of this.'

Phil takes a deep breath, exhales through his nose. 'You don't have to worry about him launching the big investigation – he wants to keep things quiet.'

'Because he thinks there might be an insider,' Martin says. 'But that doesn't matter if he's expanding the investigation overseas. He can use Interpol and almost nobody in the UK needs to know.'

'So maybe that's the right thing to do.'

'You know where I stand. I'm … *We're* the ones who are going to solve this. Nobody else would have made that big jump to Bellona.'

'Now we've made the jump, we need help–'

'No, we need time, that's all.'

'It's gonna come too late for those lads in Bristol,' Phil says. 'Maybe you should line up the photos of her victims, remember what we're trying to do here.'

'So I get emotional?' Martin turns and leans on one arm against the wall, while closing his eyes and pinching his nose with the other hand. 'Right now, I think she might be slipping. We need to keep our heads–'

Phil throws a hand up in the air. 'You never had yours! You've lost it, fella. You think you're special? Tell that to those lads' parents. Explain to them why the stepdad's down the station for questioning, why we're not splashing this woman all over the papers.'

'If those boys are dead we can't bring them back. But we can catch her, quietly, before she flies off somewhere else.'

Phil reaches out to the front door, turning the latch. 'You're not gonna catch anyone soon, fella.' He opens the door. 'I'm gonna get us the help you're too dumb to ask for.'

* * * * * * *

They'd stopped repairing the fence years before; every time the caretaker replaced the damaged wires, the local boys would prise them apart so they could play on the tarmac pitches. There were tennis, basketball, football and netball courts, all marked out, lines of different colours. That evening it was the turn of the yellow lines. Netball.

You couldn't make contact with someone while they held the ball. But you could be quicker, stronger and dirtier when you were chasing a loose ball, intercepting a pass that was too easy to read.

My knee and elbow looked like sliced salami; tiny specs of grit stung the raw skin. The other team's wing defence was a couple of inches taller than me and was probably a year older. I played for the first team, despite being only fifteen. But I had home court advantage.

The ball slipped through my hands and bounced towards the side line; the wing defence leaped after it. I gave chase and stumbled, falling against the other girl, knocking her through the gap in the fence and into the hedge outside.

I stared at my victim, half-buried in stinging nettles.

She let out a low moan.

One of the mums rushed off court with her first aid kit, running to attend to the injured girl. She pulled the player out of the hedge and to her feet. There were scarlet scratches on her arms, legs and face.

As she limped away around the outside of the court, the other team made a substitution and the game continued for the last couple of minutes.

After the final whistle, I trotted over to the injured girl, who sat on a bench having her wounds cleaned. 'Sorry,' I said with no conviction.

She looked up, eyes full of hurt and defeat.

I winked at her before running off to grab my bag and head home.

It was a warm May evening, sunset still hours away, so I decided to walk back to my village through the fields, rather than hanging around with the other girls waiting for the bus and chatting about boys. There'd be time to shower before dinner.

As I made my way past the shoulder-high crops, I thought about calling Tom when I got home. We'd kissed at the under-eighteens disco, which I'd gone to because I knew he'd be there. He was going to be my 'normal' boyfriend.

I still thought about Oliver. I wasn't ashamed my mum had known what was going on. But I'd ruined her chance to have a relationship.

Mum's response had been extreme though. Perhaps there had already been cracks in her bond with Nigel.

With Tom, I planned to let things happen slowly. He played football, but wasn't like some of the other boys who stared at me in class, who grabbed their crotches as I walked past them in the corridor, made stupid comments like: 'My dad says redheads are trouble.' He wasn't a loner, but he always seemed to be on the edge of a group, watching. And when he watched me, which he'd been doing for a while, it wasn't sleazy. He'd just smile, when I caught him looking.

'You're in big trouble now, bitch,' said a voice from behind me.

I turned to see Tracey Burgess walking along the path. She stopped an inch from my face, her warm breath reeking of cigarettes and vodka, a strange mix of anger and pain in her eyes.

'I told you to stay away from Tom,' she said. 'I told you.'

I shoved Tracey away. 'You can't tell me to do anything.'

She reached for my hair, but I retaliated with a simple judo throw, gripping her shirt collar and sweeping her legs at the ankle. She landed on her generous backside.

'Big fucking mistake.' Tracey held something black in her hand; she squeezed it and a shiny silver blade popped out. She stood up and pointed it at me. 'I'm warning you,' she said. 'Stay the fuck away from Tom. You're a year below us, you can't have him.'

I made a fist with my right hand, but kept it down by my hip. I wasn't stupid. The idea that Tracey would use the knife on me – in an argument over a boy – was a little ridiculous. But she'd been drinking, and I'd seen other girls and boys drag her away from plenty of fights.

I dropped my head down, stared at my feet.

'Stupid cow,' Tracey said as she turned and walked away.

I stood for a while.

Bullies had never bothered me before. But I knew the only way to deal with them was to fight back.

I clambered over the wooden fence into the field next to the path. If I hurried, I could catch up with Tracey and get in front of her. I'd surprise her, grab the knife and wave it in her face, show her she couldn't push me around.

Running as fast as I could, I kept an eye out for her, ducking down where there were gaps in the fence or the hedges. I ran until I was sure I must be a couple of minutes ahead of her. I climbed back over the fence and kept running until I came to the bridge over the railway lines – the supports perfect for hiding behind.

I spotted a small chunk of concrete half the size of a brick that must have fallen from the bridge. I picked it up and waited.

Will Tracey hear my heavy breathing? *I wondered.* And what am I going to do, threaten her with a rock?

A train thundered past. Then, as the noise died away, I heard the sound of a foot scraping the path. I gripped the concrete, the rough edges digging into my palm. A wave of something – not anger, more like an aggressive but controlled energy – coursed through my body.

I saw brown hair and leapt forward, smashing the weapon into the back of Tracey's head. The force sent her toppling forwards, her forehead striking the path with a hollow clunk.

'Tracey?' I said. She didn't respond.

The train was gone now, leaving me in silence.

Why did you do that, Sarah? *I said to myself.* You were just going to threaten her.

I knelt on the ground and turned her over, then checked for a pulse like they'd shown us in first aid class. She was still alive.

Further up the path, voices — two of them.

I had to move Tracey.

But what if she wakes up? *I thought.* What then?

I hit her from behind so she wouldn't have seen anything. So should I ask these people for help?

The voices came closer.

I grabbed Tracey by her collar and waistband and rolled her off the path, into a ditch, then jumped down and tried to drag her along to a spot where a bush would hide us. But she was a hefty girl.

Now the voices were close enough to hear a man and woman discussing the warm weather, hear their dog panting.

Tracey wouldn't budge.

My hands, my whole body, trembled.

I gave one last heave and almost fell backwards as she slid along the grass and behind the hedge.

The voices passed, then faded.

I felt around Tracey's neck for a pulse again.

Nothing.

Do they put fifteen-year-olds in prison? *I wondered.*

Only if they get caught.

I climbed out of the ditch and found the lump of concrete. There was no blood on it, no hair. I threw it over the hedge.

She started it, *I told myself.* But I waited for her, attacked her from behind.

I frantically brushed the grass and leaves off my clothes and ran all the way home, arriving as rain started to fall.

In the hallway mirror, I caught sight of myself; my hair was a mess. I ran upstairs with my mother's words behind me: 'Dinner in two minutes.' I splashed my face with water and tied my hair back in a ponytail.

* * * * * *

As Sarah pauses, she hears the grandfather clock ticking behind her. 'You've been very quiet.'

'I've been listening,' Karl says.

'Shall I go on?' she says, sitting up on the couch.

Karl looks over her shoulder at the clock. 'We're already over the hour. Why don't we call it a day?'

Sarah shakes her head. 'This isn't going to be the usual kind of arrangement. We finish when I say so.'

Karl's eyes flick down to the phone on his desk. Sarah glances at his left hand: he's wearing a wedding ring.

'Better call your wife and tell her you won't be home for dinner.'

He winces at 'wife'.

'Before you pick up that phone, though,' she says, 'we should probably establish a few things. I want to make sure you understand exactly how this is going to work.'

'Go on,' Karl says.

'I know you don't have to keep things confidential if you think I'm dangerous, which I can assure you I am. I know you've worked with the police, helped catch murderers. I know you're already coming up with book titles in your head. But understand this: if you speak to anyone, your family … *anyone*,' she glares at him, 'you'll watch them die.'

Karl grips the arms of his chair until they creak.

'And that's a real threat for a variety of reasons,' Sarah says. 'I already know a hundred ways to escape from prison, I've been planning it for years. But even if I don't manage to get out, there won't be a place on earth you can hide. I can't allow you to search for me on the internet – it would establish a link between us. You'll just have to believe me when I say that I work for a hedge fund and I'm worth tens of millions. As soon as I'm caught, there'll be a price on your head. Can you imagine what would happen if I offered – let's say twenty million dollars in an offshore account – to whoever butchers or skins or burns you and your family alive? What kind of dreams do you think you'd have, if you could sleep at all?'

'I … I understand.' Karl snatches the phone's handset from its cradle, almost dropping it before mashing the buttons. 'I'm sorry, something's come up …' he says when a voice answers. 'No, no, nothing serious, just need to help someone. Don't wait up.' He replaces the receiver, takes a deep breath.

'Shall I lie down so we can continue?'

'Please … please do,' Karl says.

'Where was I?'

'You … you left a dead girl in a ditch. Did you feel any guilt?'

'It was a stupid thing for her to do, threatening me with a knife over some boy.'

'You'd do it again?'

'I don't know, it all happened so fast, I just wanted to teach her a lesson.'

'But you attacked her from behind.'

'You think I intended to kill her?'

Karl is silent for a while. 'With the boy …'

'Oliver?'

'Yes. Your desire to assert yourself over him was … at the extreme end of the spectrum.'

'I suppose you could put it like that.'

'With the netball player and the bully, they tried to assert their dominance and your response was also extreme.' Karl looks up at the ceiling then back at Sarah. 'What made you come here today?'

Sarah tells Karl about the estate, the hunts, the disposals. 'Everything was perfectly planned, clean, almost untraceable. But this week … I've spiralled out of control. I nearly raped a male colleague, snatched two teenagers and killed them. I'm going to get caught.'

'The boys … Bristol. That was you?'

'I needed a quick fix, they were available.' Sarah hears a sharp intake of breath from Karl, but no words. 'Is there something you want to tell me?' she says, sitting up again.

'The … police. They're looking for you.'

'I thought they might be.'

'I'm helping them.'

'Building a profile?' Sarah is curious about what kind of guesses they made.

'Giving them a few ideas. But … you're not a typical serial killer, not the female kind.'

'What do they know?'

'Very little,' Karl says. 'When I spoke to them, it was just a theory, that you're working alone, that you're the killer. The trail is cold.'

Sarah stands up, walks to Karl's desk and leans over him. 'What will you tell them now, if they come back?'

'I'll just give them the obvious interpretation of the facts, which won't lead them to you.'

'You should record any conversations you have.'

'I will.'

Sarah examines Karl's face for a moment. 'So do you think you can help me, make me stop?'

'We'll need a lot of time together. Tonight has been … chaotic. There are gaps that need to be filled in. I have to think. Come back in two days and we'll do this again.'

Sarah takes her hands off the desk and folds her arms. 'I won't take any drugs. It has to be therapy.'

'Understood.' Karl nods like an obedient little boy.

She goes to the door, then speaks without turning back. 'My name is Sarah,' she says. 'And remember what I promised, what will happen to your family, to you, if you tell anyone about me.' She opens the door. 'Goodnight, Karl. Pleasant dreams.'

Saturday August 17th 2013

Karl spent a little more time in his office, with the bottle of Scotch, after Sarah left and before he went home to bed. But the alcohol wore off sometime around four a.m., waking him – sweating, skull aching.

Liz caught an early train to Cambridge to spend the weekend with her sister.

Now he's back at the office. He frequently works weekends – writing, seeing patients undergoing intensive treatment.

He reviews his mental notes from last night, reminding himself of the key points. But it's a waste of time; the idea he can cure this woman with therapy is absurd. She's not a prototype psychopath, but she has some of the traits, using violence to achieve her goals.

Eventually he'll have to ask why she started her story so late, in her teenage years. The way she acted with the boy, Oliver – imposing herself on him, then exerting control in a sexual way. Well, it had to be a response to some kind of previous abuse. How will she react when he asks her about that?

Occasionally, one can rehabilitate violent people. Sit them in front of their victims, their families, draw tears. Make them hate themselves, the selves they need to escape.

And addicts can learn to break out of their habits, or replace unhealthy addictions with less harmful ones.

But a serial killer?

Of course, she fascinates Karl. But he also enjoys being alive.

At least the therapy sessions will buy him some time while he decides what course of action to take.

Karl checks his computer screen, which displays the view from the camera in his waiting room. Olivia is late as always, arriving flustered. She's probably spent a good long while asking herself whether she should come to the appointment or stay in bed.

She's wearing one of her usual floaty, flowered, short dresses, flat shoes. Tragic, fragile, beautiful Olivia with those pouting lips, lightly curled blonde hair, turquoise eyes. Only twenty-two and already a therapy veteran.

He calls her into his office.

'How are you feeling today?' he says as she sits down on the edge of the couch.

'I …' is all she can say before she bites her lip. Tears well in her eyes.

She needs anti-depressants, but they can wait a little longer.

'The difficult relationship you have with your parents, I think it would do you good to spend some time away from them.'

'Like a holiday?'

'Not quite. I have facilities here, for patients. You'll have your own room. There's a very pleasant garden, a library stocked with books and DVDs. We'll have early morning therapy sessions and we can eat together in the evening if you'd like.'

'Will all this be expensive?' she says, fiddling with the hem of her dress.

'Your father won't have to pay anything extra. I do this for patients who I believe will benefit.'

'I think I'd like that.' She almost manages a smile and there's nearly a glimmer of hope in her eyes.

'I also have a room I can stay in, if you'd rather not be alone in the building. Or I can arrange for a nurse to be here, if you'd prefer.'

'It's convenient for you to stay here?'

'It's my job,' Karl says, then has to cough to prevent himself from smiling.

* * * * * *

Phil waits in the office in Wardour Street, alone.

Is this a mistake? Should I have listened to Martin?

The door downstairs slams shut and Cook hobbles up. 'My choice and I rent something with fucking stairs,' he says, limping in and sitting behind the desk. 'What you got for me?'

'I … well, it's …'

'Where's DI White?' Cook says, frowning. And watching.

'He … uh …'

'I've got an appointment in fifty-five minutes. Think you can string a sentence together before I go?'

Phil clears his throat. 'I think we've got a lead, but, well, it's a bit of a weird one.'

'I'd expect nothing less from you two.'

OK, he asked for it.

Phil tells him about Martin's conversation with Colin, the videos, the backpacker. He doesn't mention Bristol. All the way through, he can feel Cook's eyes boring into him.

When Phil stops, the DCS leans back in his chair, hands behind his head. 'So you've got a suspect for the murder of an Austrian national in Thailand ten years ago.'

'She's English, though. Could have come back to the UK.'

'Could. And it sounds like I could've made a big fucking mistake with you two.'

'Martin thinks–'

'Why isn't he here explaining what he thinks?'

'He said you wouldn't go for this.'

Cook grunts.

'He reckons she's being careful now,' Phil says, 'but maybe she wasn't so careful back then.'

'What do you think?' Cook says, apparently more curious than hostile now.

'To be honest, sir, we haven't got anything else at the moment. If we can find similar murders abroad, then maybe we can link them to flights.'

Cook purses his lips, sucks in a little air. 'That's a lot of work, a lot, for something that's a bit … off the fucking wall.'

'Like I said, it's all we've got right now.'

Cook picks up a pen, taps the end on the desk. 'I suppose … I know the Interpol boys up in Manchester. Couldn't hurt to see if this … what d'you say her name was?'

'Bellona.'

'Right. Couldn't do any harm to see if she did it again.'

* * * * * * *

Karl says goodnight and leaves Olivia in the drawing room, legs curled up on a green leather chaise longue, reading a book in her pyjamas. Her room is stocked with toiletries, dressing gowns, slippers and four sizes of plain underwear to give the impression of it being an often-used facility for spontaneous stays.

The over-salted dinner will ensure she finishes her drink and the temazepam in it should keep her unconscious until the morning.

Karl monitors her via the video feed on his office computer. Her lips move and occasionally she frowns or smiles as she reads.

Soon her eyelids droop and she falls asleep, sliding down into a lying position.

Karl has a sip of Scotch, to steady himself, then slips back into the drawing room.

He lifts Olivia's arm, lets it slump back down. He unfastens her dressing gown and carefully pulls off her pyjamas, placing them on the floor. He works the white cotton knickers down her legs, unfastens her bra. He rearranges her limbs into his favourite pose: right leg bent, left hanging off the sofa so he can see her neatly trimmed, golden pubic hair from across the room. He puts her right hand behind her head, the left rests on her belly. A live reconstruction of the oil painting hanging on the wall behind her.

He kneels, presses his nose to her neck, breathing in the sweet, citrus scent on her skin. Slowly he works his way down, kissing her all over with his lips closed, brushing the skin, leaving no saliva.

This will be a far as he goes with Olivia. One day he'll be in a position to do more. It's difficult, though; another of his patients going missing would be harder to explain.

It had been so easy with Katie. She had often spoken of, and he had noted, a desire to disappear, leave her life behind. So, of course, that provided a convenient explanation when she vanished.

He took a week off work, stayed in a holiday cottage near Kendal and kept her unconscious for days. Every day he washed her, cared for her, kissed her. He can still smell that almond and honey fragrance on her skin, taste her minty tongue, hear her shallow moans and gasps.

If only he could do that with all the girls, if only he could get away with it.

That's how this woman, Sarah, feels, isn't it? She just does as much as she can without getting caught.

My motivations are less self-indulgent, almost noble by comparison, Karl thinks. *These damaged young women, destined for a life of medication, depression and exploitation. They'll keep involving themselves with selfish men, keep obeying their domineering parents. These girls are incapable of feeling self-worth or joy or warmth. I appreciate their vulnerable beauty. I enjoy them, care for them, love them.*

Sarah is not someone to be cared for; she has to be broken, conquered. He can play her games for a little while, but there will be only one loser if he obeys her rules.

He has the facilities here. He has the drugs and the advantage of surprise.

But a small mistake would be catastrophic.

If Olivia wakes now, he can sedate her. It will all be like a dream, if she remembers anything at all. With Sarah, he'll have to kill her somehow, make it look like an accident, or at least self-defence.

Sunday August 18th 2013

Sarah runs a finger along Karl's bookcases, which cover the wall to his left. 'So you're a fan of the fictional psychos?' she says.

'It's interesting to see what people believe a killer should be, how they might think.'

'Who's your favourite?' she says.

Karl pauses to ponder the question. 'It's terribly boring, but Lecter is hard to beat. The idea of him writing for the *Journal of Abnormal Psychology* always makes me chuckle.'

'He's almost too good, though, isn't he?' she says, spotting a hardback copy of *The Silence of the Lambs* and plucking it from the shelf. 'Who wants to read about chases and the FBI when you could have Hannibal just talking?'

'Do you have a favourite, Sarah?'

She doesn't hesitate. 'Patrick Bateman. *American Psycho* is hilarious.'

'You don't object to the violence against women?'

Sarah snaps the book shut. 'I thought your profession required intelligence,' she says, then continues to examine the collection. 'It's actually a credit to women that all these boys have to be such caricatures. A girl can rip out your heart without laying a finger on you.'

'Your crimes are violent.'

'Nothing I do is gratuitous, though … well, not usually.'

Karl gives her a tight little smile. 'Perhaps we should carry on where we left off last night?'

Sarah lies on the couch. 'You wife doesn't mind you working late again? It's already eight-thirty.'

'She's away.'

I wonder if that's true. 'Where did we finish?'

'You killed the girl. I'm guessing you got away with it.'

* * * * * * *

There were no classes for a week after Tracey's death, although I went back to school with Mum to talk to the police. They were interviewing lots of my classmates, but of course I was still nervous.

As the conversation progressed, though, I started to relax. There were two detectives sitting across a table from me: a woman with hair scraped back in a ponytail who asked all the questions, and a big burly man who looked bored and stupid.

The woman asked if I'd met anyone else on the path that night, whether I'd seen Tracey hanging around with any strangers or noticed any cars parked at the edge of the village.

It was obvious they were treating me as a witness, not a suspect. The whole thing lasted less than half an hour.

The first day back at school was uneventful too, and I walked home along that path through the fields again, feeling a little pride. As the days had gone by, my view became this: Tracey tried to hurt me; I chased her down and killed her; she got what she deserved.

But this time, when I emerged from the gap in the hedge at the edge of the village, there was a navy blue car parked by the road.

The burly male detective stepped out, opened the back door and told me to get in. He had the same bored look, his eyes dopey. His tie was loose, tufts of black hair sprouting from his open collar, matching those on his balding head.

I hesitated. If he really knew what had happened with Tracey, there was no point in running. That could only make things worse, could only make me look guilty.

'Where's your partner?' I said. 'The woman?'

'I'm not here to interview you.'

'Then what do you want?'

'I'm here to help.'

I stood there, staring at him for a minute.

'I know it was you,' he said. 'So just get in.'

'I don't know what you're talking about.' I started to walk around his car.

He took two swift steps and grabbed my arm with his huge hand. 'Get in the car. Now.'

I got in the back seat; he got in the front on the other side and looked at me in the rear view mirror. The car stank of sweat and grease, like someone had been living in it for years.

'What would your mum say if she knew?'

'She wouldn't believe any of the lies you tell her.'

'I bet she wouldn't.' He smirked. 'Pretty little girl like you. Bet you're popular. Bet everyone's so proud of you. Can't imagine how disappointed they'll be when they know what you did.'

'I didn't do anything.'

He shook his head. 'Between the time you stepped onto that path,' he gestured with his thumb, 'and you stepped off, she died.'

'It could have been someone else.'

'So what were you doing in the bushes?'

I felt a jolt in my chest. 'What are you talking about?'

'An old couple, walking their dog. You remember them?'

I hesitated. He smirked again.

'They walked in the opposite direction, but they didn't see you. If you didn't pass them, you were off the path, hiding.'

'I … I was smoking.'

'What brand?'

'Marlboro Lights.'

'Who did you get them from? How much did they cost?'

'I ... I'm not telling. They'd get in trouble.'

'Right. I'm accusing you of murder and you're protecting someone who sold cigarettes to a fifteen-year-old?'

I glared at him in the mirror. I realised he wasn't bored or stupid; he just had a face that made it look that way. Behind the blank mask was a sharp mind.

'I don't think me wandering off the path is enough.'

'I've got the rock as well.'

I put my hand to my mouth; I thought I was going to vomit.

'If you'd gone for help, you'd have gotten away with it. Self-defence. But you dragged her to that ditch, left her there.'

'Don't you need a motive?' I said.

'She was a bully, that's what everyone says.' He twisted in his seat to examine me. 'Bet if I asked around, someone would remember something. Maybe a joke about your red hair. Or there's a bloke involved.'

I must have twitched when he said that because he laughed. 'Some bloke, some fifteen-year-old spotty little prick.' He laughed so hard that the car shook.

When he stopped, I said, 'I want you to take me to the police station. My mum should be with me, and a lawyer.'

'You think they can protect you? We both know you did it.'

'I don't think you can prove it.'

'So you admit that you killed her?'

'No.'

'Well, you'd better start working on your story then, find someone to say they sold you those cigarettes.'

'I'll say I ... went off the path to pee.'

I could tell he had a picture of that in his mind after I'd said it – it was the first time I'd seen any life in his eyes.

'Right now, no one suspects you. Nobody's taken your fingerprints or DNA. No one's been sniffing around for a link between you and Tracey.'

'I could say I was scared, it was self-defence, she threatened me with a knife.'

'What kind of knife?'

'One that pops out of a handle.'

'Interesting,' he said. 'How d'you know about the knife?'

'I …'

He tutted. 'Oh, dear, Sarah, oh, dear. So now we know you were there. And your story's that, in self-defence, you whacked someone on the back of the head and then dragged them into a ditch.'

'You said "we". Only you know I was there. I'll deny everything.'

'We can test your shoes, see if they match the mud from the ditch. You touched the rock, you dragged her. There'll be traces. Try your luck.'

'You tricked me.'

'That's what I do,' he said. 'You'd be surprised … well, now you wouldn't. But … most people are surprised at how easy it is. I'm a pro, dealing with amateurs.'

I looked out of the window just to avoid his smug grin.

'Of course,' he said. 'It doesn't have to be like this.'

I turned to face him again. 'Like what?'

'Taking you down the station, fingerprints, going to court. Probably won't get life, 'cos you're young, but you won't be going to university or getting a decent job. And you should see the girls locked up in those places. Might give you more than a tap on the back of the head.'

'I can look after myself.'

'Are you on the pill?' he said.

'What?'

'You heard.'

'No.'

'But you've had sex?'

'Yes.'

'When did your period start?'

'What's that got to do with anything?'

'When?'

'I was twelve.'

'No. When did the last one start?'

'So this is what you want me to do? Talk about sex and stuff?'

'When?'

I counted the days on my fingers. 'Seven days ago.'

He got out of the car, opened the back door and sat next to me. 'You'll go on the pill, go to the doctor tomorrow and say you want it.'

And before I'd had time to think about the implications of what he was suggesting, his huge hands were on my shoulders, pushing me down, sliding me under him as he lay on me, crushing me with his weight. He pulled my underwear to one side, unzipped himself and forced his way into me.

I froze.

I felt tiny, helpless. His chest was in my face; he was blocking everything out, his massive slab of a body covering me like the lid of a tomb.

I stayed there, crumpled up on the back seat after he finished. He zipped himself up and returned to the front.

'Sit up and put your seat belt on,' he said.

'Where are we going?'

'I'll take you home, then I'll be in touch. Make sure you go to the doctor tomorrow, to get started on the pill.'

He stopped the car at the end of my lane. He spoke without turning round, his voice casual: 'Telling anyone about this won't help you. The evidence is still there. Everyone'll think you let me do it because you wanted to save yourself.'

As I opened the door, he said, 'You'll be damaged goods. A murderer and a dirty little bitch. Nobody will ever want you.'

* * * * * *

'Daddy, ice cream!' Molly says to Martin. They're standing outside some kind of modern milk shake emporium, next to the swooping white concrete of London Zoo's penguin enclosure.

Despite visiting the local zoo with her grandparents three times in the past week, the first thing Molly said when Martin met her and Charlotte at Waterloo station was, 'Monkeys. Want monkeys.'

Is she allowed ice cream, he wonders? *Charlotte definitely has a thing about sugar. But then how does Molly know what ice cream is if she's not allowed it?*

'We can share one,' Martin says, persuading himself that he's treading a safe middle ground. 'Don't tell Mummy, though – it will just be our secret.'

'Ice cream! Ice cream!' Molly says, her hand breaking free of Martin's as she totters away.

He lifts her up so she can point at the snacks to be mixed with the ice cream. He counsels her against choosing things she really doesn't want, like Goji berries, and things he really doesn't want, like any kind of jelly sweet. They end up with a chocolate-heavy blend that includes M&Ms and a chocolate orange, which Martin enjoys a little too much and almost finishes.

Molly frowns at him: 'Share, Daddy.'

He lets her take the rest, then wipes most of it off her face.

Maybe everything Charlotte said is true, Martin thinks. Perhaps her parents really are attending their friend's fortieth wedding anniversary and one of her old colleagues is passing through London on her way back to Boston from Moscow. But he'd like to think his wife wants him to spend time with their daughter, that she's already decided being awkward isn't the right choice.

These days out, though, seeing Daddy at the weekend as some kind of treat, it's not the same as living together as a family, Martin thinks as Molly watches infant gorillas rolling around on the concrete while their mother lounges close by.

Martin wants this – he's glad to be out of the house, taking a break from reading endless news reports of backpacker murders from the last ten years. And he knows he's smoking too much, passing out on the sofa and waking up fully clothed every morning.

He hasn't heard from Phil, but he also hasn't heard from Cook, so at least his 'partner' hasn't wrecked things. It's too early to tell whether the killer struck again last night, but Martin is expecting some kind of climax, a further escalation. No reports yet of a bloodbath anywhere in the country, though, or an entire truckload of young men going missing.

* * * * * * *

As soon as the detective drove away, I could feel something boiling deep inside me. I knew I had to act while I was still angry, before I'd had time to think. I didn't tell Mum why I wanted her to take me to the police station – if anyone stalled me, those seeds of doubt he'd attempted to plant might have time to germinate.

It wasn't until I spoke to the uniformed officer behind a plastic screen that Mum heard me say, 'I've been raped.'

There was a long, almost silent moment, just the sound of a flickering fluorescent light, then I was ushered through a door, down a corridor and into a windowless room with a scuffed grey table and two chairs either side. I waited with my mum until the female detective who'd interviewed me at school walked in with a chubby, younger man. The female detective stared at me the way you look at someone you think you might recognise. Her mouth dropped open when I told her my story, then her cheeks flushed red and she left the room for a few minutes with her colleague.

I was interviewed, then taken to see a doctor to be examined and tested, prodded and swabbed, then sent home.

Two days later, the story made the news. My name couldn't be mentioned, but local people knew.

Other victims came forward. He'd targeted the daughters and girlfriends of more than a dozen suspects, trading time in the back of his car for losing evidence and turning a blind eye. He'd been walking around on a thin layer of fear for years, but he'd underestimated my temper. I was too angry to feel scared. And there was no trace of me anywhere on Tracey or at the scene – the rain had washed it all away.

I was a victim, not a suspect.

The only thing left unresolved was down to me. I'd been given the morning-after pill, but I kept it in my pocket for three days, slipping my hand in and touching the packet, never taking it out until it was too late.

When I realised I was pregnant, I felt an immediate, unbreakable bond with my son. I knew the baby was a boy.

I started to have fantasies. I would wait until James was grown up, then tell him how he was conceived, what his father had done. James would explode with rage, strangling the frail old ex-Detective Chief Inspector Barry Ross, squeezing the life out of him while I watched with pride.

Obviously, looking back, I know that I'd lost my mind. I thought what I'd been through made me an adult – an adult who had experienced things that few others had. I was still just a fifteen-year-old, though, collapsing under a psychological burden someone twice my age would struggle to carry.

Mum noticed that I was putting on weight. But I was eating more and not playing sport over the summer holidays. I spent a lot of time at home, sitting around in baggy clothes, watching TV.

When September arrived, I had to tell her. I couldn't fit into my school uniform and the bump had gotten too big to hide with a jumper.

She didn't say anything; there was just a twitch in her lips, and then she gave me a hug. I still remember the feeling of her pushing against my *belly. I'm sure she somehow managed to blame herself in the way that mothers often do.*

She took me to see the doctor, accompanied me to my scans. By the time I'd told her about the pregnancy, it was already too late to terminate – it was never discussed.

Back at school, nobody said anything, but they didn't talk to me either. And they stared – there was always a pair of eyes on me and my bump. I didn't care. To me, they were just children. I was going to be a mother.

A month before my due date, I woke with a dull ache in my belly. I was sitting in geography class after lunch when I felt the baby kicking frantically. I excused myself and hurried towards the bathroom, but in the corridor my waters broke. The fluid was flecked with fresh blood.

I was rushed to hospital in an ambulance and immediately examined and scanned. James was still kicking in frenzied bursts, followed by periods of no activity whatsoever.

The placenta had started to separate from my uterus and the baby was in distress. I had a blood transfusion, then an emergency Caesarean under general anaesthetic.

When I woke up, James was dead.

There'd also been further complications and bleeding – they'd had to remove my uterus.

I would never be able to carry another child.

* * * * * * *

After Sarah leaves, Karl remains in his office and makes a phone call.

Martin answers on the sixth ring. 'Hello?' he says, his voice slurred.

'It's Karl.'

'OK.'

'I was just wondering how you're getting on with the case.'

'What do you know about it?'

'You came to ask my advice.'

A pause. 'Oh ... yes. It was good advice.'

'Really?'

'Well, sort of ... I think. We're on the trail of someone. But ... it could be someone else.'

Martin has clearly slipped into old habits – drink, drugs … he's definitely on something. And maybe it's not even Sarah who he's pursuing.

Of course, Karl could tell Martin to come to his office tomorrow morning, with a hundred colleagues. But if the police botch things, Karl would quickly find out whether Sarah is serious about harming him and his family.

'Martin, when we finished your treatment, you had given up the substances.'

'I'm on top of things.'

'It doesn't sound that way. How's your marriage?'

'We're getting divorced.'

'You're seeing your daughter?'

'Sometimes.'

'And how's your mother?'

'She died a couple of weeks ago.'

'I'm sorry.' He can't take a risk and have Martin come to see him for therapy – Sarah wouldn't believe that Karl was only helping the detective with personal problems. 'I'm going to recommend that you speak to a colleague of mine. You should call her as soon as possible.'

'I'm fine.'

'When someone with your history says, "I'm fine," it's like a salesman who says, "Trust me."'

'I'm fine. Really.'

'So what are you blocking out with the substance abuse?'

Martin laughs. 'Abuse? A little smoke, couple of drinks.'

'You sound drunk.'

'I'm tired.'

'You need professional help.'

'I need to be left alone.'

'Well, are you alone now, without your family?'

There's silence on the other end of the line.

'I'm sorry, Martin. But I'm very concerned about you.'

'There's no need.'

'You have responsibilities. Your daughter, your work.' Karl says. 'The death of a family member, the end of the relationship, lack of access to a child. All of these things individually are enough to upset a person's equilibrium. It's vital that someone with your history receives help.'

'I'm not grieving. There'd been trouble between me and Charlotte for a long time. And I still get to see Molly.'

'So why are you high and drunk?'

'Karl, when I was in trouble – and back then it was obvious I did have problems, I wasn't coping – you helped me. I'm grateful for that. But I'm OK now. It's different.'

'Have you considered that you may be in a state of denial? With what's going on in your life, should you feel fine? Doesn't that suggests something's wrong? And have you considered what impact it might have on your work?'

'I'm working hard.'

'You're sitting around getting–'

'If you accuse me of being drunk one more time, I'm hanging up.'

'But you are sitting alone, in an empty house, drinking, smoking and what, watching television?'

'I'm relaxing.'

'Avoiding.'

'Goodbye, Karl.'

'Martin–' is all Karl can say before his ex-patient hangs up.

Monday August 19th 2013

Karl experiences a sense of familiarity as well as fear as Sarah lies down on his couch once again. Although he understands that the sessions cannot continue forever, he has to admit that Sarah provides a professional thrill. She doesn't make his skin crawl, like some of the other killers he's met. She's certainly not a whinger. And she appeals to his academic curiosity and desire for discovery.

'Based on what you told me yesterday,' he says, 'you're still fertile, you can still produce—'

'Eggs?' Sarah says.

'So why not use a surrogate?'

Sarah sighs. 'I was going to. I'd done all the research, met some potential candidates. Then the dreams started.'

'Dreams?'

'I don't think these will be hard for you to interpret.'

Karl instinctively reaches for a notepad, then withdraws his hand. 'Tell me. Don't leave anything out.'

'Every night I'd wake up from nightmares that would stay with me all day. The surrogate is drinking, smoking, taking drugs. I beg her to stop but she ignores me. Then the baby comes out – it has no eyes and no mouth. Or she gives birth, stands up and runs out of the room with the baby. I try to chase her but can't get close. She jumps on a train and she's gone. So I find another surrogate, we live in the same room during the pregnancy, sleep in the same bed, eat all our healthy meals together. But one night I wake to find her trying the door handle. I pin her down, tear her open with my hands, but there's no baby inside, just a hollow space.'

'Who is the father of these children?'

'There isn't one.'

'Tell me about your father,' Karl says.

'A holiday romance, my mum spent only one night with him.'

'What about your mother?'

'She's a good woman, worked hard to look after me.'

'That's important?' Karl says, once again feeling the urge to take notes, underline things. 'She worked hard? What about emotionally? Did she give you what you wanted?'

'She was always there when I needed her.'

Karl decides to return to the parents later. 'Why do you think you behaved the way you did towards Oliver, and why did you retaliate, killing the bully?'

'I have no idea.'

'You know it's unusual not to feel any guilt when you harm someone?'

'I understand,' Sarah says, 'that other people behave and think differently to me. And now, I can rationalise things. Humans aren't special. Our experiences may feel wonderful and beautiful and mystical. But everything we perceive is just electrical impulses and chemicals, passing through the bits of an animal that, in others, usually only make it into the poorest-quality pies and sausages.'

Karl chuckles. 'That's one way of describing human consciousness,' he says. 'But back then, what did you think?'

'It …' Sarah says. 'It just felt natural. She attacked me, I fought back.'

'And now, when you're seeking people out, hunting down men who have made no aggressive moves towards you, does that feel natural?'

'Have you ever been in a fight?' Sarah says.

'I stayed out of trouble in school.'

'What about being mugged, something frightening?'

'I've had confrontations with dangerous patients. And, well … there was you the other day, with the gun,' Karl says, although that now seems like something he saw in a film, which didn't really happen to him.

'And how did those things make you feel?'

'Shaken,' he says.

'Right. Adrenaline, fight or flight. Now imagine if you could stretch out that feeling for minutes, while knowing you'll almost certainly be able to overpower the other person. There's risk and danger because you can't be sure they won't surprise you, but you push that to the back of your mind. It's physical, exciting, *real*. Nothing else comes close.'

'You're feeling that now, aren't you, just talking about it?'

Sarah turns and grins at Karl over the back of the couch, the most human gesture she's displayed since he met her.

'But what about afterwards?' he says. 'When you've got a corpse, someone who had a family?'

'I don't think about them any more,' Sarah says. 'There are so many people in the world. Right now, somebody is dying in a car crash, cancer is slowly ravaging millions of bodies. Family and friends care about you, but in the context of seven billion people, you're insignificant, you barely exist. And when someone tried to hurt me, I fought back.'

Now it's Karl's turn to grin. 'Fascinating,' he says. 'Fascinating. But I repeat my question. Why did you kill the bully? Can you remember any events, violent or perhaps simply traumatic, from your early childhood?'

'I don't remember much, from before my teenage years. I mean, there are these memories, tangled up in photos and stories my mother tells, but they're just about days out at the seaside, my favourite toys, that sort of thing.'

This is it, he thinks. *The opportunity. Get the drug.*

'I'd like to run a couple of tests,' he says, his professional curiosity getting the better of him.

'What kind?' Sarah says, sitting up.

'You do them on the computer.'

'What are you looking for?'

'Do you mind if we discuss it afterwards? I don't want to influence the results.'

She shrugs. 'OK.'

For the next two hours, Sarah performs memory tasks, plays games where she loses points for incorrectly categorising cards, and describes facial expressions that flash up on the screen. She watches more pictures of facial expressions, as well as violent scenes, with electrodes attached to the back of her hand.

'One more thing and then we're done,' Karl says, giving her no indication that the results so far have shocked him. 'I'd like you to lie on the sofa and we'll do a little old-fashioned word association. Just say the first thing that comes into your head.' He holds up a digital recorder. 'I'll use this, but you can watch me erase it, once I've listened to it again.'

Sarah lies back on the sofa.

'Just say the first word that comes into your mind. It's important you don't pause to think.'

'Fire away.'

'Love?'

'Warm.'

'Child?'

'Boy.'

'Money?'

'Easy.'

'Mother?'

'Good.'

'Love?'

'Death.'

'Memory?'

'Computer.'

'Father?'

'Gone.'

'Guilt?'

'Weakness.'

Karl pauses for a second. 'Child?'

'Friend.'

'Violence?'

'Language.'

'Father?'

'Daddy.'

Karl stops the recorder. 'Interesting,' he says. 'Very, very interesting.'

Sarah sits up again. 'Are you going to tell me now? What the diagnosis is?'

Karl holds up his hands. 'I'm afraid I can't.'

'Why not?'

'Because … well, because I don't know. At least not yet.'

She frowns. 'What about the tests?'

'The tests,' Karl says, 'suggest you are not what we understand to be a psychopath.'

'Are you sure?' Sarah says with a mixture of surprise and scepticism.

'Psychopaths perform poorly on tasks that require them to learn from punishment. They also struggle when required to describe facial expressions, especially those of people in distress.'

'So what about me?'

'It appears you're able to process emotional information and threats of punishment like anyone else, but from what you've said, you choose to ignore them.'

'But … I kill people. It's all planned out.'

'A true psychopath wouldn't feel the "shakes" you refer to – they don't experience anxiety. Although … the way you behaved when we first met had a certain narcissistic quality – "You've never had a patient like me," you said.'

'That was about you, not me,' Sarah says. 'For the same reason I nearly raped a colleague. I can't stand arrogance, can't resist cutting people like that down to size.'

'I suppose that's … a reasonable explanation,' Karl says. He sits for a while, tapping his lips with a finger. 'I need to do a little reading, a little thinking. Same time tomorrow?'

* * * * * *

Twenty years ago, Karl spent a week at Arnold Nussbaum's apartment overlooking Central Park. Back then, they ate breakfast before Arnold opened the door to his first patient at eight.

Now Karl checks the time. It's twelve-fifteen, so that makes it seven-fifteen a.m. in New York. Arnold should be available. The phone rings three times before Karl hears the president of the American Psychoanalytic Association's quick, precise 'Hello.'

'Arnold, it's Karl.'

'Karl who?'

'Karl Gross.'

'Oh, yes. What do you want?'

'I'm not interrupting your breakfast, am I?' Karl says, picturing Arnold and his toast rack.

'You are.'

'Well … I wanted to ask your advice.'

Arnold sighs, sending a rush of air down the line. 'Enter into analysis and become a real psychoanalyst,' Arnold says. 'And stop publishing those distasteful books.'

'Still got that dry sense of humour, I see.'

'That wasn't a humorous comment.'

I know, Karl thinks, *I know*. 'Anyway … I have a question for you, regarding a specific case–'

'Because you're not a real psychoanalyst.'

'Perhaps. I have an intriguing patient–'

'I'm not impressed by celebrity,' Arnold says, although to Karl's ear it sounds like his interest has been piqued.

'Oh, no, she's not well known, quite the opposite, in fact. But she's fascinating, displays psychopathic tendencies–'

'How?'

Karl coughs. 'She's … she's a little violent towards men, but displays none of the classic signs of psychopathology. There's no grandiose image of herself. And she does exhibit a kind of anxiety during violent episodes.'

'Have you explored her attachments?'

'Not extensively.'

'Of course you haven't,' Arnold says. 'And her childhood more generally?'

'She has few memories. It seems the violent behaviour began in her teens.'

'That's unremarkable.'

'Perhaps,' Karl says. *I know the basics, Arnold.* 'She was raped, fell pregnant and had a hysterectomy. But she was violent and sexually aggressive before that trauma.'

'Are her stories credible?'

'For the most part. I remember the rape case – a policeman was involved and it received a great deal of media coverage. As a juvenile victim she wasn't named, though …'

'And the early sexual behaviour?'

'I suppose her story of what she did with a boy feels like a fantasy.'

'You haven't been able to unlock anything significant from her childhood?'

'I can only think there's something biological or … she's repressing memories of sexual abuse.'

'Hah. I should have known someone like you would turn to seduction theory.'

'No, no, I'm just considering all possibilities.'

'Well,' Arnold says. 'My advice to you – because you're clearly not qualified to deal with any kind of complexity – is to end your relationship with this woman. Send her elsewhere.' He hangs up.

I'm going to dig a little more, Karl thinks, *but when it comes to ending things with her … well Arnold, I think you could be right.*

Tuesday August 20th 2013

'I want to return to your mother,' Karl says. 'If she died, you would be ...?'

'Devastated,' Sarah says.

'Why?'

'Because she's my mother. She looked after me when I was young.'

'Do you still feel an attachment to her?'

'We don't see each other often, but I think about her. And I make sure she's well looked after.'

'Financially?'

'Yes.'

'Has there been anyone else? Since your teenage years? Men you've had relationships with?'

'A few, but ... their attachment to me is always stronger than mine to them. At some point, every single one of them tells me I'm nothing like anyone they've known before. It's often for the most bizarre reasons. One told me I reminded him of his father. And plenty of them seem to be encouraged by the emotional torture I can dispense, becoming cold and distant.'

Those reasons are less bizarre than you think, Karl wants to say. He understands why certain men would be unable to get over this woman.

'You were fond of some of them?' Karl says.

'I was.'

'You didn't ... ah–'

'Kill any of them? No, I prefer to keep a distance from my prey.'

That word makes Karl sit up. There are many potential meanings. 'Were there any incidents with animals when you were young?'

'As I mentioned, I used to chase the neighbour's cats, but it was only so I could stroke them.'

No, not a classic psychopath at all. Karl hesitates, unsure of what additional areas to explore. 'Did you … did you make up stories when you were younger? Or perhaps you used to imagine yourself as a character in your favourite book or on a TV programme?'

Sarah doesn't move or speak. But the silence and stillness feel like the moment in a disaster movie, just before a tidal wave smashes into a coastal town or an aeroplane crashes to the ground.

'I was wondering,' Karl says, changing tack again. 'About the – and I hope you don't mind me mentioning this – the fertility issue. I have a friend who's one of the world's foremost gynaecologists. I could put you in touch. Things move on–'

Sarah stands up and lifts her dress, exposing her scar. 'I'm missing a womb.'

'I wasn't suggesting–'

'Did I make up stories, imagine myself as … what? A comic book character, perhaps?'

'I … I'm just.' Karl shifts in his seat, then speaks quickly, 'I'm exploring every avenue. Your case is complex. And I have to admit, rather confusing.'

'So where does that leave us?' Sarah says, sitting down but keeping her eyes fixed on Karl.

He makes a steeple with his hands, gives the impression he's deep in thought. 'There is a technique that can be used, to remove inhibitions, let repressed thoughts bubble up to the surface.'

Sarah cocks her head to one side, her eyes narrowing.

'Sodium pentothal, the truth serum so beloved by Hollywood.'

'I'm familiar with it.' Sarah waggles a finger. 'But no drugs, that was the rule.'

'This wouldn't be something you could become dependent on. It would just be active a few minutes, to help unlock things.'

'You have it here?'

'I've used it with other patients. Successfully.'

Sarah takes a deep breath, then exhales. 'You want me to lie here, while you give me something that's used as an anaesthetic, that in high-enough doses is a lethal injection?'

'You *are* familiar with it.'

'Call it a professional interest,' Sarah says. 'Go and get it.'

Karl pauses. *No, don't hesitate.*

He goes to his medicine cabinet, unlocks it and retrieves syringes, a small white cardboard box and a handful of plastic packages. He sits next to Sarah on the couch. 'I'm going to put a line into your hand.'

'You first.'

'Sorry?' he says, although he understands exactly what she's suggesting.

'You'll take it so I can ask you a few questions,' Sarah says, 'make sure I can trust you.'

'I'm afraid I can't allow that.'

'Allow it?' Sarah says, smiling, almost laughing.

'This is a dangerous drug, you're not qualified—'

'Tell me what dose to give.'

Karl looks down at the packets in his hand. 'It varies. And the drug wears off extremely quickly, you have to keep topping it up.'

'Give me instructions.'

'It doesn't work like that.'

Sarah smiles and raises an eyebrow. 'Didn't you plan for this?'

'I didn't plan anything,' Karl says, but his voice is an octave higher than normal.

'You did. Steer the conversations towards repressed thought, administer the lethal dose. You thought it would be that simple?'

'I'm trying to help you.'

'Prove it. Take the drug. *Take it.*'

'OK, OK, I'll take it.' Karl fumbles with a plastic packet, tears it open. He carefully slides a cannula, connected to a narrow plastic tube, into a vein in the back of his left hand. Then he pricks a vial of sodium pentothal with one of the syringes, fills it with the drug and connects the syringe to the other end of the plastic tube. 'Give me this much,' he says, pointing to the first marking on the syringe. 'And again after ten minutes. Whatever you do, please don't give me any more than that. I can't help you if I'm unconscious.'

Sarah pushes the plunger. Thirty seconds later she says, 'How does that feel?'

Karl smacks his lips, blinks lazily. His heart feels like it's vibrating. 'I'm … OK.'

'Can I trust you, Karl?'

'Um … yes. I want to help you.'

'Do you like little girls?'

'Wha–'

'Sorry, just a little joke.' Sarah picks up the white box of vials and frowns. 'When did you get these, Karl?'

He doesn't say anything.

'They were dispensed yesterday,' she says. 'Monday. You *did* have this all planned.'

'I ... I–'

'Your eyes. They're very alert all of a sudden. I've given you a miniscule dose, haven't I?'

'No ... I ... um.'

'Too late,' Sarah says, pushing the syringe plunger all the way.

* * * * * * *

Phil slides the giant map of the world out of its cardboard tube and pins it to the wall. He could be tagging the locations on a computer, but the paper might help to make this unbelievable scenario a little easier to comprehend.

He's read faxes and emails from around the world until his eyes ache. It's not just his vision that's suffering though. The contents of the reports and the implications of what they mean when considered together make his legs shake and his stomach sink in a way he's never experienced before, even with huge amounts at stake at the poker table.

He saves the red pins for the prototypical cases. Twenty-two men, all strangled. Many had cash or other valuables in their pockets. Some of the others had no doubt been robbed in the hours before their bodies were discovered.

After the Austrian backpacker, the victims were all locals – Thai, Indian, Filipino, Moroccan. Then there's a switch to Central and South America.

Finally, ten years ago, a young man was found strangled behind a hostel in Peru near the bodies of two Canadian backpackers; someone had beaten the Canadians to death with a brick. That's where the trail ends.

There's still no link to the crimes that happened in the UK. When photos and stats on the victims are available, though, they match the type. Slim, below average height, good looking. It will take a few days to obtain any DNA profiles that the local forces managed to collect, but matches will at least confirm they're chasing a multiple murderer.

Unfortunately there's one other pattern to the crimes: almost all the locations are tropical. The victims were typically found after heavy rains; the man in Marrakesh was dumped in a fountain. Any hair or saliva from the murderer could have been washed away.

And if this is the only trail they follow, she'll have time to kill again. Because it's been three days since Cook spoke to Interpol and now the real work will have to begin.

Phil doesn't know how many people fly in and out of South-east Asia every week, but it won't be a small number. Hundreds of thousands? Millions? And if you want to draw a line, you need two points. If she didn't fly under the same name twice, at times close to the murders, then they'll waste another few days.

Phil grabs the phone. Cook answers on the second ring. 'How many probables?' he says.

'Twenty-two.'

'Fuck me.'

Phil glances at the map, the map of the entire world. 'So are we going to open this up now, get more people on it? We'll need to involve the airlines.'

'You're forgetting where I used to work.'

'She's not a terrorist, though.'

Cook laughs. 'Don't you worry about that. Send me the locations and dates, I'll get a search started. Might take a day or two, we're going back ten years.'

'I suppose I should tell Martin,' Phil says, not sure whether he wants Cook to agree or disagree.

'Too bloody right. You two kiss and make up. If I get a name, I want you both on the road before you've had your cornflakes.'

Phil is about to agree, but Cook has hung up. He tries Martin's phone a couple of times. There's no answer.

He's probably too stoned to hear it.

* * * * * * *

Karl regains consciousness, but the sodium pentothal remains in his system, relaxing him.

He sits in the centre of his office. The heavy curtains are drawn.

He takes in the sight of his naked thighs and arms with a detached sense of calm. Yes, she's stripped him down to his vest and Y-fronts and tied his wrists, ankles, waist and chest to a metal chair with strips of cotton sheet – and gagged him – but it doesn't feel so bad.

I'm not dead, he thinks. *I just made a little mistake. I'm sure, if she wanted to kill me, she would have done it, just pumped me full of the drug.*

She hasn't hurt him, either. The drug isn't a painkiller yet he feels no physical discomfort.

As it wears off, though, a dimmer switch is turned up in his mind, slowly illuminating previously invisible thoughts.

The full dose in the syringe would only have rendered him unconscious for around fifteen to twenty minutes. *She's not in the room with me. She's either checking the house or she's left to fetch something.*

A few minutes pass and he hears no sign of anyone nearby.

Liz. Has Sarah gone to find Karl's wife?

He tries to scream but the gag is tight. *Who would hear me anyway?* Two acres of gardens surround the house. The nearest neighbours are octogenarians and probably deaf.

The gag suddenly makes it difficult to breathe – he inhales and exhales rapidly through his nostrils.

Sweat runs down his forehead, mixing with the tears dribbling down his cheeks.

The breaths get faster and shallower.

Leaving on the labels with the dispensing date was a catastrophic mistake. Sarah was very clear with him: she promised to do unspeakable things to his family if Karl reported her to the police. There's no point protesting that he didn't tell anyone anything. He tried to drug her, to kill her.

It feels like hours have passed when the door swings open and Sarah appears, carrying a large rucksack, the kind people take on a round-the-world trip. She drops it to the floor with a heavy thud, before retrieving a hoover from the hallway. She's changed into a tight black tracksuit, tied her hair back. And the sight of her latex gloves makes Karl's buttocks clench.

'You have a wife and two adult children, correct?' she says.

Karl nods.

'A boy and a girl, no grandchildren?'

Another nod and a muffled whimper.

Sarah removes the gag. 'Tell me about your wife.'

Karl hurries through the story of the accident, the wheelchair, Liz's attitude to the whole thing. *Perhaps Sarah will feel some sympathy*, he thinks. *Perhaps not.*

'Sounds like a tough old boot,' Sarah says. 'How do you think she'd cope with me using this on her daughter?' She pulls a stainless steel speculum from the rucksack. 'I'll open her up and cut it all out.'

'Please–'

'Of course, it will be a largely symbolic act – she'll quickly bleed to death,' Sarah says, with a degree of regret in her voice.

Karl closes his eyes, his lips quivering.

'I wouldn't do that. It will be easier to avoid the images if you've got them open.'

He does as she advises, but he can still see his daughter on a stretcher, gown covering her torso, knees raised, legs apart …

'Of course, with your son, all the important bits are external. I can probably keep him alive for a while, stitch him up, stem the flow of blood.'

Karl squirms in his seat as much as the bindings will let him.

'Do you have anything to say for yourself?' she says.

Karl takes a deep breath, then speaks in bursts: 'I think you need me … you need someone to talk to … I don't know if you need a partner … really want another child … but … you need someone.'

Sarah crosses her arms. 'You're the first person I ever spoke to, in this way, as an adult. Then you tried to drug me.'

'I … I was trying to help you, help you to remember.'

'And you just so happened to run out of sodium pentothal the day before?'

'Not … exactly. I'd considered using it, but wasn't sure–'

'What changed your mind?'

Karl hesitates.

'That's all I needed to know, Karl. You're a useless liar.' Sarah bends down and reaches for the bag.

'No, no, it's not that.'

She straightens up again.

'I was terrified,' Karl says.

'So you decided to drug me?'

'I wanted to access your unconscious mind. You obviously believe your teenage years are the source of your … well, they made you what you are. I think there's something before, though, something more painful, even more traumatic.'

Sarah screws up her face. 'Rape, losing a baby, infertility – those aren't traumatic?'

'You were different even before all that happened. When you were younger, there was someone you trusted perhaps?'

'Sorry, Karl, this story doesn't start with child abuse.'

Keep her talking, Karl thinks. *Show her some insight, demonstrate your value.* 'When … when was the last time you had sex?'

'Interesting question,' Sarah says, almost smiling. 'A few weeks ago.'

'Who with?'

'I meet men in bars frequently, but not to hunt them.'

'Do you find these encounters satisfying?'

Sarah frowns.

'Are there things that you want to do with them, but don't?'

'What makes you think that I'm sexually repressed?' Sarah says. 'If I fancied keeping a boy in my cellar, I'd do it.' She's silent for a few seconds, staring at the wall over Karl's shoulder. Then she looks at him. 'This arrangement was never going to work, was it? I don't know what I was thinking.'

Sarah reaches into her bag and pulls out a five-litre bottle of bleach. She also takes out a syringe and a small glass vial and places them on the floor next to the chair. Then she goes over to Karl's desk, opens and closes the drawers and returns with a pad of paper and a pen. With a small, sharp knife, she slices through the cotton tying his wrists to the chair.

'Your last words, for your family. Write them.'

Karl screams.

She ties the gag back on.

He yells into the cotton. Throat-shredding cries, echoing through his skull.

'Write them or don't write them. I don't care. You have one minute.' She checks her watch.

Karl sobs.

'Thirty seconds.'

Karl scribbles: I'M SORRY, I'M SORRY, I'M SO SORRY.

Sarah snatches the paper away, reads it, smiles, and places the note on the desk. She grabs Karl's hand, which still has a line in it for the sodium pentothal. He snatches the hand away.

Sarah walks around behind him and clutches his head to her stomach. The last thing he feels is a jab in the neck.

Wednesday August 21st 2013

Crime scene tape blocks the street, restraining the reporters and gawkers desperate to get up the driveway that snakes through the garden to Karl's office. Two white vans and a tent stand outside the open gates.

Martin climbs out of Phil's car. They haven't formally made up or exchanged apologies. They've negotiated a truce in the old-fashioned man's way: a series of silent nods and a smile.

And right now, Martin needs a friend. Hearing the news of Karl's disappearance and possible death feels like someone kicking away a crutch he didn't know he was leaning on. Karl was the only one who'd heard Martin's story. While their sessions couldn't permanently change Martin's behaviour, they at least explained to him why he was what he was. He understands how his police work is an attempt to undo the wrongs in his past. And sometimes, he just needs a person in his life to point out the obvious, when the drugs and the memories and the unsolvable murders are clouding your mind.

Martin shows his warrant card to a uniform, who lifts the tape for him and Phil to pass through. 'DCI Stamp?' Martin says to a thin man in a charcoal suit, smoking next to one of the vans.

Stamp flicks his cigarette away and extends a bony hand. 'Can't go in there. SOCOs will be at it for a while.' The local DCI keeps shooting glances over to the reporters as they arrive. 'And you'll need breathing gear. The stench.'

'What?' Martin says. 'I thought there wasn't a body.'

'That's right. But somebody hoovered, then doused the floors and furniture with bleach. Doubt we'll get any DNA. Gross's computer's gone, maybe some files.'

'What *have* we got?' Martin says.

Stamp pulls a photo out of his inside pocket and passes it to Martin, who examines it, then gives the image of a handwritten note to Phil.

'Who's sorry?' Phil says.

'Handwriting looks similar to the doctor's,' Stamp says.

The local DCI is a senior rank, but he's regional. He's never – as far as Martin knows – worked on the streets of central London. 'Why did you call us?' he says.

Stamp frowns. Perhaps he was hoping Martin would know exactly who the chief suspect would be. 'You came to see him a few days ago,' he says. 'You know what all this is about?'

'We were just here for some advice,' Martin says.

'On what?'

'Unsolved case, sex thing.'

Stamp seems to be waiting for more details.

'So what happened then?' Martin says.

'Wife called the station. Apparently, he always says "nighty-night" by eleven-thirty. She said he has a few nutters on his books, and when he didn't arrive home, she wanted us to go and check on him. A PC came the next morning. Door was unlocked.'

Martin scratches the stubble on his cheek. 'You knew we'd seen him, so you've got his diary?'

'Spoke to his secretary,' Stamp says.

Martin takes his phone out of his pocket, then hesitates. 'I'll give you a call if I think of anything.' He'll get updates on this thing from Cook, if Stamp gets anywhere, which he probably won't. Martin walks back to Phil's car and dials

Karl's secretary. He goes through the usual stuff, she must be very upset, all that, then asks a few questions before hanging up.

He speaks to Phil. 'The doctor got a new patient, a few days ago, who said she'd pay cash. She used the name Emma Smith and wouldn't give an address. She was the last appointment yesterday.'

Phil looks over at Karl's office. 'You think it was her, coming to see him? You think she knew he was involved in the case?'

'Or she came to him for therapy.'

Phil shakes his head. 'I can't believe that. She just walks into his office and says she's got a problem?'

'It looks like she visited him a few times. If it wasn't for therapy, what would it have been for?'

Phil raises his eyebrows. 'You think,' he says, 'he gave her some drugs, maybe something to try and chill her out?'

'Whatever he did,' Martin says, 'it doesn't look like it worked.'

* * * * * * *

Sarah drops her phone on the passenger seat of the car, an anonymous grey Ford Focus. The call was well timed, making her look less suspicious while PCs were going door to door.

Dan was nervous again, wondering why she wanted even more time off. She told him her mum was ill, nothing serious, just needed to spend a week or two with her. He's transferred her capital to other traders. It doesn't matter anyway – it's unlikely she'll ever return to the firm.

She monitors the entrance to Karl's office from further down the road, fidgeting with the heater controls. It's the first time she's attracted this much attention.

The men who just turned up and passed under the tape: *They have to be detectives,* she thinks, *don't they? But why did they arrive in a new Porsche?*

Here they come again – one in a sharp suit, the other with his tie loosened and two days of stubble – getting back into the car.

Sarah starts her engine as they pass.

She follows them back towards London, around the traffic-choked North Circular. They eventually pull up outside a townhouse in Hammersmith where the scruffy one gets out and lets himself in the front door. Sarah makes a note of the address and follows the Porsche as it heads east along the A4, past the glitzy boutiques and restaurants in Knightsbridge, along Piccadilly and into Soho. The driver parks on a double yellow line and, next to a mobile phone shop, opens a door that probably leads to offices or flats above. Sarah drives past and waits further up Wardour Street.

When he returns to the car a couple of minutes later, she follows him past Buckingham Palace, along the river and over Battersea Bridge. He pulls into the entrance of a tall, glass apartment building. Another expensive address.

Who are these men? she wonders.

Sarah drives to her house in Holland Park. She logs on to her laptop in the kitchen and visits a site that lets her search the electoral register. There are two adults living at the house in Hammersmith: Martin and Charlotte White.

She googles 'Detective Martin White'.

A number of mentions in the press, most of them old. Murder cases, appeals for witnesses, comments after convictions. Recent reports are less frequent, all related to cold cases solved by DI White.

So why, Sarah wonders, *was he visiting the scene of a very recent crime?*

Is Martin White one of the officers Karl discussed the disappearances with?

Sarah returns to the electoral register. The apartment building by the river in Battersea has a hundred and seventy-nine registered occupants. One by one, she combines their names with "Detective" in her searches. Halfway through the list she gets an intriguing result.

Detective Phil Burton has only appeared once in the papers, commenting on a recent murder hunt in Southwark. But he also features in various poker magazines, the interviewers questioning him about his decision to join the Met: 'If Joe Navarro can go from FBI agent to writing books on how to spot bluffs, why can't I move the opposite way?'

But it's not that simple, she thinks. He'd need to have been a PC for at least two years, patrolling the streets in a stab vest, before he'd even have been considered for a detective job. *According to one of the magazines, he's won and lost millions of dollars at the poker table. What's he really doing? What's he trying to put right?*

Sarah goes through the tunnel to the mews house and retrieves a couple of basic tracking devices bought from Spymaster in Portman Square. She drives back to the apartment building and parks a couple of streets away. Putting on a baseball cap and black-rimmed glasses, she walks to DS Burton's building and waits outside the gates to the underground car park, mobile phone to her ear. After a few minutes, the gates swing open to let out a car; Sarah slips between them as they close, walking down the ramp.

Phil's Porsche is at the far end; Sarah looks through the window. The car has only done eight thousand miles. It's taxed for another four months, so it's probably between annual services. It's too new to need an MOT.

She doesn't want a mechanic finding her device. The manufacturer says the tracking website is secure, but Sarah doesn't fancy testing that claim. The battery life is twenty-one days – that should be more than enough time to get a feel for how close the detectives are to her.

Sarah lies on her side and reaches under the car. She can feel plastic protective panels – no good for attaching the tracker's magnet. This car's engine is in the rear, though – perhaps there's some steel in there. But that would probably be too hot. She doesn't want the tracker failing or causing a mechanical problem. She persists near the front of the car, passing the magnets along the underbody.

A door slams.

Sarah sees a pair of shoes, pointy men's shoes, walking towards her. She keeps moving the device around but it won't stick.

Now the feet are three cars away.

Still no sign of any steel.

One car away.

The tracker flies from Sarah's fingertips, the magnets attaching to something with a faint clunk.

The feet are in front of Sarah now. 'Excuse me?'

Sarah stands up. 'I've lost a bloody earring,' she says to Phil.

He looks at her ears. 'Where's the other one?'

'What do you mean?'

'If you dropped an earring, I'd expect you to still have the other one.'

'Oh, I lost it last night. I've looked everywhere else.' *Let's see how good you really are at detecting lies.*

Phil nods, seems to be satisfied. He reaches into his pocket and pulls out his car key. He turns back to Sarah. 'Which flat do you live in? Don't think I've seen you around.'

'Oh, I … don't live here. I was just staying with a friend.'

Phil smiles. 'I'll look out for that earring,' he says. He gets into the car, starts the engine and drives away.

* * * * * * *

Karl wakes up on a metal floor, the cold permeating his body to the bone. He sits up and touches his face, making sure that he's still solid, alive.

She didn't kill him.

Karl doesn't know how he feels about being spared. It suggests Sarah wants to continue her therapy. Perhaps she's developed an attachment to him, a dependency that she's unable to break. And he doesn't believe she's a torturer.

But that could be wishful thinking.

Against the wall opposite, there's a saggy single mattress, propped up on its side. A stainless steel toilet is nestled in one corner of the metal room, which is about ten feet square and lit by a yellowish fluorescent light. Beside Karl are twelve bottles of mineral water and a large cardboard box of canned food. There are no windows, just an air vent in the ceiling. He hears the distant hum of a fan.

He stands up and spots a telephone on the wall. He picks up the receiver. It's dead.

Karl drinks half a bottle of water and eats a can of cold baked beans with a plastic spoon. Then he lies down on the mattress and waits.

Thursday August 22nd 2013

'We've hit the fucking jackpot!' Phil shouts over the phone.

The call woke Martin - he had another smoking session last night and doesn't remember buying a lottery ticket.

'Two days after the last murder in Asia, she travelled from Singapore to Marrakesh,' Phil says. 'Killed someone there and flew to Mexico City via Madrid the next day. And she landed back in London the day after La Paz.'

'How did you get all that so quickly?' Martin says, cradling the phone on his shoulder and picking up a tie from the floor.

'Cook used to work counter-terror, this is basic stuff for them. And she was less careful than your average terrorist.'

'What's the name?'

'Hannah McInerney. But I've seen the passport application – the birth certificate's for a Hannah who died when she was seven.'

'Who signed her form and photos?'

'Economics professor at Warwick University. The address on the form is one of the student halls there.'

'Where are you?'

'In the car, five minutes from your place. But I'm not done yet. The Austrian backpacker thing was high profile, so were the Canadians in Peru. We've got DNA results from both – blood under fingernails, some dead skin on a brick – and there's a match. A woman. Probably blue-eyed and brown-haired.'

Martin is waiting at the kerb when the car pulls up. Phil hands him a blown-up passport photo as he lowers himself into the seat. Martin shakes his head. 'She's good, isn't she?'

'Fella I spoke to at the passport office said it's borderline, probably wouldn't be accepted these days.'

The girl in the photo wears thick-rimmed glasses. The picture was taken in a light that makes it hard to see the topography of her face through her pale makeup. Martin can't make out her cheekbones or the bridge of her nose. Her eyes are dark brown, almost black.

Phil drives aggressively, always at least fifteen miles an hour over the speed limit, shoving Martin back in his seat as they accelerate every time a light turns green.

'You should have gone to Traffic,' Martin says. 'They're all boy racers.'

'You don't want to catch her?'

'Ten minutes won't make a difference.'

Phil smiles but doesn't slow down.

They arrive at the Warwick University campus around twelve-thirty. Martin tells Phil to drive on past the security office – no need to get a bunch of ex-coppers involved. After asking a student for directions, Phil parks next to a single-storey concrete building with tall, narrow windows. Martin follows him as he hurries inside and shows the receptionist his warrant card.

'DC Burton, and this is DI White. We need to talk to someone about student records.'

The receptionist directs them to an office down a corridor to the right. They knock on a hollow wooden door and a voice from inside says, 'Come in.'

A middle-aged woman peers at them over a pair of reading glasses perched on a sharp nose. Martin looks at the neat desk, clear of clutter, with stationery arranged at right angles. *She's going to be awkward.*

Phil introduces himself and Martin as they sit down.

'I'm Diane Arthur,' she says. 'What can I do for you?'

'Somebody,' Phil says, 'applied for a passport using the birth certificate of a dead girl. That passport was delivered to one of your halls of residence, and the photo had been signed by a professor.'

Diane looks at him while he talks, doesn't blink.

Phil slides a piece of paper across the desk. 'Can you tell us who lived in this room in the 2001/2002 academic year?'

Diane stares at the paper for a few seconds, then adjusts it so it lines up with everything else on her desk. 'You have a warrant?'

Now Martin speaks. 'We can get one, but it'll take a little while. Meanwhile the person who took those boys in Bristol can do it again.'

Phil can't prevent himself from sitting up straight, staring wide-eyed at Martin.

But Martin doesn't expect this guardian of student records to be a gossip. And what will happen if she is?

'Show me your ID,' she says.

Martin and Phil place their warrant cards on the desk. Diane taps a few keys on her keyboard, then picks up the phone. 'Can you put me through to Detective Inspector Martin White?' Her eyes flick up to Martin, then back down. 'Can you try his mobile?'

Martin's phone rings a couple of seconds later. Diane hangs up, takes her glasses off and places them on the desk. 'Tell me about this passport.'

'The holder,' Phil says, 'flew in and out of a number of cities around the world at the time of various murders.'

Diane frowns. 'You mentioned the boys, from Bristol.'

'It's complicated,' Martin says.

'I'm sure it is …' She taps on her keyboard, her eyes narrow. She taps again. 'Ah,' she says.

'Something you'd like to tell us?' Martin says.

Diane brings her hand up to her neck. 'A few years ago,' she says, 'a young woman visited me, a lawyer. She had a lot of paperwork, court orders, that sort of thing. Anyway, she said one of our previous students had an abusive boyfriend. The student had gone into hiding, but after a short time in prison, the boyfriend was released and he intimidated her friends, broke into her parents' home, trying to find out where she was. She'd changed her name and the court order said the university had to destroy any records it held of her. Application forms, essays, exam transcripts, even her email account. Everything.'

'How could an essay help him find her?' Martin says.

'I … I didn't ask.'

'I don't suppose you noticed that the lawyer looked like the photo of the girl in question.'

'She didn't,' Diane says, glaring at Martin. 'The student was blonde, the lawyer had brown hair.'

'Can you remember the student's name?'

'It was years ago … an English name, an ordinary one. Louise or Laura perhaps.'

Martin stands up. 'We need a list of all the students in the rooms near hers and everyone studying economics,' he says. Of course, they should have a warrant for that, but now Diane's position is a lot weaker, having made a big mistake.

'I suppose I could do that,' she says. 'Under the circumstances.'

* * * * * *

Sarah sits in front of the laptop in her kitchen, monitoring the detectives' movements over the course of the afternoon. The progress is slow, but she doesn't take her eyes off the red dot.

She watches them drive through west London and onto the M40.

Maybe they've found the minicab driver, she thinks. *Should I have done something about him?*

Too late now.

But they don't turn off at Marlow.

Could they be heading to her estate? They'd have to unravel the network of offshore companies used to purchase the property, if they want to establish who owns it. It might even be impossible. And she employs the gardeners and cleaners through third parties – they've never met Sarah. Anyone who's seen her there, she's turned them to dust.

They continue past Banbury.

Perhaps they have some new evidence from last year in Stoke.

No.

The red dot stops at the University of Warwick.

Somehow they've managed to jump over the deep, wide moat she's constructed to separate the two halves of her life. She was Sarah Silver, then Sarah Smith. In between, she travelled the world and used many other names. How could they link any of her recent crimes to the student who studied at Warwick more than ten years ago?

Have you screwed up, Sarah?

Maybe they have some DNA from Thailand or India. And despite the cleaning and bleaching she did at Karl's office, perhaps she left traces there. But why would they compare those samples? She killed an Austrian, a couple of Canadians and a lot of locals. That has nothing to do with the Met, nothing to do with Karl's disappearance.

If they have her DNA, but not her hair, they may be searching for the wrong woman. She's already had her DNA tested against the HIrisPlex model, which didn't manage to distinguish her coppery red hair from the more common brown and is ineffective with green eyes. It's possible that they're seeking a blue-eyed brunette.

The passport she used back then had been sent to her room at university, though. Maybe the Austrians or the Canadians traced her path. Or perhaps someone noticed similarities between two or three of the murders and analysed airline records. They could have asked the British police to check it out.

But it's too much of a coincidence that the detectives who probably consulted Karl, looking for advice on the disappearances, have also been given the task of investigating a passport obtained with a false name.

The trail will go cold at Warwick anyway, she's confident of that. There's no record of her there; she pulled the same trick with the Universities and Colleges Admissions Service. They can talk to whoever they want – they'll just remember a blonde girl who later dyed her hair black. She never told another student where she was from, and she'd already changed her name once, in case anyone from back home was spreading the story about Sarah Silver who got pregnant by a rapist.

There is one person – Ian – who can reveal a little more, perhaps. He knows about the wrestling, about the name Bellona, but nothing after that.

Or does he?

* * * * * * *

Bookshelves cover two walls of Professor Wynn Jones' office from floor to ceiling. There are books piled ten high on his desk and underneath the chairs that Martin and Phil are sitting in. They're even stacked on the narrow windowsill, partially blocking out the sun.

'How can I help you chaps?' Wynn says, before taking a long slurp of tea from a chipped blue mug.

'You signed a passport application for a student in 2002, a female student,' Phil says.

'Did I now?'

'Well … yes.'

'What's the name?' Wynn says, then takes another slurp of tea.

'We think she might have been called Louise or Laura. She applied for the passport in another name.'

'Naughty girl,' Wynn says, winking.

'I don't suppose you remember doing it?'

'Eleven years ago?'

'Yes,' Phil says.

Martin guesses the professor could describe the contents of any book plucked at random from his shelves, but not what he had for breakfast this morning. 'How can I put this,' he says. 'If someone gives you something to sign, do you read it carefully or do you just sign it?'

Wynn holds up his hands. 'A secretary gives me something, I sign it. Otherwise it tends to get lost.'

Martin sympathises. He's careful with his case files, but bills and contracts? Well, Charlotte wouldn't leave them in his care. 'Could it have been any student, or would you only do it for someone you knew well?'

'I'd do it for someone I was tutoring.'

'Would you have any notes on those groups?'

'Just essays and dissertations, the department looks after those.'

Martin and Phil have already checked in the department's office – everything is gone and they've reallocated her grades to 'Student A'. 'Do you remember any of the female students you've tutored?' Martin says.

'I usually have a couple a year.' Wynn stares at the wall above Martin and Ian's heads for a while. '2002, that would have been the year I …' He closes his eyes. A few seconds later, they spring open. 'There was one girl that year. Pretty bright, but more of a hard worker, really. Very determined, very business-like. Blonde, she was. Then she dyed her hair black. Didn't like that so much. Anyway, she sat at the front of lectures, took lots of notes.'

Colin said Bellona had dyed black hair. 'Do you remember what her background was?' Martin says. 'Or where she went after here? Did anyone ask you for references, anything like that?'

Wynn shakes his head. 'Like I said, she was very business-like. Asked technical questions, wasn't one for small talk.'

'Anything else?'

The professor leans over his desk. 'Between us chaps,' he says. 'Well, she was in bloody good shape. Occasionally used to turn up to lectures in her gym gear.' He waggles his bushy grey eyebrows.

'Could you describe her?' Phil says. 'If we got an artist up here, you think you could help them with a picture?'

'I don't remember that much. It was–'

'Eleven years ago,' Phil says. 'Maybe freckles, full lips, long eyelashes?'

Wynn shrugs. Martin gets the feeling the professor has only retained an image of her backside.

'Moles, eyebrows, nose?' Phil says.

He shrugs again. 'Sorry, chaps.'

Martin stands up. 'If you think of anything, anything at all, please get in touch.'

Wynn takes Martin's card and places it on top of a stack of books. But even if he remembers anything tomorrow, it's unlikely he'll be able to find the card.

'If I was a betting man,' Wynn says. 'I'd say a girl like her, hard worker, studying economics, well, she's going to end up in the City, isn't she?'

'That helps,' Martin says, pausing at the door.

The professor nods. 'Or New York or Tokyo or Hong Kong, of course.'

* * * * * * *

The door swings open. Sarah looks down at Karl. 'Out,' she says.

He does as he's told and steps onto the concrete floor of a large basement. On the other side of the room, there's a cheap plywood desk and office chair; against the wall is a brown leather sofa with a large tear in one of the arms, white stuffing spilling out. There's one door to his right and one to his left.

'Strip.'

Karl frowns.

'Everything off. You don't smell too fresh.'

Karl removes his clothes and Sarah tosses him a bar of soap. She hoses him down with lukewarm water that drains into a hole in the floor while he scrubs himself. Then she hands him a towel, a grey tracksuit and a pair of towelling slippers, which make him look like a resident of some kind of institution.

Karl doesn't believe in a god or even fate. But at this moment he wonders whether the universe is teaching him a lesson. He's held girls captive, cleaned them, provided them with clothes. *Is this my punishment? An eye for an eye?*

'Why don't you take a seat at your desk?' Sarah says.

Karl sits on the chair. She lies down on the sofa.

'I'm giving you a second chance,' she says. 'Not because I believe in second chances, and not because I believe you when you say you didn't plan to kill me. But I've invested a lot of time in you. As long as you're useful to me, you'll stay alive.'

'Thank you,' Karl says, realising it's him who sounds like the patient now.

'Don't thank me,' Sarah says. 'Help me. Show your genius.'

Karl raises a hand to his temple, attempting to compose his thoughts. *Was she being sarcastic*, he wonders, *when she used the word 'genius'?*

But now is not the time for vanity.

Karl leans back in his chair. 'We weren't having much luck,' he says. 'Going back to your early childhood. Perhaps we should explore the later years, your time abroad. We might find something else there.'

* * * * * * *

I'd fantasised about hunting many times, in all kinds of scenarios.

I imagined I was back at school playing kiss chase, running down a boy, tripping him, putting my hands around his throat. I thought about following a man down poorly lit streets, hiding in the shadows every time he turned around, then dragging him into an alleyway. And more than once I dreamed of riding a horse, pursuing someone through fields and over fences, cutting him down as he tried to escape.

But until that day, I don't think I was convinced I'd actually do it.

Clients often asked me to choke them until they passed out, cutting off their air supply with my arm or thighs. I'd spent the past hour throwing a chubby little man around a hotel room. Now I sat with him on the floor in front of me with my arm wrapped around his neck. I felt his strength slipping away, his sweaty body going limp.

Usually, that would be my cue to release him, letting him slump to the floor where he'd have a little snooze.

This time, I didn't let go.

Each second felt like an eternity while I said to myself, You're killing him, you're doing it. *I willed myself to stop but, at the same time, persuaded myself not to.*

I kept squeezing.

Then, almost as though I'd been thrown back into my body with a jolt, I scrambled away, shocked and thrilled by the feeling of god-like power I'd experienced. I watched him lie there for a while, a peaceful look on his flabby face.

Eventually, he came to, the usual grin appearing as he opened his eyes, waking from a blissful sleep.

It was then I knew that, next time, I wasn't going to let go.

That evening I cancelled all my remaining appointments and booked a flight to Bangkok.

The first place in Thailand I visited was Pattaya.

I watched middle-aged men strolling through the dusty streets with teenage girls, listened to an Englishman in an internet café, talking to his wife on the phone, telling her how much he missed her, all while holding hands with a beautiful prostitute.

I thought the town would provide a hundred men I'd want to hunt, but really, I just felt sorry for them all. Obviously, I let men pay me to act out their fantasies, too, I wasn't judging anyone – or trying not to – but that place was grubby, desperate. It would have provided all the thrill of hunting diseased animals in the filthy cages of a dilapidated zoo.

I returned to Bangkok and took a bus to Krabi, where I caught the ferry to Koh Phi Phi Don.

It was like the Thailand you see on posters or in films: a strip of white sand and palm trees, stretched between two lush green peaks, all floating in a dazzling blue sea.

I hung around the beach during the day and bars at night. People approached me – boys, girls, couples. We were away from home and the usual rules didn't apply. It was like a community, one where the faces changed but everyone had something in common. So I'd sit there chatting to a Canadian or Australian or Israeli and listen to them talk about trekking through the jungles of Sumatra, going to favela parties in Rio or just getting ripped off in Bangkok.

One afternoon I was sitting at the top of a multi-tiered, open-fronted bar overlooking the sea. People came and went, taking shelter from the torrential afternoon rains or just passing the hours before they went and did nothing else in particular.

He sat at a table by himself, holding a thick paperback with one hand, occasionally lifting a beer to his lips with the other. I watched him for a couple of hours, devouring the book, oblivious to the people around him, including me.

When he left, I followed him at a distance to a hostel. There was a bar on the street, and he took a table in the corner where he continued reading. I sat nearby, keeping a discreet eye on him as a Dutch girl joined me and talked about her boyfriend back home.

I carried on like that for a couple of days, going between the cafés and bars until I found him, always watching without staring. His nose stayed in the book and I don't think he ever saw me.

On the fourth day, there was a full moon party. It was smaller than the ones elsewhere, really just people dancing on the beach outside the bars. Andreas – I didn't know his name then but I learned it later – went alone. And he'd taken something; I watched him close his eyes and dance slowly, swaying side to side, completely out of time with the music, lost in his own private world. I wonder, now, if that's why I chose him. Not because he was alone and nobody would notice his absence for a while, but because there was something unusual about him, something rare: an aura of contended solitude, and a little mystery.

I sat down in the sand, just at the edge of the light spilling out from the bars. Eventually he opened his eyes, saw me and smiled.

I beckoned him over, and as he approached, I got to my feet and started to walk away. He followed me all the way to the end of the beach where it met one of the island's green hills. The sound of the music had faded and all I could hear were our footsteps thudding in the sand. I left the beach and stopped behind a tree.

He came to me and I kissed him. Then he stepped back and gazed at me, a look of fuzzy bliss on his moonlit, delicate face.

I kicked his legs away. Before he could react, I was on the ground with him, legs wrapped around his torso, arms around his throat, squeezing so tight I thought my muscles might pop out of my skin.

With the exertion and the adrenaline and that thought in my head – You're doing it, you're really doing it this time – *it felt as if it was over in an instant and I was hurrying back along the beach to my hotel, heart racing, head pounding.*

I lay awake all night, wondering if it had really happened, if I'd dreamed it, perhaps I'd taken something at the party or someone had spiked my drink and I'd imagined the whole thing. I almost went back to the end of the beach to check, to see if there was really a boy there, a boy that I'd killed.

But as soon as the sun was up, I packed my bags and caught the first ferry, leaning over the bow as the boat cut through the water, knowing that things would never be the same again.

* * * * * * *

Martin and Phil are waiting outside in the car when Terry Knight arrives home. He sees them, waves, then lets himself in the front door of the small Victorian terrace house. He wears a tracksuit bearing 'COVENTRY JUDO' logos and has that obvious vitality you often see in people who've dedicated their lives to physical pursuits.

They follow him in and he offers them a seat on the well-worn brown leather sofa opposite a wall covered with trophies, medals and photos. Martin recognises Neil Adams – he watched him win Olympic medals for judo when he was a kid – in a shot showing him throwing a younger Terry.

'On the phone, you said something about my classes at the university,' Terry says, sinking into an armchair.

'We wondered,' Martin says, 'if you remember teaching a girl–'

'Louise Brown,' Terry says.

Martin looks at Phil, who smiles back. 'Why her?' Martin says.

'I always had the feeling I'd be hearing about her one day.'

'Not the sort of person you'd forget?'

'Louise, Louise,' Terry says, looking into the distance. 'Best fighter I've ever had, could've gone to the Olympics.'

'What happened?' It sounds like Louise could cause problems for a man, Martin thinks, sounds like she could be Bellona.

'Wasn't interested,' Terry glances over at his trophies. 'Travelled to classes in Birmingham and even London to fight the best girls in the country, but wouldn't do competitions.'

'So she must have been registered with a club before, back home?'

'Told me she wasn't,' Terry says. 'Signed up as a new member to the BJA – that's the British Judo Association. But she'd been doing it for years. It was obvious.'

'Why do you think she lied?' Martin says.

Terry shrugs. 'None of my business.'

'You didn't wonder?' Phil says.

''Course I did but …' Terry's eyes narrow. 'What's this all about?'

Phil looks at Martin, who gives him a nod. 'When she was at Warwick University,' Phil says, 'she applied for a passport in someone else's name.'

'Doesn't surprise me, I suppose. The secrecy and all that. Must have been running from something.'

'Can you tell us about her?' Phil says.

'Like what?'

'Personality, appearance, anything really.'

'What kind of trouble's she in?' Terry says.

'We just want to talk to her.'

Terry takes a deep breath and picks at the arm of the chair. 'She was a bit … this is between us, right? 'Cos I could get into trouble. It's a grey area, you know.'

'Nothing goes further than this room,' Martin says, although now he actually wants to get his notebook out.

'She was a bit messed up, I reckon. She … she'd fight one of the lads at the end of the evening and then go into the changing room with him and … you know.'

'Did you ever go with her?' Martin says.

Terry looks at his lap. 'A few times.'

'Maybe,' Martin says, 'she was just enjoying herself.'

Terry gets up and stands by his prize wall. He takes a bronze medal out of its case, breathes on it, then rubs it on his chest. 'It wasn't just that,' he says, replacing the medal and picking up another. 'She was violent. I mean, yeah, we're all there to fight, but I got the feeling she wanted to hurt people. I had to have words a few times. And when she was doing … *it*, you know … it was like … like she was still fighting. Growling, scratching … it was like trying to shag a Doberman.' Now Terry chuckles, shakes his head. 'Fucking hell. I'm starting to sweat.'

Memories, Martin thinks.

'Ever talk to her about other stuff?' Phil says.

'Tried to,' Terry says. 'But she was good at deflecting things. She'd ask you lots of questions so she didn't have to talk about herself.' He puts the medal back and leans against the wall. 'But … if you track her down,' he smiles, 'tell her Terry says hi.'

* * * * * * *

Sarah tracks the detectives as they return to London. They stop at Martin's house, then Phil returns home. The red dot isn't going anywhere else tonight.

She's getting an urge she knows only too well. But right now, there's no time for distractions, no time for planning, execution and disposal. She's already involved in a hunt, with higher stakes.

She drives over to a twenty-four-hour gym in West Hampstead and lifts weights alongside the bouncers, shift workers and insomniacs. She squats until her legs turn to jelly and then takes a long, hot shower – there's no sauna.

She doesn't drive straight home, opting to take Finchley Road towards Marylebone. She cruises around the West End for a while, not looking for anything in particular. There are still plenty of bright lights and people on the streets – she won't do anything stupid here.

She keeps heading east and it's when she lowers the driver's window in traffic on Old Street that it happens.

There's a fast food place that covers all the bases: the sign promises 'FRIED CHICKEN – KEBAB – FISH' and, alongside the drunken students spilling out, clutching polystyrene boxes and bags of chips, there's the aroma of grease and meat.

Sarah parks in a side street and hurries back to the shop. There's a huge range of junk food, all advertised with big photos.

She hasn't eaten meat for years but she orders a quarter pounder and a lamb shish kebab, then rushes back to her car. She unwraps the food, pulling the burger from the bun and stuffing it in her mouth, followed by the chunks of meat from the kebab.

She wipes her hands and looks at herself for a few seconds in the rear view mirror.

She feels strong.

She feels ready.

Friday August 23rd 2013

So far, Martin and Phil have spoken with two of the students who lived in rooms near Louise's in her final year. Both said pretty much the same thing: she was private and worked hard. And the men from her judo classes – they exchanged bodily fluids with her, but almost no words. They don't remember any distinguishing marks either; the sex was quick and clothed.

An e-fit expert is visiting everyone the detectives have interviewed. But Louise doesn't seem to have any distinctive features. All people remember are her hair colour and toned physique. Her lips weren't full or thin. No moles, a 'normal' nose. Her hair varied from almost white blonde to something more like honey and then she dyed it black. Sometimes she plucked her eyebrows to narrow lines; other times they were thicker.

Now Martin and Phil sit in a small, windowless meeting room in Holborn at one of Deloitte's offices, sipping coffee from plastic cups. A lanky man in his early thirties walks in and closes the door behind him. His black thin-framed glasses are slightly wonky and his suit trousers are too long, bunching up where they meet his ugly shoes. 'You're from the police,' Peter Fisher says. 'Do I need a lawyer or something?'

'Nothing to worry about,' Martin says. 'We just want to pick your brains.'

'About what?'

'Warwick.'

Peter sits down across the table from them. 'I finished studying there years ago.'

'We know,' Martin says. 'We're looking for someone you lived with.'

'OK.' Peter frowns, then readjusts his glasses.

'You lived in halls during your second year. That wasn't the usual arrangement, was it?'

'The place we were supposed to be renting fell through. Well, literally, the roof fell in. We got rooms on campus with third years and post grads.'

'Do you remember the girl that lived across the hall, Louise?'

'Yes,' Peter says. 'Quiet. A bit ... cold.'

'Did you ever talk to her about where she was from, or her plans after studying?'

Peter takes a silver pen from his inside pocket and starts twirling it between his fingers. 'Can't remember her ever saying much more than "Good morning".'

Martin squeezes the bridge of his nose and screws up his eyes. He's getting bored with this.

'Something wrong?' Peter says.

Phil sighs. 'We're tracking the invisible woman.'

Peter stops twirling the pen. 'What's she done?'

'We just want to speak to her,' Phil says.

'Because?'

'Can't tell you that, I'm afraid,' Martin says. Peter's is another name they can cross off their list. He's got nothing for them.

'Sounds ... mysterious,' Peter says.

Martin smiles a rueful smile, then starts to get up. 'We're going to send someone to see you, do an e-fit.'

'Oh,' Peter says. 'Don't bother.'

Martin sits back down. 'Why's that?'

'There's someone who knows her a lot better than me.'

'Who?' Martin says, fighting the urge to lean across the desk and grab Peter by the lapels.

'There was a guy on my course, history. Little guy … Ian … Ian Cox. I caught him sneaking out of her room one night. Just once. But I spotted him plenty of other times, walking from the main campus to our halls. Definitely something going on between those two. I remember thinking he was punching above his weight.'

* * * * * * *

Sarah sits outside a Caffè Nero in Shoe Lane, sipping a bottle of water. It's lunchtime and people in suits are emerging from air-conditioned office blocks, removing jackets and putting on sunglasses.

She spots the detectives leaving the Deloitte building and hurrying back to the underground car park. They weren't at Deloitte for long, but she has a good idea who they'd been speaking to. There's an encrypted folder on her laptop, a virtual incident room, with lists of names and places. They've already visited two of the people who lived with her in the third year. A LinkedIn search confirmed Peter Fisher works for Deloitte.

Sarah gives the detectives a head start as they travel east. She hails a black cab when she realises they're not stopping in the City and not visiting the Goldman Sachs office in Fleet Street where Anwar Ahmed – who lived next to Peter Fisher – works.

The red dot passes Whitechapel. 'Here's fine,' Sarah says to the driver. She pays and hurries down the escalators into the vast, crowded expanse of Liverpool Street station.

She hasn't located everyone who might be on the detectives' list. She's forgotten a couple of names. And some people aren't on any social networking sites or have moved abroad. But the man at the top of her list is Ian Cox. He lives in Colchester, which is on the A12, the road Martin and Phil have just joined.

Sarah buys a ticket from a machine; her train leaves in three minutes and will take just under an hour. She can't be sure, but she thinks that's about the journey time by car from where the detectives are now, driving past Bow.

She prays for traffic.

Sarah checks off the stations as she passes through them – Romford, Brentwood, Chelmsford – the urban sprawl receding into green fields as she gains on the red dot.

What am I going to do when I arrive? She doesn't have Ian's mobile number, just the one for his home. Should she call him away somewhere? Then what? And that's if he's home at one-thirty in the afternoon. She hasn't found out what he does for a living, but it must be something local. The police wouldn't be driving all the way out here if they could meet Ian at an office in London.

Unless they want to surprise him. Or watch him.

Although she wouldn't have expected him to know, Peter must have told them something about Ian because he should be far, far, down their list. At Warwick, they didn't live together, study together, go out in public together. She was so careful, always checking the corridor before she let Ian out of her room, telling him to keep walking past if anyone was around when he approached her door. In those days, she wasn't worried about witnesses or leads, just hated the idea that people might be talking about her, like they had at school.

At Colchester station, Sarah steps off the train, then hesitates. She needs a plan, but … Phil's car is in Colchester now. She goes to the taxi rank, gets in a cab and gives the driver Ian's street – Cambridge Road.

She tells him to stop a few houses down and walks back to Ian's home. She's already looked it up online – a large detached house worth close to a million, although he bought it a few years before, for less than half that.

There are no lights on in the front of the house. Sarah opens the gate and walks through. A low hedge and a few trees surround the front garden. In one corner, the trees and shrubs provide enough cover for Sarah to hide from view if she lies flat. She'll be able to hear what anyone says on the doorstep, but not inside.

* * * * * * *

A woman in her thirties opens the front door soon after Martin rings the bell, keeping the security chain on. She's not wearing any makeup.

'He's not in,' she says.

Phil shows her his warrant card. She closes the door enough to remove the chain, but doesn't invite them in. Behind her, the hallway is scattered with brightly coloured plastic toys. Further into the house, a child is babbling and banging two wooden objects together.

'What's he done?' she says, crossing her arms.

'Will he be long? We'll wait,' Phil says.

'He's out of the country.'

'Back?'

'Sunday afternoon.'

'Got a contact number, name of a hotel?'

'You'll have to wait until Sunday.'

'It's very important that we speak to your husband ... Sorry, I didn't get your name.'

'Kelly. Doesn't matter how important, you can't speak to him.'

Martin leans on the doorframe. 'Mrs Cox–'

'Cavendish. I didn't take his name.' She glares at Martin.

'Sorry. Anyway–'

'He's in the bloody jungle,' she says, as if that will explain her hostile mood. 'My husband fancies himself as a bit of an adventurer. Goes on these trips, trekking, climbing, canoeing.'

'Nobody in the group has a satellite phone?' Martin says.

'Apparently not.'

'Can you tell us where he's gone?'

'Somewhere in the Amazon rain forest.'

'What flight's he coming in on?'

'Listen,' Kelly says. 'In case you can't tell, I'm not too happy he's buggered off for ten days – again – when we've got a little one to look after. We didn't speak for a while before he left.'

It looks like they'll be doing Ian a favour by visiting him on Sunday, Martin thinks. 'I don't suppose,' he says, 'that he ever mentioned a girlfriend he had at university?'

Kelly looks at him like he's trodden dog shit into her white carpet. 'No. He didn't.'

'She wasn't necessarily a girlfriend,' Martin says.

'What's he involved in?'

'Nothing. We're just trying to track down this girl.'

'What's her name?'

'Louise.'

'Bastard.'

'Sorry?'

'I … he said her name once … during … you know. Then told me he didn't know a Louise.'

Phil looks away from the house. Martin shifts his weight from one leg to the other, then breaks the silence. 'We'll be back on Sunday. Thanks for your time.'

* * * * * * *

Sarah waits in the garden until dark.

She's been lying there for hours, but she's far from bored. In fact, despite the police being closer to her than she'd like, her body tingles with excitement, not anxiety. This is turning into a new kind of hunt, pursuing the men who pursue her.

She's also curious to see Ian. It doesn't surprise her that his wife is a bit of a ball-breaker.

Lights have been switched on and off in two rooms upstairs. Sarah stands up and looks along the street. She doesn't see anyone, so she climbs over the brick wall next to the house and drops down into a neat rear garden with an immaculate lawn and weedless flowerbeds. Despite the size of the house, there's another building at the end of the garden, a large wooden shed with a window. Sarah tries the door but it's locked. In the light of the full moon, she can see a desk and a large television in there. Will Ian bring the police here, she wonders, to discuss someone he's never told his wife about?

The house is alarmed, but this place just has a single old-fashioned lever lock.

When Ian comes back on Sunday, Sarah will be waiting.

* * * * * * *

It's as he's opening another can of beans that Karl has the idea.

He yanks the ring pull and tears off the lid, then examines the round sliver of metal in his hand.

A slash to the face would surely do some damage, he tells himself, at least stun Sarah for a few seconds, wouldn't it?

But what then?

He's never seen her enter or exit the basement and has no idea what's above, or which door is the one he wants. And what if that door's locked?

The police will be searching for him. He should wait.

Unless the note he left was interpreted as a goodbye before he stepped on a plane, disappeared of his own accord ...

And even if the police are trying to locate him, how will they ever find him?

Sarah's careful; she's been getting away with murder for years.

Karl switches off the light and lies on the mattress, clutching the weapon to his chest.

Saturday August 24th 2013

The lock clicks and Karl springs to his feet.

He's left the light off, hoping the darkness will surprise Sarah, perhaps make her pause for a fraction of a second. He needs to give himself any tiny advantage possible. And he's gambling on the fact that his resistance will be unexpected.

The door opens and he launches himself forward, swinging his right hand to bring the blade towards Sarah's face.

Before he sees anything, Karl feels her grip his wrist, twisting his arm behind his back, pushing him into the cell, crashing against the rear wall. She forces his arm higher and higher and pries the tin lid out of his hand. Then she grips his fingers, pulls them back and slashes him across the palm.

'A caged animal trying to bite me when I enter? You think I wouldn't be expecting it?' Sarah says as Karl collapses to the floor, clutching his bleeding hand. The intensity of the pain renders him unable to even scream. He looks at the angry red gash, stares at it with disbelief.

Sarah turns the light on and leaves with the box of tinned food, closing the door behind her.

A few minutes later, she returns with a large bucket. She shows Karl the contents, the mixture of beans, vegetables and meat that had been in cans. 'You'll get a new one in three days,' she says. 'Now come out here.' She points to the sofa and Karl takes a seat. Sarah kneels in front of him and holds his hand. She takes a curved needle and a length of wire and begins to stitch him up, a look of intense concentration on her face.

'I think there's nerve damage,' Karl says between grimaces and whimpers. 'I need surgery.'

'Learn to use the other hand,' Sarah says, and keeps stitching. When she's finished, she stands up and leads him back to the cell. 'You have nothing to do in there all day but think. Next time I let you out, I want some insight, into my situation. Justify your continued existence.'

And then she closes the door.

* * * * * * *

Sarah climbs into her van. It's the same model and colour as the previous one, but is missing traces of the boys. She has a thin camping mattress in the back, as well as a rucksack with bottled water, snacks and all the equipment she needs.

Despite setting off at eleven at night, it still takes her an hour to inch through central London, the streets clogged with taxis and buses. She arrives in Colchester after one a.m., parking a couple of streets away from Ian's house. Kelly and the child should be fast asleep now.

Sarah climbs over the back garden wall once more and walks to Ian's shed. The third key she tries opens the door; there's no sign of any alarm system.

She shines her torch around, looking for a suitable place to hide the listening device. There's no clutter in the room and the lack of any papers suggests the TV gets more use than the computer. The black leather sofa against the wall is unlikely to be moved – there's nowhere for it to go. Sarah kneels on the floor and reaches underneath. She makes a small nick in the leather and then tears it a little. It will look like an accidental rip in the unlikely event anyone goes under there. She slips the black box through the hole and attaches it to the wooden frame.

She opens Ian's laptop and switches it on but she's asked for a password. She's not that interested, anyway.

Sarah leaves the office, locking the door behind her, and returns to the van. She climbs in the back, sets an alarm for five-thirty and lies down.

Sunday August 25th 2013

Sarah wakes up naturally, two minutes before her alarm is due to go off. She eats a couple of energy bars and drinks a can of Red Bull before returning to Ian's garden. She finds another bush, this one at the end of the garden, next to the shed, and lies down behind it.

Just after nine, she hears the click. Kelly opens the sliding glass doors that divide the kitchen and garden, taking advantage of another sunny day.

At ten-thirty, the doorbell rings.

A courier will be at the door with a package for this address, but for someone who doesn't live there.

Sarah sprints across the garden and enters the kitchen. Ian's son sits on the floor in his nappy. 'Ma-ma,' he says to Sarah, grinning.

She freezes for a moment. *How old is he?* she wonders. *Can he tell his mum what he's seen?*

'Ma-ma, ma-ma, na-na,' he says.

No, probably not.

Sarah leaves the kitchen and moves into the adjoining lounge. She waits for Kelly to send the courier away and return to the kitchen. Now Sarah creeps out of the room through the exit to the hallway and up the stairs, which are solid and don't creak.

She remains on the landing for a short while, where she can hear Kelly talking to the baby downstairs.

The domestic environment feels surreal, as if Sarah's wandering around a film set.

The voices become more distant. Sarah enters a bedroom at the rear of the house. Through a window, she can see Kelly sitting in the sun while the little boy crawls around the lawn.

The house has six bedrooms, but only the ones on the first floor are in use.

The little boy's room is tidy except for a single, tiny, blue, soft leather shoe with a pirate's face on the toe, lying on the floor. Sarah picks it up and slips it into her pocket.

The two rooms in the loft have beds and other furniture, but the wardrobes and drawers are empty. If there are no visitors being given a tour of the house, there's no reason for anyone to climb the second flight of stairs. Sarah chooses the room that overlooks the street. She takes out a small toolkit from her bag and unscrews the light switch, disconnecting the wires. Now, if anyone comes up, there'll be less chance they'll see her under the bed.

Maybe Ian will arrive before the police, come upstairs to unpack and Sarah can surprise him. Otherwise, she'll listen, the knife, the taser and the gun ready in case she hears the wrong thing.

She rolls under the bed and waits.

* * * * * * *

The detectives don't fancy another conversation with Ian's wife, so they sit in Phil's car.

Martin examines a photo on Phil's smartphone. 'I told you I'd seen that face somewhere,' Phil says. The image it shows is a female TV presenter who looks identical to one of the e-fits from a former Warwick student. Another e-fit appears to be of a pop star who had a No. 1 the month before. They have been given more than twenty pictures of Louise now, but no two are the same. It feels like a vast conspiracy, or at least some kind of practical joke.

Martin's eyes are closed when a black BMW pulls up behind them in the street. Phil nudges him awake.

They rush out of the car, calling to Ian as he slides his key into the front door. He turns, eyeing them warily. 'What?' he says, placing a small, spotless rucksack on the doorstep. He's slightly overweight, dressed in beige chinos and a maroon polo shirt, and doesn't look like the outdoors type.

'Just want to ask you a few questions,' Martin says, showing Ian his warrant card. 'You're not in any trouble.' *Not with us, anyway.*

'I suppose you'd better come in then.'

'Might not be a good idea,' Phil says. 'We spoke to your wife a couple of days ago. Don't think she'll have put up a "Welcome Home" banner and baked a cake.'

Ian gives Phil a cheeky smile. 'I've got an office at the end of the garden.' He opens the front door and calls inside. 'I'm back but the police are here. We're going to my office.'

'Whatever!' his wife shouts back.

Martin and Phil follow Ian through a wooden gate next to the house. He unlocks the door to a large shed and waves them in. Despite the desk, it doesn't look much like an office, with the TV and a small glass-fronted fridge stocked with bottles of beer.

'Get you one?' Ian says, sitting behind the desk.

Martin shakes his head. The room reminds him of his study, where he goes to get away from his family. No, where he used to get away from them, before they left.

'So what brings you to sunny Colchester?' Ian says.

'We're looking for someone you went to university with,' Martin says, sitting on the sofa.

Phil leans against the wall, hands in pockets. 'A girl called Louise Brown.'

Ian's mouth opens a little and his gaze shifts from one detective to the other. 'Wh– where is she?'

'That's what we're trying to find out,' Martin says.

'Right, right, sorry. It's just … Louise.' Ian stares into the distance. 'I haven't seen her for years.'

'Not since Warwick?'

'Nope, she disappeared,' Ian says. 'What do you want with her?'

'We need to ask her a few questions.'

'Like what?'

Martin's been considering how much to tell Ian. If he had some kind of relationship with Louise, he might want to protect her. And he seems a little slimy, dishonest. But Ian also strikes him as a bit of a coward. 'About a murder,' Martin says.

Ian's mouth twitches, then he tries to smile. 'Well, I'd love to help, but like I said, I haven't seen her for years.'

'You two were … involved?'

'It's complicated.'

'Wrestling?'

Ian's eyes widen.

Weren't expecting that, were you? Martin thinks.

'How d'you know about that?'

'We're detectives.'

Ian grunts. 'You reckon she's killed someone?'

'Not sure.'

'But she's a suspect?'

'Yes.'

'Bloody hell.' Ian grins now and leans back in his chair.

'That impresses you?' Martin says.

'No … well, maybe. Look, I haven't seen her. I don't know where she is. I can't help.'

Phil takes over the conversation. 'Enjoy the jungle?'

'The what? Oh, yeah, it was great. Really good.'

'Where'd you go?'

'The Amazon.'

'Where exactly?'

'It's, er … Sort of all over.'

'Where'd you fly to?'

'Rio.'

Phil frowns. 'Really? That's gotta be a thousand kilometres from the Amazon. How did you get there?'

'Bus.'

'To what town?'

Ian keeps rubbing his jaw. He doesn't answer.

'What do you think happens,' Phil says, pushing himself away from the wall and crossing his arms, 'to people who lie to us when we're searching for a murder suspect?'

'My trip's got nothing to do with her!'

'Where were you?'

Ian shifts in his seat and drums his fingers on the desk. 'You're not gonna tell my wife?'

'Shouldn't think so.'

'Promise.'

'OK,' Phil says, smirking. 'You have my word.'

Ian leans on the desk with his hands clasped and sighs. 'I was in the US, wrestling. They've got all the best girls out there.'

'You do it a lot?' Phil says.

'Couple times a year. I can show you emails arranging the appointments – that's where I was.'

'So what can you tell us about Louise?' Phil says.

'What do you want to know?'

'How did you meet?'

Ian stares into the distance again. 'You ... you mind if I have a drink?'

Phil opens his mouth to say something, but Martin says, 'Go ahead.' *Why wouldn't you want someone to have a drink to help them loosen up?*

Ian takes a bottle of Stella from the fridge, flips off the cap with an opener on his desk and drinks half of the contents in a couple of long chugs. 'I saw her in the gym on campus,' he says, 'working out. Seemed like she was training for some kind of sport – strength and speed, you know.' He takes another sip. 'She was in unbelievable shape and had this confidence ... she would strut around. She'd catch me staring at her and not seem to care. Anyway, I figured out her routine and I used to go the same time as her. Then I spotted her going in to a judo class.' He stares into the distance for while, finishes the beer and retrieves another from the fridge.

'So one evening we were alone in the gym,' Ian says, 'and I just went up to her and said I wanted to fight. She looked at me for a few seconds, then told me to come to her room later, make sure nobody followed me. That's how it started. We used to prop her bed up against the wall so we could grapple in her room. It was' – Ian takes another long gulp of beer, shakes his head – 'unbelievable.

'I made the mistake of showing her a load of stuff on the internet, though. Videos you could buy, sites where you could find women who would fight for money. She dyed her hair, started travelling around. Called herself–'

'Bellona?' Phil says.

Ian raises his eyebrows. 'You have done your homework.'

* * * * * * *

Lying under the bed, listening to the detectives' conversation in her earpiece, Sarah agrees. She reaches into her rucksack. The barrel of the pistol touches one of the glass bottles, which emits a faint clink. She pauses and listens for any sign of movement from downstairs. But the door is closed and she's two floors away from Ian's wife and son.

The detectives are sitting with the only person in the world who should be able to link Louise and Bellona. But they've already made that connection.

How? She wonders. *Or does that even matter now?*

What's more important is what she's going to do about it.

It's clear silencing Ian won't be enough. She needs to get closer to the detectives, stop the information spreading further.

* * * * * * *

'What did you talk about?' Martin says.

'Not much,' Ian says. 'She wasn't one for chit-chat, not with me anyway.'

Martin looks up at the ceiling, runs a hand through his hair. 'There's got to be something. She must have had plans for when she finished studying, must have mentioned her school, something like that.'

'I couldn't tell you where she came from. What she did after Warwick, well, it was wrestling.'

'Did you ever see her again?' Martin says.

'I tried, believe me, I tried. She ignored my emails. Then I used a different name. But when I got close to the meeting place, she cancelled. Sent me a text.'

'Why do you think she didn't want to see you?'

'I'd love to ask her that question.'

She wanted to make a break with her past, Martin thinks. *And she did a bloody good job of it.* 'She disappeared, didn't she?' he says.

'Yeah, and I've been trying to find her ever since.'

'Did you ever tell anybody that you went to university with her?'

'No one. If anyone found her, I wanted it to be me.'

'Did you get any leads?'

'Nothing. She vanished.'

'You've got a feeling in your gut, though, where she went?'

Ian nods. 'Maybe she's just got a network of rich guys, top secret. She seemed to be going that way.'

'Her tutor at Warwick reckoned she'd end up in the City.'

Ian wrinkles his nose. 'He doesn't know about the wrestling, does he? She was like an animal,' he says, a look of wonder on his face. 'I can't imagine her spending all day in an office. And why would she? She was making a fortune.'

Martin stands up. 'Where are you going to be this evening?'

'Home, unless I get kicked out,' Ian says, then winks.

'We'll get someone round to do an e-fit. That's if you can remember what she looked like.'

'Like I saw her yesterday.'

Martin thinks about showing Ian the pictures they already have, but they might affect his memory. 'Any time you remember something,' he says, 'doesn't matter what, you call me. Straight away.'

Because we're chasing a ghost here.

* * * * * *

Ian remains in his office for a while after the police leave. He drinks another beer and eventually his heartbeat returns to normal, his hands become steady.

If they're looking for Louise, there's a good chance she's still alive. And if the Met are involved, she could be close.

Who has she killed? he wonders. *Maybe she married someone, got fed up with him. He came home from work one day and she pulled him down on the floor, wrapped her legs around him and squeezed.*

The thought makes Ian hard, straining against his trousers.

A rap on the window and his beer bottle hits the floor.

'Phone,' Kelly shouts, waving the cordless handset. 'Police.'

* * * * * * *

From the bedroom, Sarah watches Kelly cross the back garden. She runs down the stairs and slips out of the front door, clutching her mobile.

* * * * * * *

Ian watches Kelly walk back to the house, then speaks into the handset. 'You forget something?' he says.

'Hello, Ian.'

'Lou … L …' is all Ian can say. His heart rate picks up again.

'Miss me?'

Ian picks up the bottle from the floor and drinks what's left.

'I'll take that as a yes,' she says.

'Can I see you? Please?'

'I'd like that,' she says, an unfamiliar softness in her voice. 'Where?'

'I was hoping you'd have somewhere private we could go.'

'Well … there's a house across town I'm building. Not much furniture or anything, but it's got carpets–'

'And plenty of space?'

'More than enough.' He gives her the address.

'How soon can you be there?'

'Five minutes,' he says. 'But–'

'What is it?'

'The police, they want to talk to you about a murder.'

She sighs. 'It was a client. He asked me to choke him, knock him out. He didn't wake up, now I'm in trouble. You'll help me?'

'You know I will, I'll do anything. I can't believe you're back.'

'It's been a long time, hasn't it?' she says.

'It has.' He grins.

'Go to the house and leave the back door unlocked for me.'

Ian doesn't bother to tell Kelly where he's going. He jogs to the car and gets in. It takes a few attempts before he rams the key into the ignition.

He laughs, cries, whoops as he drives. More than ten years of waiting, searching, and she's come to him. He found his fantasy, lost her, now he's got her back.

He parks in front of the house and lets himself in at the side gate. He walks up the stairs to what will be the master bedroom, turning the lights on so she can see he's arrived. There are no curtains in the house yet.

He paces across the room on the balls of his feet, taking deep breaths, walking over to the window every thirty seconds to see if he can spot her.

He freezes.

The back door closes, soft footsteps ascend the stairs. And then he's looking at her.

Her face is still feminine but hard, eyes as cold as ever. Black running leggings hug her sculpted thighs and her calves that bulge above thin ankles.

She sets a rucksack on the floor, pulls off the black hood and hairnet she's wearing and shakes out her hair, a red Ian has never seen.

'Your hair,' he says.

'My natural colour. Like it?'

'It looks … right.'

'Do you have any chairs or something we could sit on?' she says.

Ian goes downstairs and returns with a couple of wooden boxes.

* * * * * * *

Sarah sits down. 'What did the police ask you?'

She heard it all, but wants to see if Ian leaves anything out.

He repeats the conversation with the detectives, without any omissions.

'How do you think they made the link between Bellona and me?' she says. 'Did you ever tell anyone?'

'Never.'

Sarah stands up and takes a couple of steps towards Ian. 'It's OK if you did. I just need to know.'

'I didn't,' Ian says, staring up at her, wide-eyed like a little boy. 'If anyone was going to track you down, I wanted it to be me.'

'Did they show you any pictures?'

'They've got someone coming to do a photo-fit.'

'Ian,' she says, putting a finger under his chin. 'Did you look for me online recently?'

'Not for ages. I'd kind of given up.'

She knocks Ian off his box, but and gets him in an arm lock on the floor. 'Who did you tell, Ian? Who?'

'Nobody!'

She applies more pressure. He screams, 'I'm telling the truth!'

Ian's forearm comes away from his elbow with the *creak* and *pop* of a chicken drumstick being separated from the thigh.

Is the double-glazing enough to muffle the sound of Ian's cries? Sarah wonders. The house is detached and she didn't notice lights on next door.

She slides one leg under his torso, one above, and wraps her arm around his neck. He bucks and thrashes, or at least tries to, but her grip on him is tight, an expert use of pressure and leverage.

'Who did you tell?'

'No … body,' he says, pushing the words out from his belly. 'I swear.'

'What next?'

'What … do … you mean?'

'A leg or the other arm,' she says. 'Who did you talk to?'

'Please! I've never said any … thing to anyone.'

All the men Sarah has killed, they've been prey from the moment she met them. She talked to some of them, listened to them, but there was only one thing on her mind.

But Ian introduced her to wrestling. And from that came the hunting.

She knows him.

There are memories.

He's a loose end, though, perhaps the only bridge across the moat she's constructed. It's possible he'd remain loyal to her, but why take the risk? She's been so careful and patient these past couple of years, but things are slipping. Time to clean up now.

There's no adrenaline or hyperventilation as she chokes him. It's more of an embrace than an act of aggression.

'Thank you, Ian,' she says, releasing her grip and standing up. Then she kneels back down, closes his eyes and places a gentle kiss on his lips.

Perhaps it's because this has been a different kind of kill, without the chase or the excitement; maybe it's due to the meat craving she's unable to shake off; it could even be a little frustration, knowing she's eliminating a witness and forcing the police to escalate their search. Whatever the reason, Sarah finds herself taking Ian's hand and placing his thumb in her mouth.

She crunches down on the bone, tasting salty blood. The sensation is like squashing a stress ball in her palm, but a stress ball with flavour.

Sarah closes her eyes and squeezes with her jaw until it aches.

She pulls the mangled digit from her mouth and lets Ian's hand slump to the floor.

Sarah stands up and grabs her rucksack. One by one, she unscrews small glass bottles of petrol. She walks from room to room, letting the bottles drop and spill their contents on the new carpets.

There's no point trying to make it look like an accident. Ian's a witness and the police will treat his death – less than an hour after the interview and just before providing an e-fit – as suspicious. They'll soon have poor-quality CCTV footage of her face obscured by glasses and a baseball cap from her train journey to Colchester, the listening device she planted in Ian's shed and, possibly, traces of DNA despite the gloves and hairnet she wore in his house. But none of that matters. They're still stuck in 2002, talking to people from her past, people who didn't know her then, might not even recognise her now. They're looking for Bellona; there's no one in the world who can tell them who she became.

Sarah opens the front door, lights a match and drops it in a puddle in the hallway.

* * * * * * *

The house is a smoking heap of charred timber and blackened brick by the time Kelly arrives, her son Ben in the back of the car. She tried Ian's mobile a few times, but got no answer.

She's crying within seconds of the scene coming into view and swings the door open before she's even brought the car to a stop. Leaving Ben in his seat, she elbows her way through the crowd of onlookers who are jostling for a peek at the smouldering shell of a house. A burly PC grabs her by the arm when she ducks under the yellow tape stretched between two lamp-posts. 'My … husband,' she says.

The officer puts his arm around Kelly and steers her over to DI Kenton from Colchester CID, who received a call when the fire brigade found the body. The DI ushers Kelly into the back of a marked car and sends a female constable to fetch the baby.

Kelly manages to tell Kenton that detectives from the Met visited Ian that afternoon.

Kenton remains in the car as he makes a few calls, but there's no record of anyone from London visiting Ian. All Kelly knows is that they were looking for a woman called

Louise. They were definitely from the Met, but didn't leave a card.

Eventually, Kenton is put through to DCS Cook, who calls Martin to confirm Ian was part of his investigation.

The local DI gives Martin and Phil a long, hard stare when they arrive just minutes later. 'You were still in Colchester,' he says.

'We wanted to have another chat with him,' Martin says, although the detectives had actually stopped at a local pub for a drink and dinner.

'What about?' Kenton says.

'It's an old case. He went to university with someone we're looking for.'

'Nothing to do with his business then?'

Martin looks at Kenton with narrowed eyes. 'Why do you ask?'

'He's pissed off a few people round here. Bought houses cheap from pensioners, closed down shops so he could build flats.'

'Pissed them off enough to do this?'

Phil coughs, but Martin ignores him.

'What about your thing?' Kenton says.

'Doubt it,' Martin says. His voice is casual even though the contents of his stomach feel ready to jump up his throat.

Someone should have been watching Ian.

If anyone wants to point the finger at Martin, tell him Ian's death is his fault, well, he couldn't really disagree. This kind of simple mistake means he's better suited to cold cases. He can sniff out new clues in an old file, reinterpret the past in a new light. A man more pretentious than Martin might even call himself 'creative'.

Whatever unusual skills he possesses, though, the other side of the coin is that, when it comes to something as basic as protecting the person closest to a suspected serial killer, he screws up.

But shouldn't Phil have considered that? Martin wonders. Or maybe Martin has infected him with his 'creativity'.

'He was going to give us an e-fit of someone he hasn't seen for years,' Martin says. 'That was about it. Didn't know anything else.' He can see Phil is desperate to speak, but his colleague manages to restrain himself. 'Did anyone see anything?' Martin says.

'Neighbours weren't home,' Kenton says. 'Old girl across the road wouldn't have heard a bomb going off.' Something catches Kenton's eye and he looks past Martin and Phil, then speaks while still looking over their shoulders. 'This person he went to university with. What do you want them for?'

Phil walks away, distancing himself from what Martin's about to say, and goes to take a closer look at the house.

'Just a lead …'

Kenton stares at Martin now. And Martin's face isn't hiding anything. He can see that Kenton understands what's going on, that, yes, there's probably a link here, but it's one of those cases he really doesn't want to be involved with. Best to follow normal procedures: go door to door, let the forensics do their thing. There'll be a bit of interest from the press, the murdered local businessman angle, but nothing that won't die down in a few weeks. If the boys from the Met know something, let them deal with it.

Monday August 26th 2013

Martin pauses outside the office on Wardour Street, takes out his phone and dials Charlotte's number.

She doesn't say hello. 'If you're calling to cancel–'

'Charlotte, listen–'

'No, I've told Molly you're coming to see her on Saturday. And I've made plans. Whatever your excuse is, I don't want to hear it.'

He's not going to get away with telling her anything less than the truth. 'Someone's been following me.'

'What?'

'A suspect. They put a tracking device on my colleague's car.'

'Are you in danger?'

'No, no … well … no. I think they just wanted to know where we've been going, who we've been talking to.'

'Oh, my God. Do you think they'll come here?'

'I really doubt that. But it probably makes sense for you and Molly to stay away from London. And …' He doesn't want to say this, but it's the right thing to do. 'Let me know if you notice anyone suspicious hanging around, a woman.'

'What are you involved in?'

'It's nothing really, just a case.'

'Murder?'

'*Charlotte.*'

'Don't you say it like that. You're being chased by a murderer, you're telling me to look out for her and–'

'I'm not being chased. *Followed.*' Martin squeezes the bridge of his nose. 'There's absolutely nothing to worry about. She's the one being chased.'

'A murderer.'

'I have to go. Tell Molly … tell her I'm sorry.'

Martin pauses before he climbs the stairs to the office. He wasn't worried when he dialled Charlotte. But now he's got an urge to drive straight over there, to pick up his daughter, take her somewhere safe.

No, he thinks, *the best way to protect everyone is to catch this woman.*

Inside, Phil and Cook sit in silence, and it's clear the DCS is about to erupt.

Ian's death has dominated Martin's thoughts since last night. But Cook's insistence on conducting the investigation in a covert manner, with just two detectives on the case … well, what did he expect? His approach is at least partly to blame.

There are few people more dangerous, though, than a senior man who knows he's screwed up.

The boss opens his mouth a couple of times to speak, but no words come out. He stares at Martin, then at Phil. 'Why didn't you tell me about this …'

'Ian?' Martin says.

'A star fucking witness that you knew about *for two days.*'

'Well, sir,' Phil says, pulling at his collar, 'we told you we were waiting for a friend of the suspect who was out of the country.'

'What did you do when he returned?'

'Interviewed him, then arranged for him to do an e-fit–'

'And you didn't think it was worth hanging around for that? You thought it would make more sense to go down the bloody pub?'

'To be fair,' Phil says, 'we had no idea she'd be following us.'

'No idea, no idea,' Cook says, looking up to the ceiling. He takes a deep breath. 'Do we know when she put the tracking device on your car? Could she be on camera?'

Phil winces. 'I … I think I saw her do it.'

'You *what*?'

'In the car park where I live.' Phil's cheeks turn scarlet. 'There was a girl searching under my car, said she'd lost an earring.'

'What did she look like?'

'It's … hard to say. She was wearing glasses and a hat. And we don't have CCTV.'

'I suppose she was average height, fucking eighteen to thirty years old?' Cook shakes his head. 'Where do you suggest we go from here?'

'We need more men on the case now, don't we?' Phil says.

'What for?'

Phil screws up his face. 'Are you joking? The psychiatrist, now this thing in Colchester. She knows we're on to her. Let's put this in the papers, get other forces involved.'

Cook smiles, leans back in his chair. 'You're obsessed with the papers. You want your picture in there? A few quotes about how we fucked up?'

At least he said 'we', Martin thinks. *At least he's subconsciously accepting some of the blame.*

'But–' Phil says.

'Right now,' Cook says, pointing a thick finger at Phil, 'she thinks she's winning. And if you were her, you'd think we haven't figured out what's going on here. Maybe we've got a bit of the picture, but the police wouldn't be behaving like this if they knew the whole story, would they?'

'And we shouldn't be behaving like this … sir.'

'That's your opinion, DS Burton.'

'We need,' Phil says, 'to get the word out. There'll be people who know her from the wrestling scene. Maybe she's working in the City and someone else from university recognises her.'

'So we keep going through the list of leads we've got. We don't need to go public for that.'

'But, sir, the investigations into the murders of the psychiatrist and Ian Cox, we're making them waste time–'

'Enough.' Cook holds up a hand. 'This is how we're doing it. We've got resources – you saw what happened with Interpol and the plane tickets. But we're going to keep a low profile. And if those other investigations turn up anything useful, we'll know about it.'

Phil stands up and walks over to the window. He mutters something to himself, then returns and leans with his hands against the back of his chair. 'Sir,' he says, then pauses.

'What is it you want to say to me, DS Burton?'

'It's just that … well …' Phil looks at Martin. But Martin has no idea what his colleague wants to say.

'The way you're behaving,' Phil says. 'It doesn't make any sense.'

Cook leans back in his chair. 'How long have you been a detective?'

'It's about three years now.'

'What about you, DI White?'

'Fifteen years.'

'And,' Cook says to Martin, 'you remember all the ones who got away? The ones who disappeared?'

Martin nods. He remembers them all.

'Well, I've got twenty-five years. And my list, it's a big one.' Cook looks into the distance, past his subordinates. 'I got all the easy collars – the wife killers, the nutters, the crooked business partners. But there's an ex-copper who got a mate to "lose" a knife. A politician who had a word in the right ear so I got a call from an assistant commissioner. And there's a pair of brothers who jumped on a plane – they're lying on a beach in Brazil while their parents are six feet under.'

Cook returns his gaze to Phil. 'And counter-terror … the fucking leaks and cock-ups. You follow someone for six months. They get wind of it and they're straight back to Pakistan or the bloody Yemen.'

Phil stands up and strokes his beard. 'With all the respect in the world, sir, this is different. She isn't going anywhere.'

You're wasting your time, Martin thinks. *Cook has two-and-a-half decades of scores to settle. You're young, idealistic. Cook – and me – are older. You want to protect the public, prevent any more lives being lost. Cook just wants to nail this woman. He doesn't care what the cost is.*

'Sir–'

'Conversation over. I mean it,' Cook says, glaring at Phil and leaning over his desk like he's ready to come over it.

Phil huffs, shakes his head. 'I'm gonna–' he begins, but the ringing of the phone on Martin's desk interrupts him.

Martin answers it. 'I remember,' he says. He listens for a while. 'What's your nearest police station? OK, go there now, we'll be right over.' He hangs up.

Phil and Cook stare at him.

'Colin,' Martin says, 'The chap who works on the wrestling site? Bellona contacted him, arranged to meet him this evening.'

* * * * * * *

The red dot travelled to New Scotland Yard earlier that morning and disappeared soon after. The police obviously found the tracker and took it apart; if it reappears, it will be some kind of trap or diversion. They'll visit the shop where Sarah bought it, but she used cash, months ago.

She's running out of options, though. They have the name Louise Brown. They're only a couple of steps away from Sarah Silver.

At six o'clock, she's due to meet Colin at the Hare & Billet pub in Blackheath. If anyone knows who's been talking about her past, it's him. He gets as much, if not more, excitement from the gossip than from the actual wrestling.

She drives to Blackheath two hours early, parks and, through a pair of binoculars, watches the pub from across the huge expanse of grass.

Just before six, she'll get a little closer and wait for Colin. When she doesn't show up, he'll leave and she'll follow him home. Sarah doesn't want to meet him in a public place; it will just act as bait so Colin will reveal himself. It will be easier to persuade him to talk after she's followed him through his front door and wrapped her arm around his throat.

* * * * * * *

Martin and Phil sit in the office, waiting. The tracker has been removed from Phil's car, but she could still be watching them. If they turn up in Blackheath, they'll blow everything, Cook said.

At half past six, Martin picks up the phone before the end of the first ring. 'She's a no-show, isn't she?'

'No sign of her yet,' Cook says.

'Probably saw the place was swarming with coppers and buggered off,' Martin says.

After all his posturing and insistence on keeping things discreet, Cook didn't hesitate to call in the cavalry. Of course, that makes sense – she's coming to them, walking into a trap, rather than being in a position to see them coming and escape. But everything falls apart if she can detect that trap.

'There isn't a uniform anywhere close,' Cook says. 'SCO19 are in unmarked vans.'

'Tell me you haven't got someone reading the paper on a bench opposite.'

Cook doesn't reply.

'She's too good for the usual methods. She's been getting away with this for years. She could be working behind the bar there and you wouldn't know it.'

'We'll see.'

'How much longer are you going to wait?'

Cook sighs. 'Give it a bit longer.'

'A waste of time. While you're sitting on your arse, she's planning her next move.'

'Which is?'

'If I knew that,' Martin says, 'I wouldn't be here sitting on *my* arse.'

* * * * * * *

For the past two-and-a-half hours, Sarah has watched the area around the pub through her binoculars.

A well-built man in his thirties has been walking a dog, back and forth, returning the way he came every ten minutes. Another man has been sitting on a bench nearby, reading a newspaper the whole time.

So Colin contacted the police, she says to herself. *He knew they were looking for Bellona.*

Sarah drives home and goes online. She browses the forum where Colin's a moderator, scrolling through all the threads devoted to her.

She turned her back on that whole scene when she left the country. No more trawling through emails from people begging to see her or threatening to beat the shit out of her or rape her.

She laughs when she discovers the bizarre drawings people have created, when she reads the stories about what she's doing now. Someone says he's been to a mansion where a billionaire keeps her in the basement, inviting friends to watch her fight teenage boys to the death. There are hundreds of other stories, fantasies: she's an assassin, a gangster, an SAS operative wearing a burka and strangling Taliban in Afghanistan.

There's a post from someone who saw her in Bangkok, but nobody seemed to take it any more seriously than the other stories. Well, nobody's posted a response anyway.

Why is Colin in contact with the police? she wonders. *Could he have put things together by himself?* He met her, perhaps got a feeling for what she was capable of. Then someone posted a message on his forum and a few days later a backpacker was strangled in the same country.

No, the links are too tenuous.

Then she realises her mistake. The detectives, when they visited Ian: they already knew about the wrestling scene. Of course they had spoken to Colin.

You're getting careless, Sarah.

She calls her mother.

'Hi Mum, it's me.'

'This is a nice surprise.'

I know, I know – I never call. 'I was just wondering,' Sarah says. 'The hot weather isn't going to last forever. Perhaps you'd like to go on holiday, a long one. Australia, Asia, somewhere like that.'

'Who would I go with?'

'Mary from next door?' *She also knows more about me than I'd like.*

'I … No, thanks. Those long flights, vaccinations, coach journeys to see some old ruin.'

'*Mum.* You can fly first class, get private tours.'

'I keep telling you, I'm perfectly happy where I am.'

'I know, I know,' Sarah says. *But I had to try.*

'The house and garden look lovely, I'm very grateful for that. You should come and see the place sometime.'

'I would, but–'

'Of course, dear, you're very busy. I do understand.'

Not quite. 'I know I ask you this every time, but are you sure you've thrown away all the old photos of me?'

'I told you I have.'

'There couldn't be any lurking around?'

'No dear, you know I understand about the photos.'

'You're absolutely sure?'

'Promise.'

'Well … OK. I have to go now. Let me know if you need anything.'

'I will, dear, I will.'

'Oh, one more thing,' Sarah says. 'The press are trying to dig up dirt on our firm. Can you call me straight away if anyone knocks on your door to ask questions?'

'You're not in any trouble?'

'No, no, they're doing it to everyone in the industry. We're not that popular, you know.'

'Well … if you're sure. I'll let you know if anyone comes round.'

Sarah would feel more comfortable with her mother far away, but that could only ever be a temporary thing. Her being on holiday might put off someone with a long list of leads, but if they work out who Louise Brown really is, they'll follow her mother wherever she goes.

Assuming the photos have been destroyed, there isn't a single image of Sarah from the ages of thirteen until twenty, when she had the disguised passport photo taken. She was off school with the flu at fourteen when the school photographer visited. And the following year, after the attack, everyone respected her wish to remain as anonymous as possible.

But the thirteen-year-old Sarah had red hair, is recognisably her.

Families in the village could still have copies of earlier class photos. Can Sarah get hold of them?

My mum lost all our photos, she's devastated. If I could just borrow the old school pictures, make copies, it would mean so much to her. And please don't mention anything – I want to surprise her.

She'll contact them by phone and send a courier so nobody sees her. Get the photos delivered to a PO box, then collect and destroy them.

* * * * * * *

At eight o'clock, long after it's obvious Bellona won't be turning up to the meeting with Colin, Martin leaves Phil at the office and travels home to Hammersmith on the underground.

He goes up to his study and opens the desk draw where he keeps his weed. It's empty.

He fires a text message to his dealer and gets a reply explaining he'll have to wait at least an hour, which means two or maybe three.

At the back of a kitchen cupboard, he finds an unopened bottle of gin and some tonic – Charlotte gave up her evening drink when she got pregnant. The fridge freezer is almost bare but Martin can use two of the three remaining items: a lemon and a tray of ice. He pours the bottle of sour-smelling milk down the drain.

As he stands staring at a picture Molly has attempted to colour in – a happy family, of course – stuck to the fridge, the bitter taste of the gin and tonic takes Martin back to that first night he met Charlotte, her approaching him as he flicked through case files in a pub across the road from her office. They swapped drinks after she laughed at his 'old man's pint' of bitter and he told her that his granny drank G and T. It wasn't long before she moved in with him and his friends and lodgers moved out. With his hours irregular and hers long, they had their own lives, meeting up for dinner or just drinks; one of them would crawl on top of the other when they got home late at night or left early in the morning.

Everything changed when Charlotte fell pregnant; they simply spent too much time together. As Martin grew to love his daughter more and more, he realised he didn't even like his wife. And he got the sense that Charlotte felt the same way.

But maybe it could be more like the old days, with her back at work.

Martin drains his drink, sits at the kitchen table, pours himself another and calls his wife.

'Is everything OK?' Charlotte says.

'Well … yes, I suppose so. Listen–'

'I was going to call you.'

'You were?' Martin smiles.

'I … I spoke to my old boss a few days ago. He's moved to the Sydney office, and–'

Martin thumps the table with his fist. 'You're not taking Molly to Australia!'

'Why not?'

'Because … she's my daughter too.'

'She is, and there's nothing I can do about that. It's been a tough decision, but you phoned me, remember, telling me to be on the look out for a murderer. And of course there's the drug problem, the documented history of psychological issues–'

'You said therapy would do me good.'

'I was wrong – nothing changed.'

Martin picks up his glass – ready to hurl it at the wall – then pauses and places it back on the table. 'I want to see Molly.'

'You'll need a plane ticket.'

'You're there already?'

'No, but I'm packing right now. We're leaving my parent's house. Most of my things are in storage anyway. We'll stay with someone else while I'm applying for our visas.'

'I'll find you.'

'I'm sure you could. And it will make you look fantastic in court. Don't fight me on this, or I'll make it even harder.'

Martin tries to speak but Charlotte has hung up.

He thumps the table again, then pours himself another drink, a lot of gin, not much tonic. By the time his weed arrives, he's two thirds of the way through the bottle.

He needs to speak to Karl, needs the voice of reason, to put things into perspective, now that there's a new problem. Together they established how Martin's work, his smoking, his tendency towards isolation are all driven by his past, his inability to stop loving a mother he should hate. But what does he do, now that he's losing the only person he still loves, his daughter? Before, he could always tell himself that, while negative emotions might motivate him, at least he was doing good. But now Ian Cox is dead, Karl could be too; all those other men and boys are dead, and Bellona has slipped through his fingers.

Clutching the bottle, he moves up to his study for some music. He starts with the blues – Howlin' Wolf – while he drinks and nods his head to the ferocious songs of love and loss. But then he switches to Johnny Cash, the later stuff where his voice is the closest a sound can come to representing the colour black. And by the time the album's finished, nothing but hissing and the occasional pop coming from the speakers, Martin is unconscious.

* * * * * * *

Karl takes a seat at 'his' desk and Sarah lies on the sofa once more.

'Everything you talk about,' he says, 'you talk about in terms of hunting.'

'Yes.'

'Why do you think that is?'

'I like to hunt.'

'Of course. But it's not a common way to view things, or a typical reason for killing. I suppose one could interpret the urge to hunt, in the absence of doing it for food, as a desire to exert power.'

'I'm not sure you're on the right track.'

Karl can feel himself relaxing into his old role – the expert, the mentor. 'What we experience consciously, well, it might not have any relationship to the subconscious impulses that actually drive our behaviour. You feel excitement, adrenaline, because you're taking risks, engaging in a dangerous activity. But there are many other pursuits which offer a sense of danger without inflicting harm on others.'

'Perhaps,' Sarah says. 'But there are plenty of men who like to fight.'

'They're often driven by anger or a desire to fight back. What are you angry about? Who exerted power over you?'

'You're drawing a blank.'

'Really, Sarah? There's nobody who hurt you, nobody who made you do things you didn't want to do?'

'I don't remember anything like that. Could it just be ...'

'Go on.'

'Could it just be some primitive instinct to hunt that's been short-circuited?'

Karl shakes his head. 'The boy, Oliver, that was about power.'

'But I didn't kill him.'

'The other men that you have relationships with, are there similarities? Do you try to control them?'

'It depends. Some people invite control, they're submissive. Others want to be the one in control.'

'Which do you prefer?'

Sarah sighs. 'I don't think, in that situation, I know what I really want. I suppose you could say I'm never fully satisfied, never lost in the moment, always wondering if there's something I haven't experienced. When I'm hunting, though, that doesn't happen. There's no time to think. It just feels natural ... right.'

'Have you ever taken things too far, in one of those relationships? Hurt someone more than they wanted?'

'Never.' Sarah pauses for a moment. 'Well … last night, I had to kill someone, I suppose you'd call him a friend. But there was no question that any kind of … feelings would get in the way. He could have lead the police to me.'

'They're getting close?'

'They were, Karl, they were.'

There's a perceptible tightening in the atmosphere, a small drop in the temperature.

'I just told you I killed a friend to protect myself. How would you expect me to treat someone, who most certainly isn't a friend, when they start digging for information about the police?'

'I'm sorry.'

'Remember the speculum?'

Karl's recalls Sarah's threat on the night she abducted him, the vision of his daughter, waiting to be mutilated.

'You'll never speak to another human being but me. Maybe I'll find somewhere more comfortable for you in time, and maybe I'll leave your family with only the pain of your absence. But you'll have to do more for me than you're doing right now.'

Karl takes a deep breath, then exhales slowly. 'I have a feeling,' he says, 'that we're getting close to the source. The hunting, the talk of "prey", there's something there. But …'

'What's the "but"? What are those instincts telling you?'

Karl hesitates. He remains convinced that there's either something repressed deep, deep inside Sarah's mind, or perhaps, even worse for Karl, there's an early event that she has no memory of whatsoever.

'Have you spoken to your mother about the … about the way you are?'

'What? You think I've told her I kill men for sport?'

'No, but you're not a stereotypical female.'

'You could say that about female boxers, CEOs, plumbers. We're not all girly-girls, wearing pink and waiting for a man to marry us.'

Karl chuckles, despite his situation. 'That's not what I'm getting at. It's not that you're masculine, or overtly aggressive. But I think even the casual observer would say there's something that differentiates you from the average human being – man or woman.'

'I'm cold.'

'There is a certain detachment, a feeling that you're assessing a situation, sizing people up rather than relating to them.'

'I hear what you're saying. But your job is to figure out why.'

'Our job, Sarah, *our* job. You're the one who has the answer. And you really, truly, honestly have no idea? The shadow of a memory, the fragment of a dream?'

'You seem to think that there's some big event from my childhood that will explain it all. Can you point to one experience that made you who you are?'

Karl purses his lips.

'There is, isn't there?' Sarah says.

'I don't see how my history is relevant to your case.'

'Maybe if you share, it will stimulate something in me.'

Karl is not persuaded. Telling his story is not the correct therapeutic approach. But then conventional techniques are unlikely to give him the kind of incredible breakthrough that ... *What, Karl? Would make her so grateful that she'd set you free?*

'My mother committed suicide after my father left her. I found her in the bath. I was eight years old.'

'So you decided to become a psychiatrist. To care for women with broken hearts.'

'Something like that,' Karl says.

'But that doesn't explain your fascination with serial killers and sex addicts.'

'There were ... other experiences, influences. My father was a womaniser. I had a cousin who was killed by a paedophile.'

Sarah stares at Karl for a while.

'So have you thought of anything?' he says. 'Any important formative experiences?'

Sarah shakes her head. 'I think I'm just a scorpion.'

Karl frowns. 'What do you mean?'

'That old fable,' Sarah says. 'A scorpion asks a frog to carry him across the river. The frog warns him: "Sting me and we both die." But halfway across, the scorpion stings the frog anyway.'

Karl nods. 'The frog's dying word is: "Why?" And the scorpion says, "It's in my nature" ...'

* * * * * * *

A year after leaving Thailand, I was out of control.

You have to understand that, as much as I'd been through, I was still only twenty-three. And I simply didn't need to be careful, or so I thought. A girl like me could get a bus into town, wander around, then leave a few days later without arousing any suspicions.

Back then, I would drink with my fellow travellers. It took the edge off this manic energy I had, the constant buzz of killing and getting away with it.

But in Mexico, I tried cocaine.

It boosted my confidence in a way I really didn't need and increased the intensity of the thrill to almost unbearable levels.

I started using it every time I hunted.

I got careless.

In Rio, during carnival, I killed three times in one night, in side streets barely hidden from the thousands of people dancing behind trucks blaring out samba music.

In La Paz the sun had only just set when I was strangling a local Peruvian behind a hostel.

It was the sharp intake of breath that alerted me to their presence. I let the local man slump to the ground and blurted out, 'He tried to rob me.'

I attacked the girl first, grabbing a chunk of brick and smashing it into her temple. The boy tried to protect her and I caught him square on the nose, then with a heavy blow to the back of the head as he went down on all fours.

I strangled the boy and the girl, then returned to my hotel to take a shower and pack my bags.

I promised myself that I'd never hunt again unless I could do it safely, under control.

And I didn't drink, or touch any drugs for nearly a decade.

Tuesday August 27th 2013

Sarah spends the day watching Martin's house from a car. This kind of surveillance is her only option now; trying to break into his home or the office in Soho is too risky.

But what am I learning, she wonders, *sitting outside? He could be on the phone right now, sending someone to Mum's house and I wouldn't know it*.

And … she's getting bored. In Colchester, it felt like she was playing a game with the detectives, something that would escalate. She had to walk away from the meeting with Colin, and now she's getting a numb backside from waiting around.

She needs to find out exactly what the police know so she can decide whether to take action. It's time to stop watching her prey from a distance.

Just after six, Martin leaves the house – looking even more dishevelled than usual, like some ageing rocker in jeans, boots and a black T-shirt – and walks in the direction of Hammersmith underground station.

Sarah has put enough money in the parking meter to get her through until six-thirty, when the restrictions end for the day. She leaves the car and follows Martin as he gets on the tube and travels to Leicester Square.

The streets there are heavily trafficked with teenagers and tourists. Steel barriers and security staff in fluorescent yellow vests surround the square, where the crowds grow thicker. *Must be a film premiere tonight*, Sarah thinks.

A cluster of over-excited girls momentarily blocks her path and she loses Martin, but she knows where he's going. She pushes between an elderly couple and cuts through an alleyway that leads to Lisle Street.

The smell of roast duck from the Chinese restaurants brings on hunger pangs. She realises she hasn't eaten a real meal today. Once again, she craves meat.

Martin has to wait for the lights to change so he can cross Shaftesbury Avenue to the northern end of Wardour Street. He passes a long queue of people snaking along the pavement outside a restaurant, smokers chatting outside bars. He lets himself into the office and Sarah walks into the Starbucks opposite. She's just had time to buy an Americano and a pastry when Martin appears again, clutching a beige paper file. Sarah follows him as he turns into Old Compton Street, Dean Street and Bateman Street. He disappears into a pub on the corner, the Dog & Duck.

Sarah waits in the street for a couple of minutes. When she walks in, Martin is sitting at the bar, a pint of dark bitter at his lips as he looks down at the open file. She orders a lime and soda from a young blonde with short spiky hair and a pierced eyebrow, then takes a seat at one of the tables further back in the pub. She sits for a while, checking her phone, trying to look flustered, like she's waiting for someone.

Martin doesn't pay her any attention. And she notices that next to the pint there's a tumbler with at least a double whisky. He drains his beer and holds up the pint glass; the barmaid comes over and pulls him another bitter. They exchange words, she pours two shots of something clear and they clink the shot glasses before drinking.

Sarah walked into the pub without a plan, but she realises this is going to be easy. Martin is drinking to get drunk and looking for company.

She walks over to the bar and orders another lime and soda. 'Does that count as work?' she says to Martin, pointing at the file.

'I'd like to think so,' he says, without looking up. He takes a generous sip of beer, then a slug of the whisky.

'Bad day?'

'You could say that.'

'What are you working on?'

Martin sighs and flips the file closed.

'Sorry. I'm so nosy,' she says.

He turns to face her, and as he does, he looks her up and down and gives her something between a friendly smile and a suggestive leer. His eyes are glazed. 'The last time this happened I ended up getting married. That didn't end well.' He takes another sip of beer.

'Oh … you think I'm hitting on you,' Sarah says. 'I was just making conversation while I wait for a friend.'

* * * * * * *

Martin wouldn't mind if she was hitting on him. In fact, he wants her to be doing it. There's something casual and confident about her: she's just wearing a T-shirt and jeans, flat shoes. And he rather likes that red hair.

He doesn't remember if he prayed for anything before he passed out last night, but if he did, it's possible a woman like this featured alongside regular time spent with his daughter and a chance to see his dad play the drums.

'It's a police file,' he says. 'But I'm afraid I don't have a uniform at home.' *Too much too soon*?

'You're a detective?' she says, eyebrows slightly raised.

'I am.'

'Wow.'

'It's not quite as glamorous as the TV makes it look.'

She points at his pint glass. 'So you're the alcoholic divorcee who gets too involved in his cases.'

'This is only my second – well, second and third drink of the day – and I find some time for things other than work.'

'A quirky hobby that helps you solve crimes?'

Martin frowns.

'I'm a bit of a crime fiction fan.' She stares at him for a couple of seconds. 'Can I buy you dinner, DCI–?'

'Only a DI, I'm afraid. Martin White. And I thought you were waiting for someone?' Martin says, eyes narrowed like he's interrogating her, when he's just stopping himself from grinning.

'Sarah. What kind of friend is forty-five minutes late without a decent excuse?'

Martin smiles. 'I have to warn you, when I said my marriage didn't end well, that was a recent thing.'

'Don't worry,' she says, 'it won't be a date. I'm making a career change, thinking about writing. You might have some good stories for me.'

'Well, in that case,' Martin says, 'how can I refuse?'

They leave the pub, then pause outside.

'What do you fancy?' he says.

'I've got a craving for meat, red meat.'

'There's a place I've heard about,' Martin says, impressed by her honesty, and the fact she didn't go for something like sushi.

They walk through Piccadilly Circus and get a table for two at a Gaucho. Martin feels a little under-dressed among the cow-skin walls and chandeliers, but Sarah is at ease in these surroundings, ordering the waiter to take them to a booth.

Martin opens the wine list. 'I never got round to learning about this stuff.'

'I don't drink anyway.'

'How am I going to get you drunk then?'

'I thought we'd agreed this was strictly professional,' she says, but her smile disagrees.

Martin orders a bottle of lager. A tall, blonde waitress, all in black, brings them a board with the cuts of meat. Sarah orders a fillet, rare.

'So you're making a career change? What did you do before?' Martin says.

Sarah looks down at the table. 'Sometimes … when I tell men, it … it makes them feel intimidated. When I know you better …'

'You've certainly mastered suspense.'

They chat over dinner, with Martin doing most of the talking. She listens to his anecdotes, tales of cases cracked, hunches followed. She's easy to talk to, likes to listen.

'What are you working on now?' she says as they leave the restaurant.

'I can't really–'

'Of course. Sorry, just being nosy again.'

There's a silence as they stand outside the restaurant.

'It's still early,' she says.

'It is.'

'So … maybe we could go back to your place? I mean if you're going to be the inspiration for my detective character, I need to see how you live.'

'I'll subject you to my music collection.'

'An important part of characterisation.'

'You've been warned.'

Martin hails a black cab and they travel to Hammersmith.

'How does a detective pay for this?' she says as Martin flicks on the lights in the hallway.

'On my measly salary?'

'Remember, I'm learning, not judging.'

'Inheritance,' Martin says. He leads her up to the loft room.

'Your place to escape the family?'

'Something like that. I've had the house for years, though. Used to rent out rooms downstairs and I needed somewhere to play those,' he says, pointing to the drums. 'The walls and floor are soundproofed.'

'Nobody can hear you scream,' she says, holding his gaze for a few seconds.

Should I make some kind of a move now? he wonders.

'You still play?' she says.

The moment has passed.

'Not in a band any more, just for my own ... well, not exactly pleasure.'

'A good release, though, like a drink, at the end of a hard day? Let me hear you play.'

'I need to get in the mood first.' Martin flicks through some records. 'You OK with jazz?' he says. 'Not many people are these days.'

'I listen to the singers, Ella and Billie. A bit of Miles.'

Martin shakes his head. A woman with his taste in music? The ultimate fantasy.

He slides an LP out of its cover – *Idle Moments* by Grant Green – and puts it on the turntable. The title track isn't really one for drumming inspiration. It's slow and there's a guitar solo, sax, even vibraphone, but not drums. He chooses it for the mood – it's slow, sounds like a late night and is fifteen minutes long. If she can sit through that without looking uncomfortable, then ...

He pulls a bag of weed from the desk and rolls a small joint, doesn't want to overdo it. He takes a few puffs and then offers it to her. She shakes her head. 'You don't drink, don't smoke,' he says. 'What's your bad habit?'

She doesn't say anything, just gives him yet another mysterious smile, full of meaning Martin hopes he'll have enough time to decode.

When the song ends, Martin lifts the needle and walks over to the drum kit. He starts slow, swinging, gradually building up his pace. He watches her eyes while she watches his hands.

She claps when he's finished. 'How can you go so fast?'

'It's not speed, really, just coordination. I hit the snare with my right hand, cymbal with my left and then the kick drum. Do each one every second and you hear something three times a second.'

'It must be satisfying to be so good at something.'

What are you good at, apart from this? he wonders. *You're very good at this.*

'This is very … teenage,' he says. 'Up in my room, playing you the drums.'

'I wish I'd met you when I was teenager,' she says.

Martin comes from around the drum kit and Sarah stands up. She kisses him, not the other way round. And it's quick; Martin's left biting the air.

He opens his eyes.

'I suppose you've got an early start,' she says. 'That case you're working on.'

'I could–'

'I'm not going to stay the night. But you'll call me tomorrow?'

'I'll try.'

'Try?'

Martin's toes curl in his shoes. 'The case ... something could happen.'

'Oh, you don't need to explain,' she says.

The thought of not seeing her again ties a knot in his guts. 'A serial killer,' he says, 'a woman, is on the loose.'

Wednesday August 28th 2013

Cook is waiting at the office when Martin and Phil arrive together. 'We're locating every single Louise Brown in the country,' he says. 'Middle names included. Anyone who changed her name to or from Louise or Brown is getting special attention. We've got a team at the university, in case there's any paperwork that's been misfiled. Maybe an old essay with a fingerprint. All her emails have been retrieved, but there's nothing useful there. She kept herself to herself, no jokes, no arrangements to go for drinks or anything like that. Only discussed coursework.'

'What about the more up-to-date stuff?' Phil says. 'The City?'

'We're talking to investment banks, accounting firms, investment managers, seeing who they recruited in the early to mid-2000s.'

All of these things will take time, Martin thinks. They can't just send a couple of uniforms to visit every Louise Brown, because if it's *the* Louise Brown, she probably won't open the door and invite them in for a cup of tea. The university thing is optimistic, box-ticking. The City firms will take their time and contribute to a very long list.

'So we're still not going public?' Phil says.

Cook grimaces.

Martin wonders what Phil expects. With the benefit of hindsight, it's clear the whole thing has been a shambles. Cook is a man who's chosen a path he knows is wrong, but he's too stubborn to turn back.

'You want us to visit anyone on the list of Louises?' Phil says.

'We can't have a repeat of what happened in Blackheath or Colchester,' Cook says.

'Monday was your fault,' Martin says. 'Anyone who's ever switched on a TV would have seen that the place was being watched. You probably had someone with an earpiece sweeping the floor.'

Cook throws his hands up in the air. 'We've all fucked up. So what? Let's not have it happen again. I want you two here, waiting for intelligence to come in.'

'I've heard enough of this bollocks for one day.' Martin walks to the door. 'You coming?' he says to Phil.

'We know the case, might be something we notice when it comes in.'

Phil could be right. But Martin doesn't think they'll get anywhere with the name Louise Brown. There's no way she – whoever she really is – would leave that door wide open. She was already starting to hide at university, must have done something to cover her tracks.

Inspiration won't come in this stuffy office, with useless information dribbling in.

And he's desperate to see Sarah again.

* * * * * *

As soon as he's back out in the street, Martin fumbles in his pocket, pulls out his phone and rings Sarah. 'Looks like I've got some time on my hands,' he says when she answers.

'You caught the killer?'

'There's some very unglamorous legwork to do. Not my speciality.'

'So … what do you want to do?'

'I need to get out of London. Go somewhere quiet, get a fresh perspective on the case.'

'Wow. And I can tag along while you read your files?'

'I thought you were interested, for your writing?'

'People usually try to do something romantic on the second date.'

'OK, OK, no files,' Martin says. He wonders whether he should have waited a day or two before calling. No – before she left last night, she asked him to call her.

'Just teasing,' she says, causing Martin to grin. 'I'll be your sidekick, give you a much-needed female view. Has she got a nickname, your serial killer?'

'Nickname?'

'Like the Red Dragon or Zodiac.'

'You've been reading too many books. She uses false names, very ordinary ones.'

'Is she a master of disguise?'

'Something like that,' Martin says. 'And shouldn't it be "mistress"? You'll need to work on your English.'

'Very funny.'

'So where do you want to go?' he says.

'I've got a friend, has this place in the Cotswolds. Said I can use it any time.'

'Bet there are some nice pubs around there.'

'Second date, remember. You have to impress me.'

'Bet there are some expensive restaurants around there.'

'That's better.'

Martin looks up to the sky and smiles. She's so assertive, but in a playful way. 'Where do you want to meet?'

'I need to get a couple of things in the West End, then I'll jump on the tube. See you at your place at three. Oh, and there's just one rule.'

'A rule?'

'For one night you're mine,' she says. 'I don't want you leaving halfway through dinner. No phone calls, no phone.'

* * * * * * *

Karl has seen Sarah smile before, but not like this. And she's bristling with nervous energy. 'You seem excited,' he says.

'I've got a date with a little rabbit called Martin.'

'Martin White?'

'You know him?'

'I ...' Karl is aware that Sarah is examining him closely. 'Well … he's–'

'He visited you, about the case. He was the one.'

'Correct.'

Sarah continues to stare at Karl for a few seconds. If he tells her more now, she'll know he initially held back.

'Well, anyway,' she says. 'We had dinner last night, and tonight he'll be at my estate. I've got him in my sights.' She smiles again. 'I don't think he'll be coming to your rescue.'

But Karl isn't so sure. Martin might have psychological problems – Karl knows he's taking a risk by not disclosing the therapeutic origins of their relationship – but he's also intuitive and an excellent reader of people. *Surely*, Karl thinks, *he'll detect that something is very wrong with Sarah.*

Unless, of course, his personal history – his relationship with another woman – makes him run to her like a little boy running to his mother.

* * * * * * *

'Inheritance couldn't stretch to a new car?' Sarah says.

Earlier, Martin filled a bin bag with all the junk from the foot wells and made a quick trip to the nearest petrol station to give the interior a hoover.

'It was my dad's,' he says.

'Ah. Like the records.'

'I bought a few of those.'

'Were you close?'

'Didn't really get to know him. He died when I was six.'

'I'm sorry,' Sarah says. 'And your mum?'

'Buried a couple of weeks ago.'

'Well, again, I'm sorry.'

'Don't be, I'm not,' Martin says, then wishes he hadn't. They don't know each other well enough yet. 'What about your parents?'

'Oh, they're … you know, getting old.' She puts a hand over her mouth. 'Sorry, that was insensitive,' she says, dropping the hand to his knee, creating a tingle in his leg.

'Was it?'

'Well, you know, it kind of reminds you that yours aren't going to get any older.'

Martin smiles, keeping his eyes on the road. 'What happened to the confident girl I met last night? You're not nervous, are you?'

'Should I be?'

'That depends.'

'On what?'

'Whether I brought my handcuffs or not.'

Sarah gives Martin another mysterious smile. He switches on the CD player, already loaded with a compilation of jazz singers he made in an unsuccessful attempt to get Charlotte interested in his music. The album gets them out of London without the need for further conversation. But the silence never feels awkward. They've already achieved a feeling of comfort and familiarity, even though they don't really know each other, in the sense of swapping facts about each other's personal lives, or sharing a bed.

They arrive at the house a little after five.

'Who is this friend?' Martin says as he stops the car outside the huge sandstone mansion. 'Not an ex, I hope.'

'Definitely not.'

Martin drops his old leather holdall in the hallway and Sarah gives him a tour of the house. He says nothing as she leads him from one room to another and another. The blonde wood panelling on the walls and old-fashioned furniture upholstered in light colours give the place a feminine feel.

He speaks when they arrive in the library. 'A lot of crime novels here,' he says. 'One pair of wellingtons and one wax jacket in the boot room, your size. Nobody else lives here, do they?'

'Shouldn't have thought I could fool a detective.'

'Why try?' he says. 'If you gave me your surname and I searched a little, I doubt I'd find anything that could put me off.'

'You could find something that made you keen for the wrong reasons.'

'Money? I don't even spend what I've got.'

'Maybe I just want you to find things out from me, not the internet.'

Martin laughs. 'Alright, I'll play the game.'

They take advantage of the warm evening, walking around the grounds, Sarah showing him the old forge and the watermill.

Later, Martin drives them to a cosy local restaurant, where Sarah asks them to combine the ingredients of various dishes, eliminating the meat.

'You're not a vegetarian,' Martin says.

'I sort of am,' she says. 'Most of the time the idea of eating meat makes me feel sick.'

They return to the house, where Sarah pours Martin a glass of Scotch in the drawing room.

'A vegetarian,' he says, 'who eats steak, and doesn't drink but has a twenty-five-year-old Highland Park in her drinks cabinet?' Martin shakes his head. 'You're … a mystery.'

He thinks he sees her smile as she turns away and clicks on a stereo – Chet Baker singing 'My Funny Valentine'.

'You mind if I?' he says, taking a small bag of weed from his pocket.

She hesitates, cocks her head to one side, thinking.

'I could go outside,' he says.

'No,' she says. 'Do it here.' She watches him closely as he rolls it, lights it with his battered Zippo, takes a couple of drags. She steps out of her shoes, reaches around and unzips her black dress. Slides it off one shoulder, the other, lets it fall to the floor.

Martin grins – which he knows is probably not the right thing to do – but he's a little drunk, getting stoned, and can't think of anywhere he'd rather be.

Sarah unclips her bra, holds it between finger and thumb and makes eye contact with Martin, daring him to let his gaze drop lower. She steps out of her underwear and just stands there, like self-consciousness is a thing that doesn't exist. *I'm naked, so what?*

And there's nothing to be self-conscious about. He had a hint of what he would find when she was clothed, but now he can see that, OK he's under the influence of a couple of things and he hasn't had sex since … he can't even remember, but anyone would agree that Sarah's body is almost flawless: toned but not too defined, still feminine – a perfect combination of curves and straight lines. Although he wonders about that scar low down on her stomach.

'Your turn,' she says.

He takes two big drags and stubs out the joint in the whisky glass. He doesn't try to be seductive, doesn't know how. He undoes his shirt, almost ripping off a couple of buttons, pulls down his jeans, nearly falling over as he takes his shorts off.

Sarah looks him up and down, then walks slowly towards him.

* * * * * * *

Commander Euan McBride's uniform is spotless, his sandy hair neatly parted, and there isn't a single sheet of paper – or even a speck of dust – on his desk. 'I've been hearing things,' he says, 'that I don't like the sound of.'

'What would those things be, exactly, sir?' DCS Cook says, feigning ignorance.

'The psychiatrist who disappeared,' McBride says. 'Two of your men visited him a couple of days before. The DCI there reckons they know more than they're letting on.'

'That's one way to explain why he's getting nowhere with the case.'

McBride glares at him. 'Then a man dies in a house fire, the day after he was visited by the same detectives. No details of the interview recorded in HOLMES, and again, the locals reckon your men are holding back.'

'He was a property developer with plenty of enemies.'

'But what did your men want with him?'

Before he'd even stepped into the commander's office, Cook knew he'd have to tell the truth. Well, a version of it anyway.

'I've put a special unit together. Investigating a number of disappearances, young males, nationwide.'

'Who else knows about this?'

'Nobody. Just the DI and DS working on it.'

McBride leans back in his chair and sighs. 'You're not working counter-terror now. And why aren't you keeping any records?'

'Well, sir. In a few of the cases … it seems evidence may have been misplaced. Witnesses have left the country before they could be spoken to–'

'They warned me about this.'

'Who did?'

McBride glares at him again. 'Phone hacking. Jimmy Savile. You think we need another balls-up? The government's cutting our numbers, outsourcing.'

'A public balls-up is what I'm trying to avoid.'

'How exactly?'

'It could be nothing, or we could have a serial murderer. It's difficult to be sure.'

McBride stands up. 'Did you hit your head at the same time you did your knee? You've got two men working on this? *Two?*'

'I've been putting things out to other forces and specialist teams in the Met, discreetly. And Interpol.'

'Interpol? Ruddy Interpol!' McBride spits as he pronounces the Ps. He clenches his fist, then takes a deep breath before sitting down. 'I've got a two-day conference in Birmingham. On Friday evening, I'll meet you back here. You'll bring records of everything related to this investigation and a written report.'

'Sir–'

'You have less than forty-eight hours. Do not let me down.'

* * * * * * *

'How's it going?' DS Rudden says, taking a stool next to Phil but barely looking at him. It's a Wednesday night and this downstairs bar in Soho is packed with students from the nearby art school, as well as staff from local media agencies, production companies, record labels and magazines. The suited policemen look out of place, but Phil knows why his friend chose this spot. There are vintage skirts and business suits, tanned skin and tattoos, girls in their twenties and women in their forties. Rudden isn't fussy and refuses to commit to a specific type. Phil picked the seats to keep his ex-colleague happy. The women have to walk past to get to the ladies' – Rudden will look each one up and down, then wink at Phil.

They used to patrol the streets of Greenwich together and have a mutual love of poker, although Rudden's more of an all-round gambler, and not a winning one.

'I'm getting hammered and it's all your fault,' Phil says. 'Over an hour I've been here.'

'Somebody's gotta keep al-Qaeda at bay.'

'Bollocks. You've had a couple.'

Rudden holds up his hands. 'Well … some of the boys were going for one.'

'Boys?' Phil says. 'Don't suppose there were any female officers there as well?'

'You know me, mate. There's a lot of things I can't say no to. I'm here now, though. So what did you wanna talk about?'

Phil gestures for the barman to bring Rudden a beer. 'You ever work with DCS Cook when he was with your lot?'

'Little bit.'

'And?'

'What's it to you?' Rudden says.

'I'm working for him.'

'On what?'

'Top secret.'

Rudden frowns. 'What, like an internal thing?'

'No, murder investigation.'

'So how's that top secret?'

Phil picks at the label on his beer bottle. 'I … I dunno, really. He's got a couple of ideas, but it seems a bit dodgy to me.'

Rudden's eyes stop darting around the room. He gives Phil his full attention. 'Whadya mean "dodgy"?'

'We're not keeping records, we're hiding things from other forces …'

Rudden goes back to his glancing around the bar. 'Makes sense.'

'Does it?'

'And it's a big case?' Rudden says, distracted. 'High profile, could make him look like a fucking hero?'

'Something like that.'

Rudden grins at a couple of blondes sharing a bottle of champagne, then turns to Phil. 'People who know him, from way back, say he used to be a good bloke. Decent footballer. Then he busted his knee and turned into a right prick. I mean, if you walked like that, you'd have something to prove, wouldn't you?'

'I suppose.'

'He used to go mental any time anyone made a mistake. Ran everything like it was some kind of … elite squad, you know. Had people he trusted and didn't want to know anyone else. Always looking for the big one, the glory, something that would get him noticed, promoted.'

'But did he cut corners, cover things up?'

'I wouldn't know. I wasn't in the inner circle.'

'Reckon you could put me in touch with someone who was?'

'What are you so worried about?'

Phil takes a gulp of his beer and grimaces. 'This thing is big, massive. Someone's killed a witness. We fucked up.'

'But you're following orders from the DCS, right?'

'Yeah.'

'And he's explained to you why you're working the way you are?'

'He reckons they could be getting inside help. And the suspect's got resources, would just disappear if we went public.'

'So what's the problem?' Rudden says, eyes following a petite girl with a nose ring as she walks past.

'I think he's got it wrong, and we're all gonna be in the shit.'

'What are you supposed to do, go to his boss?' Rudden looks disgusted at the thought. 'Nobody hates grasses more than us lot.'

Maybe, Phil thinks. *But dead witnesses, victims of a serial killer who was being investigated by only two detectives – those're the kinds of things that get picked up by the press. Calls for public enquiries, officers on trial. You can't sweep a stack of corpses under a carpet.*

'One thing, though,' Rudden says. 'A bloke like Cook, ruthless bastard like that.' He takes a handful of Japanese rice crackers from a bowl on the bar, pops one in his mouth and chews it a few time before speaking. 'He'd step on your neck if it means he gets the collar.'

Thursday August 29th 2013

Martin's eyes spring open. He sees an unfamiliar ceiling in a dark room.

He gasps for breath and feels the chill of a cold sweat on his skin.

The nightmare was vivid – a red-haired woman, leading him upstairs and then …

He turns and sees Sarah lying next to him, his vision adjusting to the darkness. There's a little light leaking in from the edges of the curtains; the sun is just rising.

Martin slides out of bed, searches for his clothes and remembers they're downstairs.

As soon as he closes the bedroom door behind him, there's a tightening in his throat, a flutter in his stomach. He opens the door a crack and takes in the view: Sarah's red hair spilling over the white pillow, one bare shoulder exposed above the duvet.

He retrieves his clothes from the drawing room floor and wanders through the house until he comes to a large conservatory. He opens the doors, letting in the birdsong and damp dawn air, and sits down on a white linen sofa. He finds the bag of weed he brought with him, still nearly full, and rolls himself a huge joint. After the second puff, the feeling in his stomach disappears.

I could get used to this, he thinks. *Living in this big house, lounging on the sofas while we listen to music, helping Sarah with the technical details of her crime stories.*

There'd even be space for Molly to come and stay – she'd love running around the gardens.

Although Sarah doesn't seem like the maternal type.

Stop picking faults, he tells himself.

Ever since Tess, back at university, Martin has sabotaged his relationship with every woman he has really liked.

Tess sang in his band, got on with his friends and was, in his opinion, about as beautiful as a woman could be.

And he was terrified of losing her. So terrified, in fact, that he drove her away with drunken, jealous rants, questions about where she was going and where she'd been, and petty bickering during the band's rehearsals.

So he eventually ended up with Charlotte, a woman he wasn't so afraid of losing, at least until that meant losing his daughter too.

He smokes and smokes, rolling twice more. His eyes close but he's not asleep, just heavily stoned. His body sinks deep, deep into the sofa – not his whole body though, just his back, as if he's being stretched into a 'U' shape.

You shouldn't be doing this, a distant voice tells him, when you're not alone. You should stay in the relaxed, warm zone, not let yourself drift over the edge into paranoia.

You're going to do something you'll regret.

Martin's mother forces her way into his thoughts, brandishing a knife, standing over him.

'Mummy loves you,' she says. 'But if you tell anyone what happened, mummy will have to hurt you.'

He sees blood on the blade and this makes him think of Sarah, her hair vivid red against the white pillow.

Sarah, Sarah …

Since he was a teenager, Martin has had recurring dreams and fantasies about a woman he'd meet one day. But when he wakes, he can't remember what she looks like. It's not as if her face is blank; it's more like he forgets it at the same time as seeing it. The perfect mate, the key to his happiness is following him around, but always in his blind spot.

Now when he's around Sarah, he experiences the same sensation as with the invisible dream girl: everything dark melts away. And when she's out of sight, he's worried about losing her.

Last night was comfortable, *right*. It reminds him of the time Charlotte insisted they take dance lessons – Argentinian tango – as a birthday present for her. Martin spent many hours shuffling awkwardly around a dance studio. But there were moments when the instructor gripped his hands and with just a pivot of her hips and a little pressure on his palms, she made his whole body move, guiding him effortlessly. When Sarah touched him, pushed him inside her, there was a feeling of inevitable pleasure and climax, no hint of discomfort or clumsiness. Afterwards, he lay next to her as she dozed, breathing in the coconut smell of her shampoo.

But there was also a strange tang, almost metallic, on her skin. The recollection of that causes a black curtain to obscure his vision. His mind rewinds to the drive along the motorway. Then back to when they met, him reading a case file. He finishes the joint and sinks deeper into the sofa.

She lives in a huge house, in the Cotswolds.

She has money.

She approached him.

He sees the CCTV footage from the club in London, but now the girl has red hair. He sees Sarah pushing him into a deep pit, bodies of other men stacked twenty deep. He sees her slicing up Karl while the doctor talks about the unconscious mind. And he sees Sarah standing outside the house where Ian Cox died, flames reflected in her eyes.

The visions come, one after another, Sarah appearing at every point in the case, at every murder scene. And there are a hundred versions of what she's doing to the men. A dungeon under the house, funeral pyres, packs of snarling dogs.

'I thought you'd gone,' she says.

He opens his eyes.

She has the slightly confused smile of someone who's not sure whether to be relieved or annoyed.

With a great deal of effort, Martin swings his legs off the sofa and sits up. 'Can you do me a favour?' he says, waving what's left of the weed. 'Flush this for me. No good.'

She frowns, then speaks as she walks away. 'I'm going upstairs for a shower.'

After giving himself a little pep talk – promising he'll make an effort to relax, not let his nerves ruin things, and remembering that the DNA tests revealed the suspect is a blue-eyed brunette – Martin follows a few minutes later. He lies on the bed, listening to the sound of running water until it stops and Sarah appears, a heavy white towel wrapped around her. She stands in front of the mirror, drawing a brush through her hair. Then she sits at a dressing table and pulls a makeup brush from a drawer.

'Do you think you could make yourself look like someone else?' Martin says.

'Getting bored already?'

'Not yet,' he says, angry with himself as soon as the words come out. 'Never … I–'

She looks at him in the mirror, eyes narrowed.

'The serial killer, the woman. We can't get an accurate description of her. Every e-fit is slightly different.'

Sarah says nothing, just goes to work, rubbing light brown foundation into her face. She pencils black eyeliner on her eyelids, gives herself bold red lips and thick, dark eyelashes. Then she disappears through a door and comes back wearing a short blonde wig.

'I think I've seen you in a couple of videos,' Martin says.

'You like it?'

'I prefer the other one.'

'But do I look like someone else?'

'Well,' Martin says. 'I suppose you do.'

Sarah goes back into the bathroom and returns with a clean, shiny face.

'You think a woman could kill men for fun?' Martin says.

She pauses, examining him in the mirror again. 'What do you mean "for fun"?'

'No other motive, just likes hurting people.'

'What does she do with the bodies?' she says, turning to face him.

'Never found one. Well, not in this country – none of the recent victims.'

'So how do you know she's killing them?'

'We don't. But we have a suspect who used to fight men for money and has a mean streak. We visited someone who knew her at university. An hour later he was killed in a house fire.'

'What else?'

'We know she went travelling about eleven years ago. She flew into Thailand and out of Peru eighteen months later on the same passport. Between those two places there's a trail of dead men.'

'And you think she's still at it?'

'She returned to the UK and men are disappearing from bars and clubs, all of them with an attractive woman.'

'How do you know the two are linked?'

'We don't for sure. But we'd like to find that travelling killer anyway.'

Sarah turns back to the mirror and plucks at her eyebrows with tweezers. 'What made you look for the traveller in the first place?'

'Detective work,' Martin says, smiling smugly.

'I haven't seen any of this on the news.'

'It's being kept quiet. Only two other detectives at the Met know all the details.'

'Why? Surely you want people to come forward with information?'

'To start with, it was because we didn't really have much more than a hunch. Now … mistakes have been made.'

'But you could show people the passport, a few of the e-fits.'

Martin takes a folder from his bag, spreads pictures all over the bed. 'These are all her,' he says. 'Which one do you use?'

She looks at the pictures, at Martin, then back at the pictures. 'What next?'

'She was using the name Louise Brown when she got the passport. Anyone with that name is getting a visit.'

Sarah turns away and picks up a black eye pencil.

Martin puts the photos away. 'I fancy some coffee. Would you like anything?' he says.

Sarah pauses, then turns in her seat to face him. 'Martin, what's with the smoking and the drinking?'

He sits on the bed. 'It's a bit soon to be asking–'

'Is it?' she says, fixing him with a long, unblinking stare. 'I'd like to know what I'm getting involved in.'

Martin lies back on the bed with his hands behind his head, eyes focused on the ornate ceiling mouldings.

Ah, what have I got to lose? he thinks. I like her, a lot. This is my chance to have a real relationship, where you share things, open up. I'm sure I'll fuck this up at some point, but let's try and get off to a good start. Keeping secrets was on the long list of things that drove Charlotte and all the others away.

* * * * * * *

When he was six years old, Martin's dad picked him up from school one day and drove him to an old farmhouse in the countryside. They were going to start a new life without Martin's mum, Dad told him. 'It's complicated,' he'd said when Martin asked why. 'Your mum has some problems, things that mean she shouldn't be looking after you.'

Martin was sitting at the top of the stairs one evening the following week. Dad was listening to The Stones and cooking omelettes for dinner, filling the house with 'Paint It Black' and the heavy smell of frying eggs.

There was a knock at the door. Dad switched off the music and Martin heard him slide the frying pan off the stove.

Dad paused before he opened the door. When he did open it, Martin could see his mum standing on the doorstep, one hand behind her back.

Does she have a present for me? *Martin wondered. He didn't get gifts on his birthday like the other kids; she just bought him things when she felt like it, when she was in the mood for celebrating.*

Dad leaned against the doorframe, arms crossed, looking down at her. 'How did you find us?' he said, but his tone was flat.

Mum said nothing, her head tilted down a little as she gazed up. She almost looked vulnerable.

'I said: how did you find us?' Dad said, still leaning on the doorframe.

Mum's arm slipped out from behind her. Martin glimpsed something silver.

Dad took half a step backwards and Mum threw herself at him, sending them both stumbling into the kitchen. They disappeared out of sight; half a second later, a deafening crash echoed through the house.

Then silence.

Martin crept down the stairs, pausing at the bottom, not sure what he was waiting for. He took two more steps and froze.

Dad sat on the kitchen floor, surrounded by broken crockery, leaning against the washing machine, eyes wide open, bulging. His mouth was open, too, halfway through a word.

The black plastic handle of a knife protruded from his chest; slick, dark blood was spreading out across his blue T-shirt and pooling on the floor. Mum stood over Dad, watching, waiting. She turned and her eyes met Martin's. He tried to run, but his feet remained where they were, pinned to the carpet. Mum scooped him up and hugged him, pulling his little head tight against her chest. 'Martin,' she whispered. 'I love you very much. Do you love Mummy?'

He couldn't speak.

'Mummy loves you so much,' she said. 'But if you talk to anybody about this, Mummy will have to hurt you. And Mummy really doesn't want you to end up like Daddy.'

* * * * * * *

Martin lies still for a minute, then slides his legs off the bed, sits up and looks out of the window.

'I've never even told my wife that story. Nobody but … nobody but a psychiatrist.'

'You didn't tell the police what really happened then?'

'I tried to tell myself it was because I was scared. But … no matter how many times I said it out loud – "*I hate you*" – really, I still loved her. I couldn't stop myself.'

'Did you ask her why she did it?'

'When I was nine – she burnt me with an iron.'

'So the police work, the drugs ...'

Martin sighs. 'The psychological term is "displacement". Until I was in therapy, I'd never consciously acknowledged something so obvious: I have to put strangers behind bars because I couldn't do it to someone I loved, no matter how much she deserved it.'

* * * * * * *

While Sarah dries her hair, Martin spends a few minutes in the kitchen pressing buttons and pulling levers, trying to figure out how to use the chrome espresso machine. Eventually he manages to make a cup of thick black coffee and takes it to the library.

He runs his finger along the shelves of books, ranging from brand new hardbacks to tatty old paperbacks. Most of them are crime novels and non-fiction. He likes her taste in music; she likes the fact that he's a detective. They have things in common.

There are plenty of children's and teens' books. *Are these hers*, he wonders, *from when she was younger, or just research?*

Martin flicks through a few of them. He didn't read this kind of stuff when he was a kid. And now, crime stories just remind him of work.

Work. The case.

I have to face facts, he thinks. *With everything that's happening — Charlotte and Molly, Dr Gross, Ian Cox, the drinking and smoking — I can't trust my instincts. They're all over the place. I mean, I meet a woman I like, and what pops into my head? Visions of her at crime scenes.*

I need to go back to the office, review all the data, do things the boring way.

But he's finishing the coffee and skimming through a Nancy Drew story when he remembers Lucy and how Maurizio called her 'Lucia.'

In the book, there's a character called Eloise.

* * * * * *

Martin drives Sarah back to London. She tells him she's meeting a friend in the City and gets him to drop her at Tottenham Court Road station so she can take the tube the rest of the way. He offers to drive her there, but she insists there's no need.

When she suggests they do something tomorrow, not tonight, he has to swallow hard. But rather than feeling the urge to be with her, it's more like he simply doesn't want to let her out of his sight. He'll have to stay at the office late, after the pubs close, so he won't be tempted to have a few drinks to take the edge off his anxiety. At least he's got a new lead to work on.

Phil's staring at his computer screen when Martin walks into the office. 'Change of heart?' Phil says.

'The university registration forms, let me see them.'

Phil brings up a scanned copy.

'Look what is says there,' Martin says, tapping the screen. 'Preferred name?'

'So this one's called Nicholas,' Martin says, 'but he prefers "Nick".'

'She could have put "Louise" there, so that's what she'd be known as.' Phil grimaces. 'Fuck. Her real name could be anything.'

'Maybe. But if my name was Eloise or Louisa, and I said it should be Louise, I might persuade people to change their records, might persuade them that there'd been a little mistake. I might do enough to break a couple of links to my real identity.'

Phil smiles, picks up the phone, explains everything to Cook and hangs up. 'He likes it. Says they're going to prioritise those names.'

* * * * * * *

'Something's happened,' Karl says.

'What are you talking about?'

'You're fidgeting. You never fidget or show any nerves. And I usually have your undivided attention. What happened?'

'Nothing's happened, nothing at all.'

'You were going to see ...' *Don't say 'Martin'*, Karl thinks. *Don't show signs of familiarity.* '... the detective.'

'I did. He spent the night, he told me all about the case, he went home.'

'You let him go?'

'He's a police officer. He'd be missed. And before you say anything, yes, Karl, I'm sure you're missed too.'

'As is everyone else you've, well ...'

'It's OK, you can call them "victims", "prey", whatever.'

There's no doubt her mood has changed, Karl thinks. *Please let her make a mistake.* 'I'm still a little surprised that you let him go. What did he tell you?'

'All about the case. About the woman he's chasing. She's a master of disguise, you know. He showed me photo-fits of *myself*.'

She's talking faster than usual.

'And you don't worry that he'll eventually make the connection?'

'I don't think he wants to.'

'Blinded by love.'

'Or lust, or something.'

'And it's impossible that you're also blind?' It's only after he's said it that Karl realises: *I'm encouraging Sarah to kill the man who's perhaps my only hope.*

'I'll admit that I like Martin, that I've never met anyone like him. But if he gets too close, or simply presents me with the opportunity to wreck the investigation, then I won't hesitate.' Sarah stands up and, despite only spending a couple of minutes on the sofa, gestures for Karl to return to his cell. He's not sure whether she's speaking to him, or just herself, when she says: 'I will not be caught.'

* * * * * * *

DCS Cook lets himself into his flat in Highgate. He now lives in a purpose-built block with a lift. He tried ground-floor flats but got fed up with listening to his neighbours' footsteps and doors slamming. He doesn't want to live in a house, with empty bedrooms unfilled by the family he doesn't have. He lasted a month of hobbling up stairs before paying to break the lease on a top-floor flat.

As a teenager, he had plenty of girlfriends and nearly made it as a footballer, playing for the Charlton youth team. But he wasn't quite good enough and ended up in the police. He kept playing and captained the Met team, until the injury.

Three surgeries have done nothing to ease the pain. He can't take a step without feeling as if his leg's going to buckle – bones, ligaments and menisci shearing, shattering and popping again. And today was the kind of day he dreads: stuck in meetings for hours while everything seizes up. More than once he had to interrupt proceedings to struggle to his feet and get the blood flowing around that knackered old hinge again.

A couple of Co-codamols or a few drinks will bring relief, but then he can't work. He can't be with a woman any more, either. The painkillers and booze make him soft, but without them, he's a clumsy, anxious man, one small movement away from howling like a kitten that's been trodden on.

He's less than twenty-four hours away from McBride's deadline. He has to find Bellona before then, has to. If he does, Commander Euan McBride will be an irrelevance. The result is all he needs.

He finally has spreadsheets with details of recruits from all the big City firms, and he's been promised the details of any Louisa or Eloise Browns as soon as they're found. Of course, it's possible that Bellona won't be on either of those lists, but he's going to spend all night finding out.

Three hours later, after cutting and pasting the City data, something jumps out. There are two Sarah Natasha Smiths with the same date of birth, with the same degree – economics – from the same university. One joined J.P. Morgan as an equity research analyst and left after nearly four years, the other joined KPMG as a trainee accountant and is still there. It could be a coincidence, but it's more than likely that one of the Sarahs stole the other's identity.

He googles 'Sarah Smith JP Morgan' and gets a few hits. It seems that she's now a hedge fund manager and a successful one, with plenty of mentions in the press. He can't find any interviews, though. She's on a *Financial News* list of high-achievers under forty, but her entry lacks a photo and the background details that all the others have given. He checks the Financial Conduct Authority's Financial Services Register and there she is, attached to RTC Capital. But she's just been marked as 'inactive', presumably because she's left the firm.

The phone rings – it's a new DC whose introduction to detective work has turned out to be the painstaking process of trying to find records of name changes. A Sarah Silver changed her name to Eloise Brown in 1998. The birth certificate shows just a mother: Rachael Silver. Cook writes down the address, then checks the electoral register online. Rachael still lives in the same house in Middlehurst, a village in Kent.

So now he has two suspects, both named Sarah – one the hedge fund manager, the other the former Kent resident who changed her identity. A coincidence? He wonders. Perhaps. 'Sarah' is a common name.

Cook grabs his phone, dials the number for RTC's London office, but there's no answer. There are no international offices mentioned on the website. *Should I go on LinkedIn*, he wonders, *find a colleague, try and get hold of them?* No, he'll call first thing in the morning, get her address in a minute and be there before she knows he's coming. He'll send Martin to Kent and take Phil with him to Sarah Smith's house. That will still leave him ten hours to the deadline, which, if it's one of the Sarahs, will be more than enough, and if it's not, well, he's not going to think about that.

He's got her – he knows it.

* * * * * *

Sarah goes to bed after midnight, but less than two hours later her eyes spring open, her chest heaves and her fists are balled knuckle-splittingly tight.

The nightmare is easy to interpret.

Sarah's walking through the grounds of her estate, towards the mill and the river, holding hands with Martin. She can feel the sun on her face, can hear the water flowing. But as they cross the bridge, Martin unbuttons his jeans. He grins while he pisses into the water, and as he does it, something black swirls in the river. Ashes turn into the men she's disposed of there. And one by one, they all point a finger at her.

She sits up in bed. Sarah let Martin leave – after the story about his mother – but she can't say exactly why. The implication was that he's not capable of bringing someone to justice if he loves them, that if he couldn't tell the police about his mother, the same would happen if he knew who Sarah was.

But there's a thought gnawing at Sarah: from what she can gather, Martin isn't a conventional detective, the type that would call for backup as soon as he suspects her. He's followed his instincts along a trail she'd hoped would be impossible to navigate. What if he's pieced it together – her approaching him, the mysterious wealth and any messages she's transmitting subconsciously? What if he's watching every reaction she has when he mentions the case? What if he made up the story about his mother, or just used the truth to give Sarah a covert message: I'm not a threat to someone I love?

No way, Sarah thinks. *Not even a maverick like Martin would play that game.*

But why do I think that? Am I just looking for a reason to spare him?

I had feelings for Ian and I got rid of him when I needed to.

With Martin, it's different, though, and he's more of a threat …

I don't believe he knows who I really am. That's ridiculous.

But can I trust myself?

Do I even have feelings for him – whatever that means – or am I just having too much fun toying with the detective, a lioness swatting a wounded gazelle with her paw, letting it creep away before pouncing on it?

Is Martin really a wounded gazelle? Or a camouflaged hunter creeping up on me?

Sarah clutches her head in her hands and is silent for a minute.

She gets up, dresses in black running gear and hurries down to the mews house cellar, where she finds a set of brass knuckles. She retrieves a couple of rubbish sacks from under the sink in the kitchen and stuffs them in her pocket.

She walks north, through the colourful streets around Portobello Road and along tree-lined Ledbury Road. She passes under the Westway as cars and trucks still thunder overhead, then crosses the moonlit water of the Grand Union canal.

Now there are no trees. The road is lined with low-rise blocks of flats and scruffier terraced housing.

She sees it in in alleyway next to a pub.

The dog – she doesn't know the breed – has brown fur with patches of black. It's not as silky-furred or slim as a boxer, but not as squat as a bulldog. It's not a stray, either – it looks cared for and has a collar.

When Sarah approaches, the dog stops chewing a bone that has been dragged from an overstuffed bin behind the pub, and trots over.

She takes out one of the black bags and stuffs an end into her collar to make a kind of bib. She kneels, and with her left hand, she pats the dog's head, then grasps its collar. She drives the brass knuckles into the side of his head three times – short, quick blows – before it has time to react. Its claws scrabble at the concrete and it tries to lift its head to bite the hand that grips it, but Sarah strikes again and again, separating its jaw from its skull and cratering its head.

Its yelps turn into wheezing, turn into silence.

Sarah stands up, takes out the other black bag and puts the dog inside. Its collar says 'TYSON'.

She tries to carry the bag under one arm, then the other. She slings it over her shoulder, but the handles won't take the weight. The dog must weigh seventy pounds and she has a long walk home ahead of her. She can dump it, which seems ridiculous, or she can hail a cab.

The taxi driver spends more time looking in the mirror than at the road, itching to ask her what's in the bag at her side.

Can he smell blood, she wonders, *meat?* She opens the window.

Back at home, in the main house, she lugs the bag down to the basement, then goes back up to the kitchen, returning with a cleaver and a boning knife. She hacks off a hind leg, then slides the knife under the furry skin to expose the thigh muscle. She slices off a thick fillet of meat, laying it on the thigh. She wipes her hands on her hoodie, then removes her bloody clothes, leaving them in a pile next to Tyson.

Now wearing a dressing gown, she returns to the kitchen where she chops onions, garlic and mushrooms, then fries them with the finely diced chunks of the meat.

The dog's flesh is like beef but less fatty – she stuffs forkful after forkful into her mouth, washing it down with gulps of bottled water.

For half an hour, she lies awake, staring at the clock.

Then she rushes to the bathroom and vomits.

When she returns to bed, she doesn't fall asleep. She passes out.

Friday August 30th 2013

Phil arrives at the office to find Cook and Martin waiting. The boss sits upright, smiling and fidgeting with some papers. 'Sit down,' he says. 'But it won't be for long. By the end of today, we're going to have her.'

'Eloise?' Martin says.

'Could be,' Cook says. He tells them about the name change, the mother in Kent. 'Martin, you're going there. Just need to find out where Sarah Silver is now, what she's calling herself these days.'

'Sarah?' Martin says, like he's never heard the name.

'That's what I said. Why?'

'Noth … nothing.' Martin scratches his temple. 'What do I tell the mother?'

'Tell her … tell her you think she witnessed something on her travels, some organised crime thing, something she might be too scared to talk about. And feed her some bullshit about not telling her daughter, compromising the investigation. In fact, if you think she's the one, you stay with the mum until you've spoken to me so she can't alert her.'

Martin nods. 'Why am I going alone?'

'If the mum tells you her daughter's in London, or up north, we'll get over there.'

Martin sits for a while.

'What are you waiting for?' Cook says.

'I … I'll go. Now.'

Phil wonders why Martin looks dazed. Probably smoked a joint this morning.

Cook waits for the door downstairs to slam, then speaks. 'Right, we've got another lead. Sarah Natasha Smith, hedge fund manager. Well, *was* a hedge fund manager until a few days ago. I spoke to one of her colleagues this morning – said her departure was very sudden, she sounded pissed off. And she's recently taken time off sick, which she never did before.'

'Is that all?' Phil says. It doesn't sound like a hot lead. Not enough to explain why the DCS looks set to bounce around the room.

'She's secretive and got more than enough money to pull this off, make people disappear. They said she's a bit of a ball-breaker as well. And her name, date of birth and education are an exact match for another Sarah Natasha Smith. She's borrowed someone else's identity.'

'We're gonna bring her in?' Phil says, remembering his conversation with Rudden. 'We'll need backup.'

'Let's watch her for a bit.'

Phil raises a finger and thumb to his chin. 'Why didn't you tell Martin this?'

Cook clenches his jaw a couple of times. 'I picked you two for this case for good reasons. He came up with the Eloise idea, the wrestling stuff, things nobody might have thought about.'

'But?'

'He's unreliable. You want him next to you in a potentially violent situation?'

'Well ...'

'Exactly,' Cook says.

'But what if he finds something, down there in Kent?'

'Then he calls us and we deal with it. Now we're gonna go in separate cars. I'll park a bit further down the road and we'll check things out.'

Cook gives him the address and then Phil follows the DCS in an unmarked Vauxhall Astra – if this was the real killer, she'd recognise the Porsche she tracked. They stop in a leafy street in Holland Park lined with three- and four-storey Georgian houses. Every building has freshly painted woodwork, windows polished like mirrors and a well-kept front garden. The target address is a huge semi-detached with a garage and trimmed hedges. *Certainly got a few quid*, Phil thinks.

Cook calls him. 'Don't reckon she's home. Still, go and knock on the door. Then take a couple of steps back and look up, stay visible.'

Phil reluctantly does as he's told; nobody answers. He returns to the car and rings Cook. 'What now?' he says.

'If we don't see any signs of life by midday,' Cook says, 'we're going in.'

* * * * * *

The address Cook gave him takes Martin to the end of a terrace of six cottages on the edge of the village. They're red brick, two storey, probably built in the fifties. No. 6 has a freshly trimmed lawn; the paintwork on the door and windows is glossier than that of the neighbouring homes.

Martin opens the gate, which swings open on well-oiled hinges. He walks up a recently weeded path – there's freshly disturbed earth between the paving stones. He knocks on the door but there's no answer.

He walks over to the window to the left of the front door and peers inside. He can see through the small lounge and kitchen and into a conservatory at the back. There's a stylish, modern sofa, sleek kitchen units and vases of fresh, exotic flowers. Martin raps on the window, but it's obvious nobody's home.

He steps back and catches the eye of a middle-aged woman peering at him over her reading glasses from the window next door. He walks around the hedge to No. 5, the neighbour now waiting at her open door.

Martin flashes his warrant card. 'I'm looking for the Silvers – it's about Sarah.'

'God, no,' says the woman in an Irish accent. 'That family's been through enough already.'

'I'm not coming with bad news, just want to ask her a few questions.'

The old woman's face relaxes. 'Sarah? She hasn't lived here for years.'

'Where is she?'

'Surely you'd know that?' the neighbour says, eyes narrowed. 'What did you say your name was?'

'DI White. It seems Sarah changed her name. We're having a little trouble tracing her.'

'You know why she did that, don't you?'

Martin shakes his head.

'Heaven help us if you're the best the police have to offer. You'd better come in then. I'm Mary, by the way.'

Martin hesitates on the doorstep. 'Will the Silvers be back soon?'

'There's only Rachael and she'll be at the hairdresser in town. Probably home in half an hour,' she says over her shoulder as she walks into the kitchen. 'Get you a cup of tea?' Mary flicks on an electric kettle. 'I'm having one so don't be worrying about the hassle.'

'Splash of milk and no sugar. Thanks.'

'Take a seat and I'll be with you in a minute.'

Martin perches himself on a chintzy sofa and scans the room. There are family photos everywhere, from formal, black-and-white portraits to colourful holiday snaps. Plenty of wedding pictures, graduation shots. Beaming, gap-toothed children, chubby-cheeked babies, proud parents.

'That's all I see of them these days,' Mary says, setting down a tray with a teapot, cups and biscuits. 'Lot of them involved in a family property business, penniless now.'

'The crisis,' Martin says, nodding and wondering how much small talk he should make.

'A wicked thing,' she says. 'If only I had a daughter like Sarah.'

'Why's that?'

'Have you not seen the place?' Mary says, pointing next door. 'Like something from a magazine. The girl pays for a gardener, cleaner, plus new furniture and a new kitchen every few years. Rachael wants for nothing.'

'Do you know where the money comes from?'

'It's all above board, if that's what you're thinking. She's into hedge funds or something.'

'In the City?'

'That's where they usually are, eh, detective?' But she says it with the smile of an indulgent aunt.

Martin takes a sip of tea. It sounds like this Sarah has plenty of money. Enough to pay for, say, a huge house in the Cotswolds. 'You were worried earlier, said the family had been through a lot, that Sarah had a reason for changing her name.'

Mary's mouth makes an 'O'. 'Terrible business it was. Girl in the village was murdered. A detective tried to pin it on Sarah, then said he could protect her and forced himself on her. Terrible business.'

'Did they find the real killer?'

'They didn't.'

'How old was Sarah?'

'Fifteen as I recall.'

Martin takes out his notepad and writes: 'A FIFTEEN-YEAR-OLD GIRL "FALSELY" ACCUSED OF MURDER.' He looks up at Mary. 'And she changed her name?'

'I think she wanted to leave things behind when she went to university. They didn't mention her name in the papers or anything, but … people around here knew what happened. She got pregnant, lost the baby and had a hysterectomy. Who wouldn't want to start again after all that?'

A hysterectomy? Martin thinks. *The scar.*

He's heard enough. He has to get in the house next door now. If he didn't think Mary would be watching him, he'd be tempted to break in.

Although he could, of course, make a start by asking Mary what Sarah looks like, what colour her hair is. But he wants to see a photo; he wants to be left without any doubts. 'Have you got a number for Mrs Silver, a mobile?'

'She'll be back soon.'

'All the same, I'd just like to make sure.'

Mary looks at him, then gets up and walks to the kitchen, returning with an old Nokia. She holds it at arm's length, peering through her reading glasses and prodding the keys with her index finger. 'That's the one,' she says, showing Martin the screen. 'You'll use your own phone to make the call?'

Martin smiles.

He taps in the number, eager to hear the mother's voice, wanting her to sound completely different from his Sarah. But he hesitates before pressing 'CALL'. *Why are you calling the mother*, Martin asks himself, *giving her a chance to alert her daughter?*

You're trying to track down a murder suspect and you're behaving like a lovesick little boy.

He pockets his phone and waits by the window while Mary clears the cups away.

A dark blue Audi hatchback pulls up in the lane and a woman steps out. Her dyed black hair has been freshly blow-dried. A cashmere sweater and crisp tailored trousers show off her slim figure. She looks out of place walking down the garden path.

'Thanks for the tea,' Martin says, hurrying out of the front door. He catches up with Rachael Silver as she's letting herself in. Rachael turns to face him. She looks familiar, but then she has a face that could be in a magazine, an advert for skincare or hair products perhaps. Her nose is a little larger than Sarah's, but she has green eyes.

'Who are you and what do you want?' she says, hand on the door jamb, blocking the entrance.

'Detective Inspector Martin White. May I come in?'

'Let me see your ID.'

Martin hands over his warrant card. Rachael examines it carefully, then hands it back. 'You can come in if you tell me what this is about.'

'When was the last time you spoke to your daughter?'

'You didn't answer my question.'

'We're looking for Sarah, but it seems she's changed her name.'

Rachael stares at Martin, her gaze searching his face before settling on his eyes for a few long seconds. 'Why are you looking for her?'

'We believe she may have witnessed something.'

'What you're saying doesn't make sense.'

'Excuse me?'

'You want to know when I last spoke with her, but you only know her by an old name. If she saw something recently, you'd know what name she's using now.'

'It's an old case.'

Rachael stares at him again. 'Do you know what she does for a living?'

'Your neighbour said she works in the City – "in hedge funds or something".'

She lowers her hand from the doorframe. Whatever Martin's said, she seems to be satisfied with it. 'I suppose you'd better come in.' She walks into the lounge, flicks a switch; lamps around the room come on. The place looks like a boutique hotel room – expensive and a little impersonal. There are no photos.

'Nice place you've got,' Martin says, sinking into a comfortable armchair.

'The benefits of having a rich child,' Rachael says, sitting across the room on a sofa. 'Although she's always trying to persuade me to move. Spain, California, somewhere hot.'

'You don't fancy it?'

'I have friends here. I'm sure I'd get lonely elsewhere. She doesn't seem to understand that.'

'When was the last time you spoke to her?'

'Yesterday.'

'You talk often?'

'Now and then.'

'And you get on OK?'

'Fine, but she's not the type for girly chats, you know. Very practical, makes sure the house is well maintained, I'm looked after.'

'And her father?'

Rachael purses her lips. 'He died before she was born. Hunting accident.'

'I'm sorry,' Martin says.

'Don't be. He was a violent man, obsessed with killing animals. He got what he deserved.'

'There are no family photos,' Martin says, looking around the room.

'Correct.'

'Can I ask why?'

'You're asking some strange questions.'

'I'd just like to get to know Sarah a little better.'

'Because?'

'It will help with the investigation.'

Rachael leans on the arm of the sofa and supports her chin with a fist. 'You didn't tell me what that was about.'

'It's … complicated.'

'Indulge me.'

Martin coughs into his hand. 'Sarah went travelling after university?'

'She did.'

'Well,' Martin says. 'It's possible she knows what happened to a backpacker in Bangkok.'

Rachael pauses, thinking. 'Why are you investigating a murder in Thailand?'

'We believe it's linked to crimes in the UK,' Martin says. 'She never mentioned anything to you?'

'Never. But what on earth has this got to do with family photos?'

'Sometimes,' Martin says, speaking slowly, in the measured manner of a teacher, 'witnesses don't come forward. It's good to know the reasons why. If they're just afraid, then of course that's a perfectly good reason.'

'I still don't see where this is going.'

'Forgive me, Mrs Silver, but I've been a detective for a long time. I get a feel for people. In this case, I'd like to build a picture of Sarah. Is she the sort of person who could keep a secret, or would she go straight to the police if she saw anything?'

Rachael taps her lips with a finger. 'I see. Well, Sarah is a very private person.'

'But you're her mother – why wouldn't she want you to have photos?'

Rachael tucks her legs under her on the sofa. 'When she was fifteen–'

'Your neighbour told me.'

'Good old Mary,' she says, looking in the direction of the house next door. 'Well, Sarah wanted to start a completely new life, erase everything that had happened.'

'You don't have a single photo?'

Rachael doesn't say anything.

'Can I see them?'

She taps her lip again. 'Wait here.'

Rachael goes upstairs. There's the sound of furniture moving on a wooden floor. Something heavy falls.

She returns with a tatty green shoebox. She sits down, takes the lid off and flicks through the photos. 'Baby photos,' she says. 'Primary school, holidays … ah, this is one of the last pictures I got, a few weeks before the attack.'

Martin feels as if there's a hummingbird trapped in his ribcage, its wings whirring furiously.

Rachael hands him the photo: a red-haired girl staring directly at the camera.

His Sarah.

He sinks back into the sofa.

'Are you alright?' Rachael says. 'You don't look well.'

'I … I've made a terrible mistake.'

'What would that be?'

Compose yourself, Martin. Don't make her suspicious, don't make her call Sarah. He sits up straight. 'Mrs Silver, would it be possible not to mention my visit to your daughter?'

'Why?'

'The girl we've been looking for doesn't match her description.'

'So why can't I tell her you came?'

'It … it could compromise the investigation.'

Rachael frowns. 'How quickly do you expect this thing to be resolved?'

Martin's mouth is moving on autopilot when he says, 'By the end of the day.'

* * * * * * *

Sarah wakes late, an unpleasant taste in her mouth.

She acts without thought, without consciously pondering the meaning of what she's done. Now is not the time for reflection.

In the basement, she strides over to the panic room, where Karl will be waiting for their next session.

She pauses for a second before switching off his air supply.

Back upstairs, Sarah goes online and books a first-class flight to Hong Kong, departing at ten p.m. that evening.

* * * * * * *

Martin sits on a bench next to the village green, his hands shaking as he rolls a joint. He already feels stoned, sitting here watching ducks floating on a pond, while he considers his romantic involvement with a possible serial killer.

He has a lot of questions.

Has he given her new information, or just confirmed things she already knew?

And their night in the Cotswolds – that was the perfect opportunity to get rid of him. But she didn't. Should he be encouraged by that? Or is she waiting to see if she can get more out of him?

Martin, there's nothing to think about. You're too close to this, to her. You've located a woman suspected of killing something like thirty men, but you didn't call it in immediately because you enjoyed her company? There's no way you can establish how she feels about you. She took an interest in your work because she wanted to find out what you know about her. And so what if she has a similar taste in music, if it isn't just made up? Why wouldn't she sit through your drumming, pretend she's not bored by a little jazz, even sleep with you, if it meant she could find out how close the police were getting?

But Martin is a good judge of people, of actors and liars.

He's spent time with Sarah, talked to her, touched her. And he can't believe she's killed anyone. He can't even picture her being violent. But … his opinion is irrelevant. A sample of her DNA – if it matches those samples from Thailand and Peru, from the woman he was told *probably* has brown hair, *probably* has blue eyes – would provide a definitive answer.

What if, he wonders, *what if she was like that back then? What if she did kill people, but now she's stopped?*

OK, she killed Ian Cox, but that was to cover her tracks.

Maybe she killed Karl too. Or maybe not.

Could it be … she's the one, but the escalation in the crimes that Martin observed – taking a chance among all the cameras in London when she'd previously stuck to quieter areas; snatching two boys in broad daylight – could it be that she was having some kind of breakdown so she sought treatment from Karl?

Does she want to stop?

* * * * * * *

The phone rings while Phil waits in his car, but it's Martin, not Cook. He lets it ring.

What the DCS said has been weighing on his mind. Yes, Martin's a stoner. But he's done more than anyone to crack this case, living up to his reputation for spotting the things nobody else does.

You can take chances, act a little weird when you're following clues, though. But when you're in a potentially violent situation, there's no room for error.

The phone goes to voicemail, then starts ringing again. This time Phil answers.

'I need to tell you something,' Martin says.

'Have you spoken to Cook?'

'No.'

'So it's not her, Sarah Silver?'

'Er … No.'

'How do you know?'

'She's got alibis for a few of the nights, and … she had a good reason for the name change.'

'What's that?'

'She ...'

Phil spots someone coming out of the house. No, it's the house next door – an old woman with a Labrador. 'So what was it you wanted to tell me?'

'Why I joined the force.'

Phil laughs. 'Are you high?'

'What's that got to do with anything?'

'Just seems like a funny time for a heart to heart.'

Martin doesn't seem to hear that last comment and launches into a story about his mum killing his dad while Phil listens in silence.

'She got away with it?' Phil says, already knowing the answer, understanding why Martin never accepts the obvious explanation for a crime.

'It was easy. My dad had snatched me from her. She said she went to confront him and he attacked her, so she grabbed a knife. He was six foot two, and had convictions for possession and assault. She was five foot. Didn't even go to court.'

Phil grimaces. 'Why are you telling me this? Now?'

He hears Martin take a puff, hold it in, then breathe out.

'The week before we got this case,' Martin says, 'she died. Cancer.'

'I suppose I don't need to say I'm sorry for your loss.'

'I'm quitting,' Martin says.

'What do you mean you're quitting?'

'My motivation is dead, literally.'

Phil runs his hand forward through his hair and over his face. 'Cook was right about you.'

'What does that mean?'

'You're unreliable.'

'When did he say that?'

'You think he's wrong? We're chasing a serial killer and you're giving up – for what? Personal reasons? Like it's all about you?'

'I don't trust myself any more, to make the right decisions. My instincts are shot.'

'So ironically your judgement's not completely off.'

'You wouldn't have got close without me.'

Somebody knocks on the car window. There's a red-haired woman standing in the street.

'I have to go,' Phil says, ending the call. He lowers the window. 'Can I help you?'

'Did Dan send you?' she says, her arms crossed.

'Sorry?'

'Dan, my boss. The one who fucked me. The fat bastard that's trying to ruin my career.' She looks up and down the street, agitated. 'How much is he paying you? You're from the papers? I'm calling the police.'

'No need,' Phil says, pulling out his warrant card.

'Oh,' she says. 'What are you doing here?'

'I'm afraid I can't talk about that.'

She looks up and down the street again. 'Well … while you're here, I want to show you something.'

'I need to stay in the car.'

She leans on the window frame. 'It will just take a minute. Please.'

'Sorry,' Phil says.

'He's been harassing me, sending me things. I want to show you, I want a witness.'

She's not going to back down, Phil thinks. *It will be quicker to humour her for five minutes. There's obviously been a misunderstanding about her leaving her job – a simpler explanation than being a serial killer.* 'OK,' he says. 'Let me check. Please go back inside.' Phil watches her return to the house and calls Cook. He tells the DCS that Martin's lead was no good, but doesn't disclose his crisis of confidence. Then he explains what just happened.

'Fuck,' Cook says. 'So that's why her colleague said she was acting weird.'

'Should I go in?'

'I suppose so, can't do any harm.'

Phil strolls up to the house and knocks on the door. She answers, looks up and down the street yet again and then lets him in.

The door slams behind Phil.

Something strikes the back of his head.

* * * * * * *

Phil wakes up with goose bumps, cold metal stinging his buttocks. He's naked, tied to a chair in a large basement. In the corner there's some kind of steel structure with a door. There are more doors at each end of the room and also some kind of office: desk, chair and sofa.

The red-haired woman, Sarah Smith, stands in front of him, a pair of long-handled bolt-cutters in her right hand. On the grey concrete floor, there are darker patches where stains haven't been quite scrubbed away. She's folded his clothes and placed them in a corner.

Phil tries to estimate his odds of getting out alive. He gives a rescue by Cook a one-in-five chance and by Martin one-in-a-thousand. Or maybe she'll use Phil as a hostage. But … someone will have to raise the alarm for that to be noticed.

'Who knows you're here?' she says.

'Just … DCS Cook.'

'And where's he?'

'In a car down the road.'

She rests the bolt cutters on the chair between his legs, the blades on either side of his balls.

At some point, Phil will have to use his bluffing skills. He'll have to tell her a lie that might save him. But right now, he's going to give her everything she wants.

'What about Martin?' she says.

He's about to ask how she knows the name, then remembers she's been tracking them. 'Cook doesn't trust him.'

'Why not?'

'Bit of a loose cannon, you know.'

She smiles, like they're talking about a close mutual friend. 'Think you can persuade this Cook to knock on my door?'

The sharp blades press against his balls.

'I'll try. His number's in my phone.'

Sarah holds it up to Phil's ear and Cook answers. 'It's definitely not her,' Phil says, trying to sound casual. 'But she knows a lot of women in the City who started out when she did. I reckon it's worth spending time with her.'

Cook speaks quietly. 'I know it's her. I'm armed. Just stay calm.'

'OK,' Phil says, his voice tight. 'See you in a minute.'

'He didn't sound suspicious?' Sarah says, applying just a little more pressure to the bolt cutters, drawing a gasp from Phil.

'Don't … think so,' he manages to say. 'But he's … hard to read.'

'Describe him.'

'He walks with a limp … some old football injury.'

Sarah pulls away the bolt cutters and paces across the room a few times. 'Can he run?' she says.

* * * * * * *

Cook unzips his rucksack, reaches inside and pulls out the pistol, a Browning HP that found its way home from Iraq or Afghanistan and ended up in a drug dealer's flat. He screws in a homemade silencer.

He gets out of the car and crosses the road, right hand holding the gun in his coat pocket, left holding the rucksack.

He takes a deep breath, then knocks, standing to the right of the door. If he hears a gunshot, he'll fire back.

The door opens and there she is, no flicker of recognition or surprise in her eyes.

'Come in,' she says. 'We were just chatting in the kitchen.'

Cook closes the door behind him. The hallway is wide, with a grand staircase on the left and light flowing in from a skylight two floors above. He speaks as Sarah walks towards the first door on the right: 'Turn around slowly.'

She darts through the door.

Cook doesn't have time to fire. He moves over to the wall and leans against it.

Her voice comes from the other room. 'I'd leave the way you came in, if I was you.'

'Can't do that.'

'My house. And I'm quicker than a crippled old man.'

Cook grips the gun a little tighter and smirks. 'You don't remember me, do you, Bellona?'

* * * * * * *

Soon after he'd moved from the uniformed service to CID, Terrence Cook felt he was missing something. He missed donning the helmet and shield for riots; missed chasing down muggers, tackling them, pushing their arms behind their back, rubbing their noses in the concrete.

He tried a few martial arts and quickly got into judo. With karate and taekwondo, you couldn't really hit someone, you had to hold back or wear pads. But judo let him actually fight, grappling with all his strength and determination.

He found himself staring at the girls and women at the classes. Some of them arrived and left in skirts and jewellery and makeup, but on the mat, they were strong, determined, aggressive. He couldn't help wondering what it would be like to fight them in a different environment. And it would be OK, to fight a woman, if she wanted to, if she could look after herself, wouldn't it?

He didn't know where that urge had come from – his parents rarely argued, let alone hit each other. But he'd had one volatile relationship after another, characterised by screaming, throwing blunt objects, and rough, violent sex.

He was friendly with the girls at the judo classes, but they were wary when the subject of fighting away from the mat came up. So he turned to the internet and discovered the mixed wrestling scene.

Finding the right girl was tough. There were bodybuilders, some of whom were bigger and stronger than him. A lot of them wouldn't really fight, though – they were too worried about injuries disrupting their training. And there were smaller girls who were experienced fighters, but he was close to six foot and skilled. He wanted to fight someone feminine, but without holding back.

He arranged to meet Bellona in a hotel. It didn't take long for her to prove she was the girl for him. He was stronger than her, but she was fast, wild and had plenty of dirty moves. She'd dig her thumbs into every soft spot, push her forearms into his face, stick a knee or elbow into his crotch every now and then. When she got him in a choke, she'd take him to the point of passing out, smiling when she finally let him go. And it was all part of a plan, the oxygen deprivation tiring him, a dead leg slowing him down.

But by the end of the hour, he'd learned some of her tricks. He got her in an ankle lock, then a choke; he returned the favour, holding on for a few seconds when she tapped out, taunting her, 'How does that feel?'

She stood up after that, stared at him blankly. He saw her move, but he didn't react fast enough.

It was a short, sharp kick, her heel connecting with the side of his knee. There was a popping sound and then he screamed, collapsing to the floor.

She didn't look at him, just hurried into the bathroom to pick up a bag, then slipped on a pair of shoes and a coat and walked out the door.

It was easy to hide what had happened from friends and family – he wouldn't be the first person to damage a knee playing football. But it was a lot harder to get over the fact that someone had crippled him.

He saw the post about her being in Thailand, and all the other crap. He attempted to track her down in his spare time, but he got nowhere and now he can see how ineffective he was – he didn't even make the link with the Austrian backpacker. But he did keep an eye out for cases that might involve female violence against men. That's why he'd noticed the pattern of disappearances and ended up seeing the grainy CCTV footage taken at a bar in Nottingham. The face was disguised, unrecognisable. But he just knew it was her. Something about the way she moved.

At the time, he was on track to head up SO15, Counter Terrorism Command, but the head of Murder and Serious Crime was feeling the heat from an earlier involvement in a phone hacking investigation. Cook discreetly expressed an interest in switching back to murderers and away from terrorists.

The plan he was starting to formulate was risky but a hundred times more likely to succeed if he had a genuine reason for investigating missing persons. All he needed were a couple of outsiders – detectives who might actually be useful on an unusual case but, just as importantly, wouldn't gossip about it or worry too much about the career implications if things didn't work out. He knew Martin White's reputation – everyone did – and he remembered the fuss a few people had made about the poker player and his ambitions.

They made faster progress than he could have hoped for, discovering the wrestling stuff themselves and finding out what she was really doing in Thailand. Then she burned down the house in Colchester, and Cook knew they were on to something. But it also started the clock ticking – he couldn't keep the investigation a secret for much longer.

He'd had the two plainclothes officers make themselves obvious outside the pub in Blackheath. Catching her there would have sped things up, but he didn't want her in police custody.

He wanted to get her at home.

* * * * * * *

'Give me a clue?' she says.

'Why do you think I'm limping?'

A pause. 'A kick to the knee did that?'

'You can't imagine what I've been through.' Not that he expects her to care, of course.

'Shouldn't have tried to beat me, should you?'

'All I wanted was a fair fight.'

'Very noble. But I hate to lose.'

'I know you don't have a gun,' he says.

'I can get my hands on one before you can put a bullet in me.'

'I doubt that.' Cook wonders why she answered the door unarmed, why she's waiting on the other side of the wall.

'You know, you've come at a bad time,' she says. 'A day later and I'd be a few thousand miles away.'

'You can still get on that plane.'

'You plan to come with me?'

'I just want what you owe me.'

'A new leg?'

'Compensation.'

'How much?'

Based on the value of her house and the hedge fund job, he's arrived at a figure he thinks is realistic. And looking at the huge abstract painting hanging in the hallway, he thinks he's being conservative. 'Five million pounds should do it. I've got an account set up. You transfer the money, I'll mess around with our files on you, leave in the dead ends, destroy the real leads.'

'It will take a few days.'

She's stalling. 'You must have cash, offshore, that you can transfer.'

'I do, but most of my money's tied up in shares. I've only got two million cash, if you want it right now. But … your plan doesn't make sense anyway.'

'I think it does.'

'Not to me,' she says. 'I transfer the money, then what? We both try to kill each other.'

It sounds as if her voice is coming from the same level as his, meaning she's standing up on the other side of the wall. He could empty the gun in that direction at knee height and probably maim her, leaving her alive to transfer the money. But if he shoots too high or misses, there'll be no deal.

'I just want to take my knee to a warmer climate.' Cook can see himself, relaxing in a bar overlooking the sea, sipping iced cocktails, chatting to a tanned local girl.

'It's that simple?' Sarah says. 'You've been hobbling around for ten years, feeling sorry for yourself. I just give you a few mil and you're on your way?'

'If you didn't have money, things might be different.'

'You'd still like to hurt me, though.'

'I would. But I'd rather spend the rest of my life on a beach without worrying about being a murder suspect.'

'I'm sure the Met will still want a word.'

'Maybe, but they'll take a murder more seriously.' He smiles as he imagines Euan McBride sitting in his office this evening, checking his watch, wondering where the hell Cook is.

'What about your detectives, Martin and Phil?'

'I figured you'd take care of them.'

'Why not do this over the phone?' she says.

'You forced my hand, coming out to talk to DI Burton. I just wanted to watch you for a while.'

Cook is lying. He was always going to come in, take a risk on what's a borderline kamikaze mission. Hurting Sarah is all he really wants, although getting away with a few million will be a nice bonus.

'I don't buy the files thing,' she says. 'There must be computer records.'

'I've kept them isolated–'

'The office in Soho.'

'Only three men know everything. Well, only two who know your current name, this address, and we're both in the building.'

'How did you find this place?'

'I spoke to someone at your office.'

'Who?'

'Svetlana, I think she was called. Told her I was your personal trainer, you hadn't turned up for a session and I only had your work number. I needed to send you a bill.'

'Where's Martin?'

'Out of town following up a lead that's no good. I can give you his address.'

'I have it. So how are we going to do this?'

'You can instruct a transfer online?'

'I can.'

'Where's your computer?'

'I've got one in here.'

'So I come in, we make the transfer, I leave.'

A phone rings on the other side of the wall.

'I'm going to take this,' Sarah says.

Cook tries to tell her not to, but she's already talking.

'Martin? Hi. Why don't you come over to my place in … two hours?' She gives him the address and hangs up.

'Martin White?' Cook says.

'We've been seeing a lot of each other.'

'Jesus. He knows about you?'

'No. We met in a pub. He's … nice.'

'You're a piece of work.'

'I know,' she says and he can tell she's smiling. 'Anyway, we have business to take care of before he gets here.'

'The transfer.'

'Change of plan. I'm going to do your other leg.'

Footsteps.

Cook bursts through the door, gun raised. A door swings shut at the other end of a long drawing room that stretches to the rear of the house. He hurries over, but now he can hear her running upstairs.

She'll want me to follow, he thinks, *won't she? So I should go downstairs. I might find Phil, then there'll be two of us.*

He opens the door a crack. A narrow staircase, going up and down, probably used by the servants in the old days. He creeps down; at the bottom, he opens the door.

Phil is naked, tied to a chair, gagged. Cook tries the door opposite the one he came through but it's locked. The door to the big metal room isn't. He reaches inside and finds a light switch.

The fluorescent bulb flickers and then casts a yellow glow onto Karl's corpse. Cook stands, staring for a while until Phil's muffled cries remind him of their situation. He removes the cloth from Phil's mouth and uses the bolt cutters to release him from the chair.

Phil pulls his clothes on. 'Where is she?' he says.

Cook puts his finger to his lips, then points upwards.

'We have to get out of here,' Phil whispers, eyes wide.

Cook shakes his head. 'We've got her.'

'It's her house. We should get out,' Phil says. 'Maybe just cover the exits.'

'*No*. We take her now, we take her *down*.'

Phil narrows his eyes a little, appears to be thinking. 'OK.'

They creep up the stairs, back the way the DCS came, into the large room. Cook gestures for Phil to push an armchair in front of the door to the stairs while he keeps his gun pointed at the entrance to the room.

Now they creep to the front of the room, stopping to listen every couple of steps. Cook opens the door a few inches and checks the hallway.

Nobody there.

He slips through the doorway, gun pointed at the stairs. From behind him, Phil moves, making a dash for the front door. He has his hand on the lock when Cook fires two shots into the back of his head.

Phil drops to his knees, slumps left and lands on the floor with a thud.

Cook goes to him and checks his pulse. Nothing.

'You can't afford to walk out of here now, can you?' Sarah shouts from the top of the house. 'You've badly misjudged the situation.'

'We can do the transfer,' Cook says. 'It's not too late.'

'You expect me to trust you now? You shot a colleague.'

'What choice did I have?'

'It doesn't matter. I want this, to hunt you down, to hurt you again.'

'You can still walk away,' Cook says. 'Be sensible.'

'Everything's locked,' Sarah says. 'The windows have security glass. And see that keypad by the front door? The only way out of here. I'm going to hurt you.'

'I'll smoke you out.'

'It will attract too much attention. You're going to have to try and hobble up these stairs and then I'll get you.'

'I'm not talking about a fire.' Cook takes a canister of teargas out of his rucksack and throws it to the top of the first flight of stairs. He gets out a gas mask and pulls it over his head.

Upstairs there are footsteps, then a door slams.

By this evening, he thinks, *I'll have tortured the account details out of her. Phil's body – and Martin's – will be in the basement. I'll fly business class in the morning, be lying in the sun this time tomorrow.*

The teargas has created a dense fog on the staircase. Without a mask, there's no way she could be there. He throws another canister up, just to make sure.

Cook climbs the stairs slowly, straining to hear footsteps or creaking floorboards over the sound of his own breathing in the mask. He continues up to the top floor and pauses on the landing. He thinks the sound of a door slamming came from the right. There are two rooms either side of him, one more door in the middle.

He crouches by the first door on the right, slowly turning the handle, opening it just enough to roll a canister in.

No coughs come from the other side of the wall. He does the same again for the next room. Again, silence.

He opens the central door and puts another canister through there, hears it clank down the stairs. So that's where the staircase comes up. She can't surprise him from down there now.

Cook sits with his back to the wall. *Why did she come to the top of the house?* he wonders. *Misdirection? Has she already taken those stairs down to the basement?*

When he went down to find Phil, what did he see? The room was empty, nothing but the furniture and the bolt cutters. But the other door down there, what's behind that? A cupboard, weapons?

He rolls canisters into the other two rooms and again hears nothing. *Could she escape the gas by hiding in a wardrobe?* He checks the rooms but they're all unfurnished, floorboards bare.

She must have gone down the back staircase.

He makes his way down. There's a turn where the first floor is, but no entrance to a room. He goes down again; the armchair still blocks the entrance to the ground floor.

She's in the basement.

Cook goes back up, then down the main staircase. His knee is throbbing now, but the adrenaline pushes him on. He checks the other rooms on the ground floor. The kitchen has a door leading onto the garden, but it's locked. *Should I just wait?* he wonders. *Maybe deal with Martin, then figure out a way to flush her out of the basement?*

He takes a chair from the dining table in the kitchen, carries it to the top of the stairs and puts it in front of the entrance to the back staircase. It won't completely block it, but he'll hear her at least.

He's back in the kitchen when a beep comes from the front door, then a click.

She's leaving.

Cook hurries to the hallway as fast as he can.

A police officer in body armour and a helmet is entering the house. 'Who called you?' Cook says, noticing too late that the police officer, like him, carries a silenced pistol.

The first shot hits him in the thigh, the second in the shoulder. Cook collapses and the police officer walks over, then stands on his wrist so that he releases his gun.

The helmet comes off and Sarah looks down at him. 'This,' she says, 'is going to take some cleaning up. I'm expecting a visitor.'

'Please,' Cook says, grimacing.

'Stop moving, you're getting blood everywhere.'

'I'm … sorry. I … I can still help you, we can work … something … out.'

'Martin's already coming over. If I need anyone to help me, it will be him.'

'Just put a bullet in my head then.'

Something catches Sarah's eye. 'You see that?' She points the gun at the wall. 'Blood on textured wallpaper. I've got an hour and a half to get that out. I'm not going to make more mess.' She taps her lips with a finger, thinking. 'You don't know how to get rid of the smell of teargas, do you?'

'What …? No.'

'So you really are no use to me,' she says, then sighs. 'Actually, this could work.' She kneels down and pulls the helmet onto Cook's head. She puts the gun in his mouth and fires two shots, then stands up and looks at him. 'Very clean,' she says.

* * * * * * *

Martin hesitates outside the house. All the windows are open and so is the front door. Air conditioning fans hum. He walks up the steps and says, 'Hello?'

Sarah appears in the doorway, wearing a white towelling robe, her hair wet. 'Sorry,' she says. 'I'm running a bit late. Had to tidy up – the place was a bloody mess.'

'Everything OK?' Martin says, stepping inside. 'It–'

'The smell? A bit of a vermin problem, I had to get the place fumigated.'

'It gets your eyes, doesn't it?' he says. He'd love to know where the teargas came from. 'You're sure it's OK?'

'Don't worry,' she says, rubbing her hair with a towel. 'You're safe in here, I promise. How's the case? Any breakthroughs?'

'Not yet,' Martin says, conscious of the tone of his voice. *Coming here without a plan is a monumental mistake.*

He's already glancing at her pale neck, fighting the urge to reach out and touch her cheek. *She's a killer*, Martin tells himself. *It really doesn't matter what she looks like, how comfortable she makes me feel. Those are the reasons she gets away with it.*

'Shall we go upstairs?' she says, and Martin knows he's going to get himself into trouble.

He closes the front door, then follows her up to a bedroom where everything is white. She takes off her robe and drapes it over the metal bed frame.

This is how she does it, Martin thinks. *Who would predict what comes next?*

Downstairs in the hallway, a phone rings.

It keeps ringing.

They look at each other, smile. 'When I get back,' she says pulling the robe back on, 'you'd better be naked.'

* * * * * * *

Sarah picks up the phone and takes it into the kitchen before answering. 'Hello,' she says, knowing only one person has the number.

'I tried your mobile,' her mother says, 'but you didn't answer. And the office, they said you don't work there any more.'

'I'm taking some time off. I might go away for a while.'

'What's wrong?'

'Nothing, Mum. Nothing at all.'

'You're sure? It's just that–'

'What?' Sarah is suddenly conscious that there's a detective in her bedroom, alone.

'I'm not supposed to tell you this,' Rachael says. 'But … I had a visit from the police this morning.'

'And they said you shouldn't tell me about it?'

'They said they'd made a mistake.'

'What kind of mistake?'

'I don't know, I showed them–'

'What? You showed them what?'

'I know you asked me not to … I kept a box of photos.'

Sarah clenches her fist. 'I can't believe this.'

'You're my daughter. I need those memories. I hardly see you.'

Sarah closes her eyes and leans against the wall with her forehead. 'When was the photo taken?'

'You were fourteen.'

'It looks like I do now?'

'He seemed to recognise you straight away.'

'What was his name?'

'Martin–'

'White.' Sarah says.

'You know him?'

'I do.' *I know him intimately.* 'What did he say? Exactly?'

'Not to call you for at least twenty-four hours.'

'You did the right thing, Mum, calling me. Thank you.'

Sarah goes back upstairs. Martin is in bed, a sheet pulled over him.

'Where were we?' Sarah says, walking over to a wardrobe. She opens the door and takes out a pair of handcuffs.

Martin frowns when he sees them, but he doesn't move as she climbs on the bed and secures one of his wrists to the frame. She gets off the bed and sits on a white leather armchair in the corner of the room.

'So that was–'

'Your mother,' Martin says.

'You told her not to call me.'

'I did.'

'You expected her to ignore your request?'

'No, but I knew it was her when the phone didn't stop. Only a parent lets it ring and ring like that.'

Sarah makes a steeple with her fingers. 'So, Martin. Detective Inspector White. What exactly are you doing here?'

'I know who you are.'

'And you still came.'

'I think … I think I can understand what you've done.'

'And I'll forget what you do for a living?'

'I'm quitting. You can too. You were seeing Dr Gross, weren't you? You want to stop.'

'I think so,' she says. 'I think so. This can't work, though. One day we'll have an argument. The thought I could do something will cross your mind. And I'll worry about you turning me in.' She shakes her head. 'We're different. Your history drives you to catch people like me, people who learned the opposite lessons from their past.'

'You don't have to be like your father.'

Sarah narrows her eyes. 'What do you know about him?'

'Only what your mum told me: a violent man, died in a hunting accident.'

Hunting? Sarah thinks. *He was a hunter?* For a long moment, she feels as if he's in the room with them, watching.

'Come over here,' Martin says.

She doesn't move, just examines his face. He's wide-eyed, eager. Martin's the only person who knows about her – well, the only person alive. And he's come back to her.

No matter what he says, though, he's a detective with a knack for uncovering the things no one else can. But … perhaps that means he's capable of believing that she wants to stop.

Sarah walks over and slips under the sheets. Martin's body is warm and she feels his heart thumping against her breasts.

They kiss and clutch each other and Sarah is lost in Martin's arms, her mind empty of thoughts. There are only physical sensations – torso against torso, hand on face, lips brushing, teeth biting.

But soon she realises he isn't lost in the same way; he remains limp against her thigh.

'This never happens to me,' she says and lifts her head to look at him. He smiles, but not with his eyes. 'Why are you nervous?' she asks – then throws off the sheet, rushes over to the window and pulls back the curtain a couple of inches.

The street is cordoned off. There are snipers on the roofs of the houses opposite; armed police crouch behind cars.

'Why?' she says, turning around.

Martin sits up in the bed. 'When I walked through the front door, I didn't have a plan, I just wanted to see you. But then you left the room to take that call, and … I saw what it would be like. I'd always be wondering where you're going, what you're up to. I tried to call Phil, then Cook. They didn't answer and I started to panic. The teargas–'

'They're in the basement,' she says. 'It was Cook who killed Phil, though.' She tells him what happened.

'Phil's dead and … Cook was just settling a score?'

'Some people can't let go.'

'But Phil …'

'You don't seem worried you'll end up like them.'

'I think … I think, with us, initially it was an act, but then you started to feel something.'

'And that will stop me killing you?'

'I think you're lonely.'

Sarah is still for a moment.

It's Martin who has turned out to be the scorpion, not me.

She hurries out of the room, goes down to the basement and through the tunnel, emerging in the cellar of the mews house. She puts the body armour back on and feels inside the helmet. She sponged out Cook's blood and it's still a little damp. She pulls it on over a balaclava, then takes an MP5 machine gun, like the ones the police use, from a cabinet.

They're waiting for her, perhaps waiting for a signal from Martin, who's still chained to the bed. A couple more minutes won't make a difference.

* * * * * * *

Martin lies alone. He knows he made a sensible choice, but that doesn't stop him regretting it.

Heavy footsteps thunder up the stairs. *Are they in the house already?*

And there she is – armoured, carrying a machine gun, a defiant look in her eyes.

'No,' he says. 'They've got the place surrounded.'

'I have a tunnel into the house behind.'

'They'll be in that street too.'

She taps her helmet. 'Worst I'll get is a bullet in the arm or leg.'

'Take me as a hostage.'

'You'll get in the way.'

'So what did you come back for?'

She walks over to the bed, taking off the helmet and balaclava. 'You trapped me … well, almost,' she says, smiling. 'I'm impressed. I enjoyed chasing you, playing the game. And maybe I …' She leans over the bed, puts a hand behind his head and kisses him. 'I'll give you some time, to miss me, to live with your regrets. Then I'll come back for you.'

And then she's out of the room. He hears her walk down the stairs until the footsteps fade away.

In the distance, a man shouts.

Three shots are fired.

Silence.

Friday September 20th 2013

Martin rises at six without an alarm – a regular habit since he stopped the weed.

He pulls on jeans, hiking boots and a fleece. It may only be September, but it's always a few degrees cooler in this part of the world.

He boils the kettle in the cosy kitchen and waits for the sound of paws padding through from the lounge. He wanted solitude up here, but after a couple of days, loneliness set in. The dog – a seven-year-old collie called Archie – came from a shelter for strays in Aberdeen.

Martin ruffles the fur on the back of Archie's neck, then fills a thermos flask with hot tea.

They hike across the moors for an hour and a half, a man and his boisterous companion dwarfed by the vast, gently undulating landscape under an infinite sky, never seeming to get closer to the green mountains on the horizon.

Martin stops to lean against a dry stone wall, where he pours himself a cup of tea, between sips throwing an old tennis ball for Archie to fetch. Then they head back to the cottage.

The weather's clear – there are few clouds and little humidity. Perhaps after breakfast they'll jump in the Land Rover and drive deeper into the Cairngorms, maybe take a walk halfway up a mountain.

This is what Martin's days are like now, and he can't imagine tiring of walks along craggy coastal cliffs or around the deep, dark lochs, taking refuge in one of the many pubs and distilleries when the rain comes.

He fries a couple of rashers of thick streaky bacon and two of the eggs his nearest neighbour – three miles away – delivers every few days on her way to … He never listens to where she's going. He's too busy enjoying her unsuccessful efforts to steer the conversation around to who he is and what he's doing up in the Highlands.

Martin is just about to click on the radio for the news when the metallic bang of the door knocker echoes through the cottage.

There's no gun to reach for – he opens a drawer and pulls out a carving knife.

But there's no way it could be her.

Probably a journalist. He knows they'll track him down eventually.

He replaces the knife, then opens the door. A red-faced delivery man thrusts a heavy box into his arms.

'Bloody Amazon,' he mutters as he descends the steps and returns to his van.

Martin opens the box and takes out the books. They should keep him away from the television in the evenings after he speaks to Molly on Skype. He's chosen to start with *Basic Psychology, The Psychopath* and *Freud: An Introduction.*

He sets the books on the table, then returns to the kitchen and switches on the radio.

While Sarah remains in a coma, more suspected victims have been identified. The interest in her remains elevated.

Of the three shots fired by a police marksman with a Heckler & Koch G36 assault rifle, two struck Sarah's helmet. The impacts fractured her skull, causing severe swelling of the brain. She remains under twenty-four-hour guard in University College Hospital's Critical Care Unit.

Her victims' families are split roughly eighty/twenty between those who hope she never wakes and those who want her to answer their questions and face a life behind bars. One hundred per cent of the media are praying for the chance to interview and photograph the world's most prolific female serial killer. And Euan McBride is clinging onto his job, although Martin gives him a one-in-a-thousand chance of doing so, despite DCS Terrence Cook, now deceased, being a perfect – and legitimate – scapegoat.

Martin switches off the radio, slips the bacon and eggs onto a plate and returns to the lounge where he takes a seat at the small pine table.

While he digests the substantial breakfast, he starts reading one of the books – *Freud: An Introduction*. After a few pages, he arrives at the following passage:

> *Freud believed the mind is like an iceberg. Most of it lies beneath the surface, a subconscious universe of thoughts we can't observe. It contains memories too painful to remember, elicits emotions we don't want to feel, and makes us do things we don't understand.*

Martin closes the book, opens the back door and follows Archie out into the morning.

Acknowledgements

I'd like to thank the many people who read various early versions of this story and provided feedback: my wife, Karen – thanks also for putting up with this scatterbrained dreamer for the last fifteen years; my sister Zeynep; Lisa Griffiths; Karen Runge; Adam Jenkins; David McLeod; Alan Jordan; C.M. Taylor; and everyone at the LitReactor workshop who reviewed chapters, including the late, great R.Moon.

Thanks to Kit Foster for designing a great cover. And Nancy Duin for the proof edit.

I studied psychology but needed to improve my knowledge of psychoanalysis and psychopaths. Details and inspiration came from: *Basic Freud* by Michael Kahn; *The Psychopath: Emotion and the Brain* by Blair, Mitchell and Blair; and *Psychoanalysis: The Impossible Profession* and *In the Freud Archives*, both by Janet Malcolm. Michael O'Byrne's *The Crime Writer's Guide to Police Practice and Procedure* served a role that needs no explanation. Any mistakes are my own.

About the Author

V.R. Stone lives in London with his wife and two children. He has a degree in psychology and, like Sarah Silver, he works in the investment business. But he's never killed anyone he met in a bar. Or anywhere else for that matter.

You can follow V.R. Stone at:

www.vrstoneauthor.com

facebook.com/vrstoneauthor

twitter.com/vrstoneauthor

goodreads.com/author/show/15643947.V_R_Stone

18849062R00183

Printed in Great Britain
by Amazon